"This is much better. But how do I aim this thing?"

"First you got to relax," Longarm told her. "If you try to hold a gun too tight, you'll freeze up and that'll make the muzzle wobble."

Charlene relaxed so completely when Longarm pulled her wrists back that he suddenly found himself holding her in a close embrace. His hands were still on hers, but his forearms were pressing against her billowing softness and her back was pushing against him from shoulders to knees. Charlene's full buttocks were plastered against Longarm so tightly that he could feel the warmth radiating.

Longarm followed his instincts...

TABOR EVANS

AND THE
STEER SWINDLERS

A JOVE BOOK

LONGARM AND THE STEER SWINDLERS

A Jove Book/published by arrangement with
the author

PRINTING HISTORY
Jove edition/May 1984

ISBN: 0-515-06266-9

Jove books are published by The Berkley Publishing Group
200 Madison Avenue, New York, N.Y. 10016. The words
"A JOVE BOOK" and the "J" with sunburst are trademarks
belonging to Jove Publications, Inc.

PRINTED IN THE UNITED STATES OF AMERICA

Chapter 1

"Hey, Long!" one of the men in the box canyon shouted.

Longarm took the last few puffs on the stub that remained of the long slim cigar he'd lighted when the light got bright enough to hide the flare of a match. He ground the stub under the heel of his boot while he debated whether or not to reply. He hadn't realized until now that the outlaws holed up in the canyon had recognized him in the few seconds when he'd been visible during their brief exchange of shots the evening before.

"What's on your mind?" Longarm called back.

"Figured we might make a deal with you," a different voice replied. "No harm trying, is there?"

Longarm couldn't identify the fugitives by their voices; he didn't know whether Coulter or Messer had spoken first.

"If you know my name, you know the only kind of deal I'll make you," he told them. "Lay down your guns and walk out with your hands up. If that's the deal you got in mind, I'll listen."

"Hell, Long, that ain't no deal! That's giving up!"

"And we ain't about to do that!" the second outlaw added.

Longarm didn't bother to reply. He bit off a piece of hard jerky from the sliver he held in one hand and followed it with a few kernels of parched corn. While he chewed, he studied the mouth of the box canyon in the increasing dawn light. When he'd arrived the previous evening he'd been too busy to examine the area closely. In fact, he'd been too busy even to choose the spot where he'd spent his night-long vigil. During the brief period between dusk and dark he'd had more on his mind than the scenery, and had stopped behind the massive rock simply because it was the closest shelter handy.

Longarm had discovered the canyon in the eye-deceiving light that always follows a desert sunset after four long days in the saddle trailing the outlaws from the vicinity of Fort Douglas. They had been days of zigzagging across the arid, broken country southeast of the Great Salt Lake, staying on

1

the trail of the fleeing killers by spotting an occasional pile of horse dung or a broken spot on the hard, sun-baked soil where the disturbed earth showed that a scavenging coyote had scratched up the shallowly buried remnants of one of the fugitives' hurried meals.

Just before sunset the previous day he'd been guided to the outlaws' hideout by a tiny thread of smoke sent from the cooking fire that Messer and Coulter had incautiously kindled. The ridge from which he'd seen the smoke rose to a high shoulder, too narrow for a horse to walk along. Dismounting, Longarm made his way on foot to the highest point, where he could look downslope and see part of the canyon's floor.

He assured himself first that his judgment about the canyon had been correct: it was a true box, its only entrance the gash in the face of the cliff. Then he settled down to watch. There must be a spring in the canyon, he decided when he saw a touch or two of green vegetation in the already fading daylight. There were hundreds of such canyons in the desert country, their locations circulated over the grapevine telegraph that existed between the lawless hands preying on the scattered towns of the sparsely settled Western states and territories.

He'd waited and watched on the ridge until he'd seen both men as they moved around, settling in for the night, and had observed them long enough to identify them, though he'd never had any doubt about the pair being the murdering outlaws he was after. They were far beyond rifle range, so he'd taken time to survey the boulder-strewn, broken country that lay between him and the rising wisp of smoke. The terrain had been ideal for a surprise approach, and Longarm had painstakingly dodged from one patch of cover to the next until he'd gotten to within a quarter of a mile of the canyon's mouth.

His hope of surprising the fugitives ended and the shooting started when his cavalry remount heard one of the outlaws' horses whinny in the canyon and replied to it. The whinny had alerted his quarry before Longarm could reach the cover of the boulder behind which he was now sheltered, and they'd come out shooting.

He'd headed at a gallop during those last minutes of waning daylight, dodging from boulder to boulder, trying to avoid the rifle slugs sent his way by Coulter and Messer while at the same time getting the outlaws in the sights of his own Winchester.

2

He'd been lucky to be close to the house-sized rock when the outlaws' ragged bursts of hurriedly aimed shots began kicking up dust around the horse and whining as they ricochetted off the big boulders that dotted the area around the canyon's mouth.

Messer and Coulter had been too cautious to show themselves long enough to enable Longarm to get an effective return shot at them. They'd popped up to shoot without taking time to aim, and the only damage their shooting had done was a shallow crease in the rump of Longarm's mount.

Even that shot had been lucky for him, he thought. Stung by the slug, the horse had made a huge forward leap that placed Longarm safely behind the house-sized boulder. He'd waited there through the long night, his ears straining to catch any noise that might indicate the two outlaws were trying to make a getaway under cover of darkness, but Messer and Coulter hadn't stirred during the night. Longarm hadn't slept in spite of his exhaustion. He'd invested too much time cornering the outlaws to let them sneak away while he dozed.

One of the fugitives now broke the silence that had followed their last few angry words. "Listen, Long, we figure what we got here's a Mexican standoff. Let's talk about a deal."

"I've already told you the only kind of deal I'll listen to," Longarm answered. "And I don't figure the way you do. We ain't got a standoff at all."

"You can't come in, we can't come out," the reply came. "I don't know what else you'd call it."

"I'll come in after you when the notion strikes me. Don't make no mistake about that," Longarm said calmly. "It wouldn't be the first time I've busted into a canyon."

"We'll be ready when you get that notion. There's two of us and just one of you. I don't call them good odds."

For the second time, Longarm ignored the challenge. He ate the last bit of the jerky and finished the corn he had in his hand and stood up. Moving to the horse, he reached for the canteen that hung from the saddle strings on the cantle. The moment he lifted the canteen Longarm realized that it was too light. He'd filled it the morning before, and it should still be three-quarters full.

Lifting it to eye level by the straps, a single quick glance was enough to show him what had happened. Metal glinted from a nick not much bigger than a pinpoint a third of the way down the canteen's circular rim. The rifle slug that had grazed the horse had first touched the canteen's edge and scraped off a tiny speck of the blanketing layers of wool and canvas, opening a hole smaller than a needle's eye on the canteen's rim. The hole was not big enough to release a stream, but during the night a steady seepage had drained most of the water from the canteen.

Longarm shook the canteen carefully, then shook his head. Instead of being three-quarters full, the canteen was now three-quarters empty. He had little more than a cupful of water to last him until his siege of the canyon could be brought to an end.

Well, old son, Longarm told himself silently, *looks like you're up shit crick without a paddle. It'll be hot today, just like it's been all along, and that little piddling mouthful of water you got left ain't enough to keep you and the nag from getting mighty thirsty.*

Hanging the canteen back on the cantle without drinking, he lighted a fresh stogie. He was in no hurry to talk further with the cornered outlaws. No matter how high the cards might be that they held, hidden from his rifle sights in the canyon, all the aces in the waiting game Messer and Coulter had started playing were in Longarm's hand.

Between the mouth of the canyon and the massive boulder that shielded him and the horse there was a stretch of fifty or sixty yards of open ground. Even if the slit through which the two fugitives had to leave the mouth of the canyon was wide enough to allow both of them to gallop out at the same time, they'd still have to cross that barren ground, snapshooting from their saddles, while he cut them down with aimed shots from the cover of the boulder. Hunkering down, Longarm puffed his cigar and waited patiently.

This time their next proposal was so long in coming that he was thinking seriously about making good his threat to ride into the canyon after them. This time the outlaws gave him the clue he needed to identify their voices.

"Listen, Long, me and Coulter've been talking," the speaker said, tagging himself as Messer. "We got damn near ninety thousand dollars from that Army payroll we taken and a bank job we pulled over in Montana Territory before we moved west. How'd you feel about a three-way split?"

"About the same way I'd feel if your proposition was to let

4

you go scot free," Longarm replied.

"Thirty thousand's a hell of a lot of money," Coulter said. "You stop and think how long it'd take you to have that much in cash on what the government pays a deputy marshal."

"I draw my government pay clean, Coulter," Longarm pointed out. "That money you and Messer stole has got blood on it. You killed three men when you ambushed that Army pay wagon."

"You didn't have nothing to do with that," the outlaw said persuasively. "And it don't bother us none. Blood washes off gold real easy."

"Not when it's in my pocket, it don't," Longarm snapped. "Anyhow, if you know enough about me to recognize me by sight, you oughta know I ain't for sale."

When neither of the outlaws replied, Longarm decided the time had come to quit talking. He edged to the side of the boulder and peered around it, concentrating his attention on a fissure that split the cliff's sheer wall some distance away from the mouth. After studying the break for a few moments he decided it offered a better bet than storming the canyon's narrow entrance. By bracing his feet on one side of the long vertical crack and his back on the other, he could climb to the rim in a few minutes and have a clear field of fire down into the canyon.

Old son, Longarm told himself, *if them bastards are watching for you to make a move, this is a fool stunt you're about to pull. But if they're watching, you'll find out soon enough, and if they ain't, it's your best chance to get 'em outa their hidey-hole without wasting so much time waiting.*

There was still no sign of life from the canyon mouth. Lifting the flat stone with which he'd weighted down the reins of his horse, Longarm swung into the saddle, slid his rifle from its saddle scabbard, and started for the crack in the cliff's face.

He walked his horse, holding it in check, knowing that any drumming of hooves on the hard soil would reach their ears. In spite of Longarm's hope that the outlaws weren't maintaining a watch, they must have been keeping an eye in his direction. He'd covered perhaps two-thirds of the distance to his objective when both outlaws burst from the canyon mouth, rifles ready.

Longarm's vigilance robbed their move of any element of surprise. At the first flash of a moving form in the canyon mouth, he had his rifle up and was waiting. When one of the

5

outlaws came into sight, his rifle already shouldered, Longarm fired a split second before the moving man could aim. The slug found its mark and while the renegade was still swinging his own rifle his body was slammed backward into the stone face of the cliff by the force of the bullet.

He got off his shot, but missed Longarm and took the remount horse in the chest. The horse reared, spoiling the aim of the second outlaw as he followed the first from the canyon mouth. Like the first, he had his rifle shouldered and ready. The crack of his shot broke the morning stillness. Longarm's wounded horse neighed shrilly when the second bullet found its belly. The animal had been dancing on its hind legs, but now it moved less wildly.

As long as the horse under him was still gyrating wildly, Longarm could not aim from its saddle. A second shot came from the outlaw standing in the canyon mouth, but it went wild, the slug buzzing angrily past Longarm's head.

As his horse's dancing turned into a slow downward sag, Longarm moved with the sure instinct honed by countless gunfights. Lowering his rifle, he closed one big hand around the forestock and began firing as fast he could lever fresh shells into the chamber. The second outlaw dropped to the ground beside the first, his rifle falling from his hands as he lurched down.

Longarm's horse stopped its frantic gyrations. It still stood erect, but it was trembling now in its death throes. It danced into a half-turn as it collapsed and Longarm saved himself from falling with it by sliding his feet from the stirrups and jumping free. He landed hard as the horse finally fell to the ground and its twitching stopped abruptly.

Grabbing for his rifle, Longarm rolled behind the carcass of the dead horse. He brought up the Winchester and leveled it at the mouth of the canyon. The sun had started to rise while the quick gun battle was taking place. Its rim was already showing above the horizon and its bright rays were flooding the desert.

Longarm studied the canyon mouth for a full minute before he realized the reason for the nagging worry that had begun pulling at his mind when he'd first looked at the canyon's mouth.

Instead of two bodies lying on the ground there was only one. The outlaw who'd come out last had managed to make

6

his way back into shelter. Longarm clamped his big strong teeth around the butt of a fresh cheroot. He did not light the long, thin cigar, but began refilling the magazine of his Winchester. Then he started purposefully toward the mouth of the canyon.

Chapter 2

Even before he got to the mouth of the canyon Longarm had identified the dead man as Messer. He stopped just outside the narrow fissure that opened in the cliff's face and called, "All right, Coulter, come on out! I know you're hit and hurting, so you might as well give it up."

"Like hell I will!" Coulter called back. "If you want me, the only way you'll get me is to come in after me."

"Don't make me kill you," Longarm urged. "If you stand up in court, there's a chance a jury might only send you to the federal pen."

"Chance, hell!" Coulter snorted. "I know I got a rope waiting for me if I stand trial. I'd sooner take a chance right here in a shootout with you, Long!"

"You can't stand up to me, Coulter," Longarm replied. His tone was not boastful or challenging; he spoke in a coldly level voice, stating a fact. "You're hurt, you ain't able to move fast like you'd generally do," he went on. "I ain't got a scratch on me, and I'm fresh as a daisy."

"Maybe you're right, Long," Coulter said. "I might not be able to stand up to you, but I can sure as hell try!"

"Well, I'll give you a minute or so to think about it, anyhow," Longarm told the outlaw.

Moving to one side of the canyon mouth, taking a position that would force Coulter to turn before firing if he should come through the opening, Longarm found a small boulder a dozen yards from the break in the cliff face and sat down on it without taking his eyes from the spot where Coulter would emerge if he came out. He was feeling thirsty now that the sun had begun to warm the air, but his canteen was on his dead horse a hundred yards away. Moving slowly and deliberately, Longarm lighted a cheroot and forgot his thirst.

He'd settled down on the boulder without lowering the muzzle of his rifle, and now he sat with the stock's fore end resting on his knee, the weapon pointing at the canyon entrance, his

8

right hand gripping the neck of the stock, his finger still on the trigger. Except for the thin gray thread of smoke rising from the tip of his long cheroot, Longarm might have been a statue. He sat motionless as the boulders which dotted the ground all around him, his face expressionless, his eyes fixed on the canyon's mouth.

Minute after minute passed as the sun crept up in the sky and Longarm's elongated shadow grew ever so slightly shorter. Only when the flicker of another shadow passed across his did Longarm move. He looked up and saw the buzzard wheeling into a turn at the rim of the cliff, and a smile broke the impassivity of his features. His eyes followed the buzzard's shadow as the big black bird made another circuit, dropping steadily lower.

When it completed its turn, the buzzard had dropped below the top of the cliff. It tightened its circle as it sailed on motionless wings above the carcass of the horse the outlaw's bullets had brought down, and for a moment Longarm thought the scavenger bird was going to drop on the horse.

Frowning, Longarm started to raise his rifle, but before he could move the gun the buzzard planed out into level flight and passed above the carcass. It kept moving, tightening its circle of flight still more as it dropped. Then it flared its huge outspread wings and came to earth a few feet from Messer's body. For the first time since he'd been keeping his strange vigil, Longarm moved. He shifted his position on the boulder a fraction of an inch and a grim smile twitched the corners of his lips. He knew he would not have to wait much longer now.

Moving clumsily now that it was on the ground, its huge wings folded to its body, its tailfeathers dragging and leaving a wide line in the dirt, the buzzard waddled slowly toward Messer's corpse. It stopped beside the dead outlaw for a moment, its head with its great curved yellow beak swinging from side to side as it studied its surroundings with red-rimmed yellow eyes. Then, with an ungainly lurch, the buzzard closed the short distance between it and the body and landed on Messer's motionless chest.

An inarticulate scream of rage sounded from the box canyon, followed by the sharp bark of a pistol. The slug kicked up a spurt of dust a foot beyond the buzzard. The bird hopped off the body and began moving away. It unfolded its wings and started flapping the great black pinions as it moved. Then it took off and with long, sweeping wing strokes mounted steadily into the cloudless blue sky until it became a distant dot.

From the canyon Coulter shouted, "All right, Long! You win! I'm throwing out my gun!"

Longarm had not moved from the boulder. He stood up now and tossed away the stub of his cheroot before replying. "I want to see three guns on the ground before you come out, Coulter. Your rifle and pistol and Messer's rifle," he ordered.

One by one, the weapons sailed from the canyon mouth and clattered to the hard ground beyond Messer's corpse. Coulter called, "Can I come out now, Long?"

"Come ahead. Keep your hands up," Longarm answered.

Coulter emerged from the canyon. He held his hands above his head, but his right arm sagged, and Longarm saw the wide blotch of blood that stained his shirt on that side of his chest. He waited while the outlaw moved slowly toward him, and when Coulter was still two or three paces distant Longarm motioned with the rifle muzzle for him to stop.

"How bad are you hurt?" Longarm asked.

"It ain't but a scratch, except it's stiffened up and I can't shoot like I oughta."

"A little work'll take the stiffness out," Longarm told the outlaw coldly.

"What d'you mean, work?"

Longarm jerked his head toward Messer's body. "You want to leave your pal for buzzards' meat? Seemed like the one that was about to start on him a minute ago sorta upset you."

"Damn you, Long!" Coulter raged. "You'd have left the buzzard alone, wouldn't you? Watched the damned thing rip his face up and not made a move to stop it!"

"Messer wouldn't've minded," Longarm replied unfeelingly. "He wouldn't've known about it."

"No, but I would! Maybe Messer wasn't much, but him and me partnered for a long time, going on four years now. I wasn't going to watch that buzzard work on him!"

Longarm thought of the civilian teamster and his two soldier escorts left dead by Coulter and Messer when they'd ambushed the Army pay wagon two weeks earlier. By the time he'd gotten to the scene, the three men hadn't been very pretty to look at after the work the buzzards had done on them. He felt no pity for Coulter.

"You can drag Messer in the canyon and pile some rocks on him after we get my saddle gear off that horse you killed," he told the outlaw. "I don't owe it to you, but I'll give you that much time. But you still got to do a few more jobs before we can start back to Fort Douglas."

Noon had come and gone before they were ready to mount and leave the box canyon. Longarm had transferred his saddle to Messer's horse and was leading Coulter's mount. The sub-dued outlaw was handcuffed, wrist irons lashed to the saddle horn. The gold the two men had taken was safely in Longarm's saddlebags. As they started riding silently for Miles City, Long-arm leaving a trail of smoke from a freshly lighted cheroot, the buzzard wheeled in huge circles in the cloudless sky, wait-ing with the persistence of its kind.

Although his train pulled into Denver's Union Station more than an hour before noon, Longarm did not go to his office and report in. After he'd turned Bones Coulter over to the provost marshal at Fort Douglas and signed his name to fifteen different forms covering the loss of a U.S. Cavalry horse when it was on requisition to a deputy federal marshal, he'd just had time to board the train to Denver.

He was bone-tired after having been in the saddle travelling over rough country for almost two weeks. His long black coat was dust-streaked and his twill trousers felt stiff as boards. For a week Longarm hadn't stopped long enough to shave or bathe. A week's growth of stubble itched on his jaws and his usually neat, well-groomed moustache was ragged and drooping in-stead of sweeping upward in a bold curve like the horns of a longhorn steer. There were only three things he really wanted: a good swig of his favorite Maryland rye whiskey, a hot bath, and a barber's shave, in that order.

Instead of walking from the station, Longarm hailed a hack and gave the driver his address, on the unfashionable end of Cherry Street. When the carriage had rumbled through the busy business district and past the newer houses, the driver reined up in front of his rooming house. Longarm tumbled out on the street side and lifted his saddle off the seat beside the driver. He paid the fare and was bending over to pick up the saddle when the door of the rooming house burst open and his landlady came scurrying to the curb.

11

"Well, laws a-mercy, Marshal Long, it's you!" she exclaimed as she peered at Longarm over the gold rims of her narrow oval spectacles. She frowned. "Are you sick or hurt or something?"

"No, just a mite tired," Longarm replied as he picked up the saddle and started toward the door.

"If I didn't know you better, I'd say you'd been looking for the elephant and listening to the owl," she told him, opening the door wide to let him swing his saddle through.

"All I need is to clean up," Longarm told her over his shoulder as he started up the narrow flight of stairs to his room on the second floor. "I'd be mighty grateful if you'd pour a kettle of hot water in the tub of the bathroom down the hall from me. I aim to soak away this crust of dirt just as soon as I can get my boots off."

"I've got a kettle boiling on the stove right now," she said. "You go on. The bathtub'll be ready for you, and Hoh Quah brought your laundry back the day after you left, so you'll have nice fresh clothes to put on after you've bathed."

His room was dim, the shade still drawn as he'd left it on the morning he started for Utah. Longarm didn't bother to raise it. He leaned his Winchester in the corner, dropped the saddle beside it, and made a beeline for the dresser, where a half full bottle of Tom Moore stood.

He tilted the bottle and gulped. Then, after lighting a fresh cheroot, he took a second mouthful, which he swallowed more slowly. He pried himself out of his boots, picked up a freshly laundered pair of balbriggans and a flannel shirt from the bundle on the bed, took clean trousers off the nail in the corner beside the bed, and headed for the bath.

Two hours later, surrounded by the pleasant scents of bay rum and macassar oil, Longarm looked at himself in the wide mirror of George Masters' barbershop. His cheeks were their usual smooth bronze hue, his brown hair brushed back in a single clean sweep, his moustache neatly trimmed and combed into its customary symmetrically upswept curve. Even the lines at the corners of his eyes did not detract from the look of mature youthfulness reflected in the mirror.

"Guess that'll hold me till next time, George," he told the barber. He took a quarter from his pocket and slid it into Masters' hand. "Keep the change, like always."

12

"Looks like you're going out on the town tonight," Masters commented, dropping the coin in the till drawer.

"Not tonight. This is my poker night at the Windsor, so I'll be there for a little while. But unless luck's really good to me, I'll be quitting early. Chances are Billy Vail's going to have a case waiting when I report in, so I'll likely be starting off again tomorrow."

"You'd better get right on into Marshal Vail's office," the pink-cheeked young clerk told Longarm in a whisper when he entered the outer office from the hall. "He's a little upset because you didn't report in right after you got back yesterday."

"How the devil did he find out I got back yesterday?" Longarm frowned.

"Bob Edwards saw you leave the depot. He'd gone down there to get a new key for his telegraph sender," the clerk said. "The chief marshal gave him a wire to send you at Fort Russell, and Bob spilled that he'd seen you before he thought."

Bracing himself for the storm he was sure would be coming, Longarm opened the door to Vail's private office. The chief marshal was sitting behind his desk, which was heaped with the usual mass of paperwork. Vail's lips compressed when he saw Longarm, and his ruddy cheeks grew a shade pinker as he motioned for him to come in. Longarm pulled up the red morocco-upholstered chair, the only one in the office he found comfortable, and sat down. He waited for Vail to speak, but the chief marshal was pawing through the stacks of paper on his desk.

"It's nice of you to honor us with a visit," Vail said with an overdone mildness when at last he looked up. "Did you forget that it's a standing order for you to report the result of your case the minute you get back to Denver?"

Longarm matched Vail's mild tone. "No, Billy. But I didn't want to make you ashamed of me yesterday, coming to the office the way I looked. By the time I got cleaned up it was too late, the office was closed."

"If it makes you feel any better, I waited here an hour after closing time to talk with you about your new case."

"Well, now, how in tunket was I to know that, Billy? Seems to me if it was all that important, you'd've sent a messenger after me to my rooming house."

13

Vail extended a hand across his desk and said, "Since you got back early yesterday, I suppose you've written up your report?"

"Now, be reasonable, Billy!" Longarm protested. "I just this minute walked in the door."

"After an all-night poker game at the Windsor, I suppose?"

Longarm answered before he thought. "Not on your tintype! I quit early, while I was a few dollars ahead. I—" He saw the frown growing on Vail's face and stopped short, then went on, "Well, after I spent all that time out on the Utah desert with no company but a damned murdering renegade, I needed to talk to somebody decent again."

To Longarm's surprise, Vail smiled. "I can't say I blame you. And when you come right down to the nubbin of this new case you're going to handle, it's not all that urgent. Important, don't make any mistake about that, but a day's not going to make much difference."

Longarm relaxed. "I thought for a minute there that you was really mad at me, Billy. Not that you didn't have a right to be," he added hurriedly. "I know I oughta checked in, but I'm telling you the truth when I say I couldn't stomach my own stink another minute longer after I got off that train."

Vail nodded. "All right, Long. Run down your report for me now. You can write it up later."

"Sure." Longarm nodded. "Well, I caught up with the two that ambushed the Army pay wagon. Messer and Coulter— we've had Wanted fliers on both of 'em. Had to kill Messer, turned Coulter over to the provost marshal at Fort Russell. Left the Army money with him, and another twenty thousand they'd stolen from a bank up in Montana. That about sizes it up."

"I remember the names of those two outlaws." Vail frowned. "Be sure you tell the clerk to notify everybody who's got a flyer out on them that they can cancel them now." Then, his voice severe again, he added, "And when I said you can write up your report later, I didn't mean after you get back from this new case. I mean before you leave on it."

"Don't worry, Billy. I'm turning over a new leaf."

"Seems I've heard you say that before," Vail said wryly.

"I guess. But this time I mean it," Longarm told him. He fished a cheroot out of his pocket and lighted it. "Well, I'm ready to go out again, I guess. What's this new case you got for me, Billy?"

14

Vail glanced at the big gilt-cased Vienna Regulator clock that stood on its own shelf on the wall at one side of his desk. He said, "Cattle swindling. But I don't want to start going into it until Jim gets here."

"Which Jim're you talking about?" Longarm asked. "Between us, I'd guess we know three or four of 'em."

"I don't think you've met the one I asked to come in this morning, Long. I'm talking about Jim Fraser, the managing director of the Colorado Cattlemen's Association."

Longarm whistled. "He's quite some muckety-muck, ain't he?"

"Well, he's an important man in the state," Vail agreed. "The Cattlemen's Association is a big organization, and it's got a lot of members who know the right people in Washington."

"Billy, this ain't one of them cases where I got to play nursemaid to some high-up politician, is it? Now, I didn't mind a bit when you put me to looking after President Grant, he's a real fine man, and he acts just like ordinary folks. But some of—"

"Set your mind at rest," Vail assured Longarm. "Jim's just like real folks, too. He's one of the men I play poker with at the Association's private clubrooms two or three times a month."

"I'll take him on your say-so, then," Longarm said.

"He should be here by now," Vail said. "Even though our game last night didn't break up until pretty late."

"Now, that'll do to hang a picture on!" Longarm exclaimed. "A few minutes ago you was getting ready to jump on me for sitting in a friendly game for a little while, and now—"

Vail broke in to say, "I get to the office on time even when I've been in a poker game the night before. And I remember quite a few times—" He broke off as a knock sounded on the office door to call, "Come in."

"Mr. Fraser's here, Chief Vail," the pink-cheeked young clerk said, putting his head in the door. "Do you want me to ask him to wait, or shall I bring him in?"

"I'd imagine if you just open the door all the way, Jim can bring himself in," Vail replied.

He stood up, and Longarm followed suit, as the clerk swung the door wide and a tall, heavy-set man in his middle forties came in. His suit spoke mutely of an expensive tailor, and the rosebud in his buttonhole was dew-fresh. His dark hair was

15

combed immaculately, and his clean-shaven cheeks bore a healthy tan that was a match for Longarm's deep bronze.

"Sorry I'm late, Billy," Fraser said, extending his hand to the chief marshal. "I had a few things at the office that had to be taken care of right away."

"Of course," Vail replied. "Jim, this is the man I told you about, Custis Long. He's my top deputy, and I'm putting him on the steer-swindling case."

Fraser thrust out his hand and shook Longarm's. He said, "Billy's told me quite a bit about you since this case began to develop, Long. I understand you've got a nickname that's known all over the West. Longarm, isn't it?"

"Folks call me that," Longarm admitted.

"Well, if you're as good as he says you are, I know our members won't have to be worried much longer about their herds," Fraser went on. "And I don't mind telling you there are a lot of them who're worried right now."

"I'll do all I can to ease 'em," Longarm replied. "Only I still don't know what this case is all about."

"I was just beginning to explain it when you came in," Vail said. "If you'd rather—"

"No, no!" Fraser protested. "It's your case, Billy. I'll just pull up a chair and listen while you go over it with Marshal Long, and then if he has any questions, I'll answer them."

After the three men had settled down into their chairs, Vail picked up the papers he's squirreled out of the piles on his desk and straightened their edges. He said, "What's happening is that there are a lot of outlaw steers being sold right now."

"You mean rustled?" Longarm asked.

"I guess some are rustled," Vail agreed. "That's not our job, of course, unless we just stumble onto a case."

"It's not rustling I'm worried about," Fraser broke in. "Since Colorado's cattle country, I suppose you've heard of apthos fever, Long?"

Longarm hesitated for a moment, trying to recall his days as a cowhand. Then he asked, "Ain't that what's called hoof-and-mouth disease?"

"Yes," Fraser replied. "Hoof-and-mouth, foot-and-mouth, bad-foot—hell, it's got a lot of names."

"There wasn't none of it around when I was cowhanding, so about all I know is second hand," Longarm said. "And I had a sorta half idea the ranchers had knocked it out by now."

16

"So did the ranchers," Fraser told him. "But they were wrong. It's been spread by the damned steer-swindlers. And I'll say this very seriously, Long. If we don't stop them, the cattle industry could be totally wiped out. And I don't mean just in Colorado. I'm talking about the entire western United States!"

Chapter 3

Fraser's sober face left no doubt in the minds of Longarm and Vail that he was dead serious. They sat silently for a moment, then Longarm said, "I ain't been around cattle ranches all that much since I taken up marshaling, Mr. Fraser. Back when I was cowhanding, there wasn't such a thing as hoof-and-mouth disease. I don't know anything about it except the name."

"That's my situation, too," Vail put in. "I heard a lot of ranchers mention it a little while after I came here from Texas, but the talk died down."

"That's because the first outbreak wasn't bad, and was confined pretty much to Colorado," Fraser explained. "It came in on British cattle, and wasn't very widespread back in the seventies. This time, it's a different story. Infected steers are showing up all over the place."

"Jim tells me he's pretty sure this gang of swindlers is selling infected steers, telling the buyers they don't have anything wrong with them." Vail frowned. "Is that what your members say, Jim?"

"Right, Billy. But the steer-swindlers aren't just operating here in Colorado," Fraser went on. "The Texas Cattlemen's Association warned us about it first. They've had some cases of hoof-and-mouth down there lately."

"Suppose you tell me a little bit more, so I won't be going off half-cocked when I set out on the case," Longarm suggested. "I don't remember hearing much about hoof-and-mouth disease, except that nobody's come up with a way to cure it."

"Nothing's been found yet," the cattleman said. "All we know to do is to shoot the infected cattle and burn the carcasses as quickly as possible. There's a theory that hoof-and-mouth germs stay in the ground or the grass unless it's burned."

"You mean there's no way to treat the cattle or clean up the range either?" Vail asked.

"That's right," Fraser said. "When a herd of steers gets

18

infected with apthos fever, every animal that's been exposed to it has to be killed."

"Even if they haven't got the fever?" Vail asked.

Fraser nodded, and Longarm observed, "Looks to me like that's sorta doing things the hard way. Ain't there a chance some of them sick steers might get well?"

"A few probably do," Fraser said. "But they'll carry the germs in their bodies and get sick again sooner or later."

"They don't just die all at once, then?"

"A steer with hoof-and-mouth disease might live a couple of months," Fraser replied thoughtfully. "It'd be skinny and not worth much on the market, even if it didn't show any other signs of being infected."

"A man oughta be able to tell whether a steer's sick just by looking at it, I'd say," Longarm remarked thoughtfully.

"He can tell a steer's sick, but not that it's got hoof-and-mouth," Fraser said. "There's no way to detect it until it begins spreading, and then it's too late."

"I don't know all that much about steers," Longarm went on, "but I think *I'd* know when one's sick just by looking at it."

"Of course you can tell a sick steer," Fraser said a bit impatiently. "But cattle in a herd where hoof-and-mouth is just starting can look healthy one day and overnight half the steers will start losing weight. The next day or so they'll begin developing sores at the tops of their hooves and around their mouths. By then the rest of the herd will be infected."

Vail's voice betrayed his shock when he said, "Then hoof-and-mouth would just about wipe out any rancher with an infected herd, wouldn't it?"

"That's about the size of it, Billy," Fraser answered. "I've seen ranchers start with a thousand head in a herd and after a month of cutting out diseased steers, wind up with maybe forty or fifty head that have stayed healthy."

"A man sure can't stand much of that," Longarm observed. "I don't guess there's any way he can make a dime outa the sick ones? What'd happen if they was butchered and cooked?"

"Well, anyone who ate the meat from one of those sick steers might not get very sick themselves, but they'd be carrying the infection in their bodies." Fraser frowned. "To tell you the truth, the doctors don't know too much about that part of it."

Longarm turned to Vail and said, "So what I've got to do

19

in this new case you've put me on is to find out where them sick steers is coming from and stop 'em from going to the slaughterhouses. I guess you know that might take me a long time."

"We've got a few leads to start you off with," Vail told him. "I'll go over those with you in a minute."

"We can give you some help through the Association, too," Fraser offered. "Our inspectors are always out, checking brands for rustled cattle. They'll be looking for hoof-and-mouth at the same time, now."

"Well, now, that'll be right handy," Longarm said.

Fraser glanced at the clock and stood up. "I think I've given you and Marshal Long all the information I can right now, Billy," he said to Vail. "I'd better be going along. I've got a busy day ahead."

After the Association manager had left, Vail picked up the sheaf of papers he'd laid aside when Fraser had come in.

"Did you ever hear of a man called the Real McCoy?" he asked Longarm.

"There's two men I've heard called that, Billy. One's a prizefighter, and I've never met him. I'd guess you mean the other McCoy. He used to be in the cattle business."

"He still is, from what I've gathered. Do you know him?" Vail asked.

"Depends on what you mean by knowing. I've shook hands with him a time or two."

"Would you know him if you saw him now?" Vail persisted.

"Well, he wasn't no spring chicken when I got acquainted with him. That was right soon after the War, when I'd got the itch to be a cowhand and headed West."

Vail smiled. "That was a while back, and he'd be a pretty old man by now, I suppose."

"Well, one damn sure thing, none of us gets younger. But I guess I'd know McCoy now, even if he's changed some. Why?"

Vail held up the thin sheaf of papers he'd been holding. "A lot of these waybills have his name on them as the shipper. McCoy's got an office down in Kansas City, and he seems to be brokering a lot of steers to the Indian Bureau and the Army."

"That's how we got pulled into the case?"

"Yes. The government's spent a pile of money this past year buying cattle that have turned out to be infected with hoof-

and-mouth. They've had to shoot the infected ones, of course, and then buy more to replace the ones that were killed."

"Seems like it'd be easy to trace back the waybills to find out where the bum steers come from and stop whoever it is that sells 'em, then. Is that all I got to do on this case?"

"That's the easy part."

Longarm was lighting a fresh cheroot. Between puffs he said, "I figured it sounded a little bit too easy to be true. Where's the catch, Billy?"

"Those infected steers have to come from somewhere. All we have to go by is McCoy's waybills, and whatever other waybills there are from different cattle brokers."

Longarm puffed his cigar in silence for a moment, then said thoughtfully, "You mean it just ain't reasonable for a bunch of different cattle brokers to buy infected steers all over hell's half-acre at the same time. The brokers would all have to be buying from the same place."

"Something like that."

"Ain't it the Agriculture Department's job to keep track of such stuff, Billy? They'd be bound to know where hoof-and-mouth disease breaks out, wouldn't they?"

"Yes. They thought about that in Washington. You'll find reports here from some of the Agriculture Department inspectors who've tried to locate the places where the infected steers have been coming from."

"When you say *tried*, I take it they ain't had much luck?"

"None to speak of. That's why they passed the buck to us. They say it's our job to investigate," said Vail.

"Meaning me." Longarm nodded.

"Meaning you," Vail agreed, handing the papers across the desk to Longarm.

Longarm riffled through the sheets, not reading them, just flicking his eyes quickly from one page to the next. He asked Vail, "You went through all this stuff pretty careful when it first come in, I guess?"

"I looked at all of them, sure."

"It might save me some time if you got any ideas about where I oughta start."

Vail thought for a moment, then said, "There's a report on infected steers delivered to the Indian agent over at Sand Creek Reservation. It's one of the latest ones."

"Sand Creek?" Longarm frowned. "You mean there's still

some Cheyennes stayed on after Chivington done all that killing there fifteen years or so ago?"

"I don't suppose you'll find many left," Vail replied. "I haven't been there for a while, and it wasn't much more than a big camp the last time I saw the place. But there'd have to be enough to make it worthwhile for the Indian Bureau to keep an agent there."

"It's as good a place to start as any, I suppose," Longarm said thoughtfully. He dropped the butt of his cheroot in the brass cuspidor that stood at the corner of Vail's desk and walked across the office to the big map that covered more than half the wall. He studied the map for a moment, then turned back to Vail. "I guess your map's up to date, ain't it, Billy?"

"Now, you know damned well it is. You've used it enough."

"I was just thinking about that new spur the UP's been pushing down into the farm country east of the mountains. It runs along Big Sandy Creek quite a ways, but that reservation's a good bit south of the railroad, the way this map looks."

"If that's what the map shows, that's where the reservation is," Vail said. "Why?"

"Oh, I was kinda hoping I'd be able to ride the train right to where I was going. I had my fill of forking a horse the last two or three weeks, and it looks like it'll take me most of a day on horseback to get from the railroad to that reservation."

"I imagine you'll get there without your butt hurting too much," Vail said unfeelingly.

"At least it's close to home," Longarm said. He glanced at the map again, then returned to pick up the reports he'd placed on the corner of Vail's desk. "I tell you, Billy, after all the chasing around I had to do when I was running down Coulter and Messer, I'm plumb tired of travelling. I'm right glad I won't have to go kiting off five or six hundred miles on this case."

"So am I, Long," Vail replied. "Because when you get out of this office, keeping up with you is just as bad as trying to catch a flea on a hot griddle. I'll tell my clerk to fix up your travel vouchers while you're gathering up your gear. I suppose you'll be leaving on the late train this evening?"

"I suppose," Longarm said. "And you won't have to worry about keeping up with me this time, Billy. If I have any luck, I oughta be back here in a few days."

• • •

On both sides of Big Sandy Creek plump heads of wheat stood belly-high to Longarm's horse as he rode along the almost obliterated trail that followed the shallow watercourse. The wheat undulated like small ocean waves in the fitful breeze that took the sting out of the sun's hot glare. The country was more like Kansas than Colorado, he thought, looking across the wind-rippled wheat fields. It had looked much the same since he'd left the train that morning at the little settlement named after Kit Carson and set out, riding a livery horse.

At noon he'd seen a farmhouse close enough to the trail for him to reach easily, and though he'd offered to pay for a meal, the family had refused his money, and had invited him to stay and eat as their guest. The bacon and turnip stew and homemade cornbread had reminded Longarm of family meals when he was a boy back in the hardscrabble hills of West Virginia, and he was at peace with himself and the world as he puffed a cheroot and watched the trail ahead for the first sign that he was getting close to the Cheyenne Reservation.

He saw it after he'd covered another eight or ten miles. The wheat fields ended abruptly. Ahead of him the ocher soil stretched barren except for some clumps of grass as yellow as the earth, the creek a shining streak between banks void of vegetation to the point where a score or so of shabby shanties huddled along both sides. A horse or two wandered along the banks, and beyond the houses he could see a few steers nosing at the bunchgrass. On the banks of the creek were a few small gardens that looked to be in need of attention. Their rows were straggly and showed long, bare stretches where plants had been picked, while the remaining growth was scattered and sparse.

As he drew closer, Longarm could see people moving in the area of the houses. Closer to the settlement he recognized them as Cheyennes by their hawklike noses and long, square jaws. Most of them were old, and there were more women then men. Only half a dozen were his own age or younger. He noticed at once that they were neater and much better dressed than Indians he'd seen on the reservations in the Nation. Most of the clothing they wore looked fairly new. They glanced at him incuriously and a few nodded greetings, but most of them merely looked at him and then ignored his passing.

In the center of the randomly spaced shanties there was one white-painted house. It was small, not more than two rooms,

23

and at close range Longarm could see that the paint was cracked and peeling. He wove between the ramshackle dwellings until he reached the house. A crudely hand-lettered sign was nailed over the door: U.S. INDIAN BUREAU. SAND CREEK RESERVATION.

Before Longarm could dismount, a rangy young man wearing faded duck jeans that had been washed but not ironed came out onto the small veranda. He said, "Swing down, mister. I'm Jack Lawson, the agent here, and I'm right glad to see a new face. We don't get many visitors."

Longarm swung out of his saddle and took the agent's extended hand. He said, "Glad to meet you, Lawson. My name's Long. Deputy U.S. marshal."

Lawson dropped Longarm's hand as though it had suddenly gotten too hot to hold. His eyes grew troubled and his face clouded. "Oh, Lord!" he exclaimed. "Don't tell me it's going to happen at last!"

"What's going to happen?" Longarm asked.

"They've decided to close the reservation, haven't they? I guess you're from the Indian Bureau headquarters, back in Washington, aren't you?" Lawson said. "You've come to herd the Cheyennes that're left down to Indian Territory. Is that right?"

"If it is, this is the first I've heard about it," Longarm told the agent. "I ain't from Washington. I work outa Denver, and I ain't got a thing to do with the Indian Bureau."

Lawson's face lost its look of apprehension. He said, "In that case, I'm glad to see you. Did you just stop in because you were passing by, or did you come here to arrest somebody?"

"All I'm doing is looking for information," Longarm assured the agent.

During the brief period the two had been talking, a handful of the people whom Longarm had seen wandering around the settlement had moved up to the office and were standing watching them. Lawson turned to them and said a few words in Cheyenne. The deep bronze faces of the Indians broke into smiles, and they moved up closer to the veranda. Lawson turned back to Longarm.

"This happens every time they see a stranger stop here," he explained. "Come on inside, Marshal Long. There's what's left of my noontime coffee, if you'd like a cup."

It was cooler in the office. The agent's headquarters was

24

divided into two rooms by a partition across its center. A long pine-topped counter stretched from end to end of the square room, the counter and the desk which stood behind it against the partition wall taking up perhaps a third of its space. A pot-bellied stove was in the corner opposite the desk, and a shallow cabinet hung on the wall at one side of the stove. A pine table and several chairs occupied what space remained in the center of the room. Through a door in the center of the partition wall, Longarm saw a rumpled bed in the back room.

He gave the office only a perfunctory glance, for the two young Cheyenne women sitting at the table drew most of his attention. Their faces were typically Cheyenne—aquiline noses, full lips, long, rounded jaws. He had no way of judging their figures, for both wore the long unbelted dresses Longarm had seen on every Indian reservation he'd ever visited. Their mid-night-black hair was braided into twin strands, one braid on either side of their breasts.

A deerskin jacket was spread out on the table between them and they were weaving decorations of colorful dyed porcupine quills into its lapels and back. They looked up when Longarm and Lawson came in, but said nothing.

"This is Rising Morning Star, Marshal Long," Lawson said, indicating the woman holding the jacket's back. Then, turning to the younger Cheyenne, "And this is Dawn Flower."

Longarm touched the brim of his hat, then took it off. "I'm right pleased to meet you ladies," he said.

"We are glad to meet you, too, Marshal Long," Dawn Flower replied. To Longarm's surprise, her English was excellent. It had only a trace of the throaty Cheyenne language in it. She looked at Lawson and asked, "Shall we get coffee for you?"

"Please do, Dawn Flower," the agent replied. "Then you and Star should take your work outside. Marshal Long and I will want to talk privately."

Dawn Flower went to the stove and lifted one of the lids. She took a handful of corncobs from a box in the corner behind the stove and dropped them into the firebox. Her companion began to gather up the porcupine quills and make a bundle of the jacket. She laid the bundle beside the door and moved the chairs, placing one on each side of the square, unpainted table.

Lawson motioned Longarm to one of the chairs and sat down in the other. Longarm took a cheroot from his pocket, lighted it, and sat silently while Dawn Flower placed cups in front of him and Lawson. At that moment the coffee pot began to bubble, and Rising Morning Star hurried to lift it from the stove and fill their cups.

"You're going to stay the night, I hope?" Lawson asked.

"That'll depend on how long it takes us to get our business done," Longarm answered.

"I still don't know what's brought you here, Marshal, but I suggest you stay," the agent said. "Whether you're going back to Kit Carson or south to Lamar, you couldn't reach either one by dark even if you started right now."

"I'll stay, then," Longarm said. "If it won't put you out any."

"Not at all." Turning to the woman, the agent said, "You heard. We'll have Marshal Long as our guest for supper. Now, let us talk in private for a few minutes." After the Cheyenne women had left, Lawson turned back to Longarm and said, "We don't have many visitors here. I guess you can tell that."

"It is a mite off any trail," Longarm said. "But I sorta looked for this place to be a lot bigger than it is."

"It was bigger not too many years ago," Lawson told him. "But the young people don't stay here any more. The two girls who look after me are an exception. And two or three of the older ones die every year."

"How many Cheyennes you got, all told?"

"Thirty-four."

"All of 'em here when Chivington pulled his dirty sneaking raid, I guess?"

Lawson nodded. "All but the girls and two or three of the older people."

"How come the Indian Bureau lets 'em stay?" Longarm asked. "Seems to me they'd've been moved down to the Indian Nation on the regular Cheyenne reservation."

"I think the Bureau was afraid to move them when they began moving all the tribes down to the reservations," Lawson said. "Of course, they did force most of the Cheyennes to move to the Nation, but those who survived the Chivington massacre refused to leave with the others. They said they wanted to stay here and look after the grave their tribesmen were buried in."

"Just one grave?"

Lawson nodded. "A mass burial."

"They probably figure this is medicine ground," Longarm said thoughtfully. "That being the case, I'd guess the Indian

26

Bureau was afraid to do anything that'd stir 'em up again."

"I've more or less come to the same conclusion, Marshal. I was assigned here six years ago, and my supervisor advised me to handle the Cheyennes carefully. He hinted that those who'd come back here to Sand Creek after the massacre weren't going to be forced to go with the rest of the tribe to the new reservation in the Nation."

"Then they've let things alone here pretty much, I take it."

"Maybe too much. There'll be a committee from Congress come out and look around every two or three years, and maybe once a year I'll see one of the Bureau men from Washington. That's about all the attention Sand Creek gets, though."

"I guess they still feed 'em, don't they?"

"Oh, yes. That's a funny thing. Somehow . . ." Lawson sat down, frowning, as though he'd forgotten what he'd been saying.

"You was just about to tell me something funny," Longarm prompted him. "Go ahead."

"Oh, yes. Well, the records in Washington haven't been kept up to date, so every three months the Bureau has a hundred steers driven here from the railroad."

"I'd say you got the best-fed reservation of any of 'em, then," Longarm said. "Last time I was in the Nation, none of the tribes was getting enough beef to get by on. But I sure didn't see many cattle when I rode up."

"Oh, I don't keep the surplus steers," Lawson said. "I've been—" He stopped short, an expression of panic growing on his face. "Oh, God, now I've ruined myself!"

Chapter 4

Longarm said nothing for a moment, but puffed his cheroot as he kept his eyes on Lawson. The agent was staring across the table at him. His panic-stricken look had changed to one of dismay.

Longarm said, "Son, you don't have to finish what you was going to say. I got a pretty good idea what you was about to let slip out, but it ain't my business. I got enough to do minding my own affairs, so I don't aim to butt into yours, and I don't owe the Indian Bureau a single solitary thing."

"You just stopped off here on your way through, then?"

"No, I was headed here, all right. I'm checking up on range stock. There's been a lot of hoof-and-mouth disease going around, and a bunch of steer-swindlers seems to be at the bottom of it. That's the case I'm on right now."

"I really did talk out of turn, then," Lawson said. "Look here, Marshal Long, I don't think I've done anything wrong—"

"Now, wait a minute," Longarm interrupted. "If you're worried about me reporting anything to the Indian Bureau, you can rest easy, unless it's something bad, like you been stealing government money."

"I don't get enough government money here to make it worthwhile to steal." The agent smiled. "But I guess you could call what I've been doing a kind of stealing."

"Maybe you better open up, now you've gone this far," Longarm suggested.

"Well..." Lawson hesitated for a moment, then squared his shoulders and said, "You act like the kind of man who'd see the reason for what I've been doing."

"All you can do is try me out." Longarm smiled.

"What I started to say is that the Bureau's records in Washington haven't been kept up since this reservation was set up after the massacre. There were over a hundred Cheyennes here at Sand Creek then, so the Bureau's been sending me enough

28

steers every quarter to provide beef for three times as many people as I've got here now."

"And you been selling the extra cattle to buy clothes and stuff," Longarm said. "I noticed the ones I saw when I rode up are pretty well dressed."

"Clothing and food, mostly." Lawson nodded. "They've got too much beef and not enough flour or sugar or salt, things like that. But I swear I haven't taken a penny for myself."

"I'll believe that," Longarm said promptly. "I've seen too many crooked men not to know a straight one when I meet him."

"You won't mention what I've told you to anybody in the Indian Bureau, will you? I haven't been selling the surplus steers to stockyards. The farmers around here are glad to buy one or two out of every shipment, and they keep quiet."

"I won't even remember you said anything when it comes time to make my report," Longarm promised. "But I do have to report on what your cattle look like—whether or not they're sick. Can we go take a look at 'em?"

"There aren't many from the last herd to look at, Marshal. The new herd's due in about a week. The only steers from the last bunch I've got left are a few I've been holding back from slaughtering, hoping they'd put on weight."

"You mean they're lean and scrawny and don't move around a lot? Look sorta sickly, maybe?"

"Yes. How did you know?" Lawson asked.

"Because that's how steers act when they got hoof-and-mouth disease. And the way it sounds, yours has got it. Let's go take that look right this minute!"

As the two men wove between the scattered shanties, walking toward the bank of the creek where the steers were grazing, Longarm asked, "Did you and the Cheyennes eat any of the sickly looking steers that were in that last herd?"

"Two or three. I had to let them start slaughtering the ones that didn't look so good. They were all we had left. It takes about two steers a week to keep the people fed. They're beef eaters, you know."

"All the Indians I ever seen eat lots of meat," Longarm agreed. "You said you ate some of the beef from them sickly steers, just like the Cheyennes did?"

"Of course," Lawson replied. "I eat just about the same things the Indians do, except I cook my meat longer than they

29

like it. They want theirs just about half done."

"You feel sick or puny after you ate it?"

"No. I don't recall that any of the Cheyennes did, either. Even if they did, they probably wouldn't have mentioned it to me. They still don't trust white men's medicine. If any of them had felt sick, they'd have gone to their own medicine woman."

They'd passed the last of the shanties by now. Just ahead Longarm could see where a shallow ditch had been dug to divert a flow of water from the creek into an old buffalo wallow. Around the little pond was a narrow belt of green grass on which three scrawny longhorn steers were grazing near the water's edge.

A shorthorn steer that had the white face of a Hereford but the coloration of a longhorn *grulla* stood almost belly-deep in the pond. It had the long legs and narrow body configuration of a longhorn as well as the telltale coloration in its coat. The two men stopped and Longarm peered at the hooves of the animals on the ground.

All four of the animals were thin, their coats rough, their ribs showing, and their hip bones protruding to form deep hollows between their rumps and their bellies. They looked at the men and after a few moments started moving slowly, almost lethargically, to the creek. They stopped on its banks and resumed their grazing on the sparser grass that sprouted there.

Longarm walked around the pond in a wide circle, giving the animals plenty of room. Lawson followed him. As far as Longarm could see, there were no sores or old scabs around their legs above their hooves. He looked at their mouths and muzzles and saw no signs of sores there, either.

He told Lawson, "The three on the ground look all right to me, but we better chase that steer outa the water so I can get a good look at its hooves."

Moving to the opposite side of the pond, Lawson scrabbled a stone out of the ground and tossed it at the steer in the pond, shouting and waving his arms at the animal. For a moment the steer turned and looked at the man with its opaque, white-rimmed eyes. Then it plodded to the bank, veering away from Longarm. He watched its hooves, dripping now, their ridges distinct and shining wet. The steer's *grulla* markings, dark dappled dots on a greyish-tan hide, extended down its legs. Peering closely, Longarm was not surprised to see a few red sores among the dots.

30

"Take a look at this critter's legs, right at the top of its hooves," he told Lawson, who'd walked back to join him. "The red spots look to me like the signs of hoof-and-mouth."

"I wouldn't know," the agent said, shaking his head. "I can see the sore spots, all right, but I wouldn't know what they mean. I've never seen a steer that's had hoof-and-mouth disease."

"Neither have I," Longarm said. "All I'm going by is what I been told it looks like." He turned his attention to the animal's muzzle, but saw no lesions in the white hair that surrounded its pale pink lips. He shook his head. "I just plain don't know about this one here. It don't act no different from the others, but it's sure got sores just above its hooves."

"What do you think I ought to do?" Lawson asked. "I was planning to slaughter one of these steers tomorrow."

"Now, a question like that sorta puts a man up shit creek without a paddle," Longarm said. "About all I can say is, if you and the Cheyennes ain't got sick by now from eating beef off the other steers outa this bunch, it oughta be safe to turn this one into beef, too."

"I might wait an extra day," the agent said thoughtfully. "If the places on its hooves don't look any worse late tomorrow or the next morning, I'll go ahead and slaughter it."

"That's about as sensible a thing to do as I can think of," Longarm agreed. He looked at the sun, dropping toward the horizon in the west. "Now, soon as I get my horse staked out for the night, I'll ask you to get out whatever waybills or Indian Bureau papers you got with that last shipment of cattle. I need to find out where they came from."

"I'm not sure what I have will be much help to you," the agent said. "I sign four or five forms when I get a consignment of steers, but I only get one to keep. But I think this last bunch came from a stockyard in Kansas City, and the shipper was called McKay or—no, I remember now, McCoy."

"Sam McCoy?"

"I think so, but I can't be sure. We'll look before supper, but I don't remember whether the shipper's name's on the one form I kept."

"Well, we've got plenty of time, I guess," Longarm said.

"We'd better do it before we sit down to supper," Lawson went on as they came in sight of the house. "I didn't mention it, but we eat early and go to bed early. Coal oil costs so much

31

these days that we can't afford to burn lamps any more than we have to. I imagine the girls will have started supper by now, so I'll get my files out and we'll have a look while they finish setting the table."

"Them Cheyenne girls seem like pretty smart young ladies," Longarm remarked as they walked. "They looking after their kin, or just staying here because they like it?"

"They came here to look after their grandparents," Lawson replied. "The old people died, and the girls stayed. I suppose they're still here because they really don't have anywhere else to go, except to the big reservation down in Indian Nation."

"I'd imagine this seems more like home to them."

"Yes, it does. I've taught them English and tried to get them accustomed to our ways." Lawson hesitated, then went on, "I hope you don't have any objection to them eating at the table with us this evening. They usually eat supper with me."

"It won't bother me a bit. This ain't the first time I've shared my victuals with an Indian, and it likely won't be the last."

"That's fine, then. I'm trying to equip them to find a place in the white world when the Bureau finally closes Sand Creek down."

They went into the office. Rising Morning Star and Dawn Flower were busy at the stove. Lawson stepped at once to the file case. After a moment of thumbing through the papers that crowded its top drawer he extracted a sheet of flimsy tissue and, after glancing at it, passed it to Longarm.

"I was right," he said. "The cattle came from the same cattle broker that provides most of our stock—McCoy, in Kansas City. But there's no clue where the steers came from."

"I can find that out from McCoy," Longarm said, memorizing the broker's address as he scanned the requisition form. He handed the flimsy back to Lawson. Now, I'll lead my horse down to the creek and stake it for the night, and call it a day."

"Fine. From the looks of things, we'll be ready to sit down by the time you get back," Lawson replied.

Supper had been eaten with the reddening rays of sunset staining the floor inside the door, and dusk was bringing the soft blue-grey that preceded darkness when they finished their meal. It seemed to Longarm that his presence at the table had been more embarrassing to Rising Morning Star and Dawn Flower than theirs was to him.

He'd noticed the girls watching him covertly several times, but they'd both been very quiet, almost shy, in spite of the efforts both he and Lawson made to draw them into conversation. They answered Longarm's questions and volunteered a few remarks of their own, but for the most part they ate in silence.

Puffing his after-dinner cheroot, Longarm looked out into the deepening dusk and said to Lawson, "That creek sure looks good to me. If you don't mind, I think I'm going to go take me a quick bath. I got so much sweat salt on me after all night on the train and all day in the saddle that I'll sleep a lot better if I rinse it away."

"There's a place where I bathe, upstream from the village," the agent said. "It's got a pebbled bottom, so you won't be bothered with sand in your boots if you put them at the edge of the creek where you can step into them when you come out of the water."

"That sounds good to me," Longarm replied. "How far up do I have to go?"

"It's just around the first upstream bend, about fifty yards. There's—" Lawson stopped and frowned and shook his head. "I don't guess there's any landmark I can give you to help you find it, Marshal. You'll just have to walk along the bank and watch the bottom till you come to it."

"I will be glad to go with Marshal Long and show him where the place is," Dawn Flower volunteered. "I know it well." She looked questioningly at her sister.

"Go." Rising Morning Star nodded. "I will wash the dishes. It is a good thing to help a guest."

Darkness was settling down fast when Dawn Flower indicated a rifle in the shining water of the creek after she and Longarm had walked a short distance around the bend that hid the settlement from view.

"There is the place," she said. "As John said, it has a pebbled bottom. You can feel it with your feet."

"Thanks a lot, Dawn Flower," Longarm said. "I'll be back in just a few minutes. All I want to do is rinse away the crust of salt I got all over me."

Dawn Flower turned away and started back. Longarm levered his boots off and placed them at the water's edge, then stepped back a pace and stripped quickly. He waded into the refreshingly cool water. The pebbles on the creekbed were no

33

bigger than a fingertip, and scrunched into hollows under the pressure of his bare feet.

Along the bar formed by the tiny stones the water was only a bit more than knee-deep when he reached the center of the stream. Longarm sat down; the water came almost to his armpits. He began splashing it over his back and shoulders. A flicker of motion in the dim light drew his eyes to the bank. Dawn Flower stood at the water's edge. She was reaching for the hem of her dress and as he watched she pulled the garment over her head. She wore nothing under it.

For a moment she stood motionless, letting the dress trail from her hand. There was enough light for Longarm to see her body clearly. When she'd pulled her dress over her head, the twin braids of her hair had fallen down her back, and her jutting breasts were very large, with dark rosettes that looked almost black in the failing light. Her hips spread generously from her narrow waist and between sturdy thighs the vee of her pubic brush formed a dark triangle.

"Would you be offended if I joined you, Marshal Long?" she asked.

Longarm had recovered quickly from his initial surprise. He knew the moral code of the Cheyennes gave a woman as much right as a man to choose a partner to whom she was attracted.

"I'd be more offended if you didn't," he told her.

Dawn Flower let the dress fall and waded to where he sat. She rubbed her palm over his moist shoulder, then knelt beside him and began lifting water in her cupped palms and letting it trickle over his shoulders. When she began rubbing his biceps and ribcage as the wager ran down, her warm hands were a sharp contrast to the cool water.

"It is good for a man and woman to be clean before they are together," she said, a smile of promise parting her full lips to show her flashing white teeth. "Why don't you help me as I am helping you?"

"That'll be my pleasure," Longarm assured her. He was already feeling a stirring in his groin.

Rising to his knees, Longarm began doing as Dawn Flower had suggested, cupping his palms, raising them filled with water, and letting it trickle down her shoulders while he followed the tiny cascade down her satin skin with his warm hands.

34

He could see her response to his ministrations almost at once. The golden skin over Dawn Flower's breasts pebbled gently, her rosettes puckered up and the tips emerged stiff and firm. He bent to kiss her breasts, his tongue travelling over their dark buds. Dawn Flower extended an exploring hand and found that Longarm's response was as positive as hers, though hidden under the water's surface.

"Oh, my!" she whispered. "You are bigger than most men, I think. Let us go quickly to shore! The water is cool, but I am burning inside!"

They waded to shore. Dawn Flower's dress had fallen on the hard-baked sand at the stream's edge, and she released Longarm for a moment to spread it out. Jackknifing her legs, she sank down on the dress, pulling Longarm to his knees as she settled down, her buttocks resting on her heels. She turned her face up to him, her full lips parted invitingly. They kissed, their tongues entwining as the caress lengthened.

In one swift move Dawn Flower unfolded her legs and dropped back. She still cradled Longarm's throbbing erection in her hands and he felt her warmth as she positioned him. He drove in with a strong, steady lunge. Dawn Flower gasped, a throaty sigh of pleasure, and clamped his hips between her thighs. Longarm began stroking, engulfed in her body's moist warmth, feeling the muscles of her legs grow taut each time she lifted her hips to meet his thrusts.

Dawn Flower's gasps became small bubbling moans, then rose to shrieks of pleasure as Longarm continued stroking. She locked her sturdy legs around him, trying to pull him deeper, as her cries mounted and became one crescendo of sound until her body stiffened and convulsed and then relaxed. Longarm did not move until Dawn Flower's climax passed and she lay quiet beneath him. He looked down at her face, passive now, her eyes closed. After a few moments she opened them and looked up at him.

"Did you feel nothing, Marshal Long?" she asked.

"Of course I did." Longarm smiled and added, "But ain't we well enough acquainted now for you to stop calling me that?"

"What should I call you, then?"

"I got a sorta nickname that people who know me well use. It's Longarm."

"Longarm," she repeated, trying the word. Then she smiled

35

broadly, showing her white teeth. "You are long other places, too. I feel the length of you in me, and it's good. It makes me want to feel it even deeper."

Longarm stirred and moved as though to start thrusting again, but Dawn Flower tightened her legs around him and stopped him from moving.

"No," she said. "Let me mount you this time."

"Sure, if that'd please you," he agreed.

Longarm lifted himself away from her and lay on his back. Dawn Flower crouched above him, straddling his hips. She made no move to take him in, but bent forward, trapping his erection between their bodies. After a few moments she started swaying her shoulders from side to side, brushing her tautly protruding tips against his moustache. Longarm tried to capture them in his mouth as she moved, but Dawn Flower's agile twists kept him from succeeding.

"You're just teasing me," he said, after he'd made several unsuccessful efforts.

"Yes," she agreed. "You are not eager enough yet."

After a few moments, while Dawn Flower continued to tease Longarm by keeping her nipples out of the grasp of his lips, he felt her hand slip between their bodies and close around his erection. She raised her hips to free him, spread her knees wider, and began rubbing Longarm's tip against the warm moisture of her crotch. Longarm lay quietly, but his nerves grew tauter as Dawn Flower continued to tantalize him with her body.

Soon he was straining up to meet her, trying to thrust into her, but always she evaded him. Just before Longarm reached up to grasp her hips and hold her motionless while he thrust into her, Dawn Flower raised herself on her knees and brought her torso up. With a swift motion of her hand she positioned Longarm and dropped with all her weight on his throbbing shaft. She pressed down on him with all her strength, twisting her hips, her head thrown back in ecstasy.

"*Ai-ee!*" she cried, her head turned to the stars, and followed her exclamation with a few words in Cheyenne which Longarm did not understand.

Bending forward once more, Longarm's face pressed into the warm fragrant valley between her full breasts. She began gyrating her hips, raising and lowering them in quick, uneven moves, her inner muscles clamping Longarm's shaft, squeezing

36

him with the firmness of a hand, all the time continuing her wild, spasmodic movements.

Dawn Flower's tantalizing had done what she intended it should. Longarm no longer tried to control their moves, but lay with tightening nerves as she twisted and bounced until he let himself go and jetted while Dawn Flower's cry of release rose to the stars. She raised her body, pushing down on his hips with its full weight, while Longarm throbbed and drained. After a long while her muscles, too, grew slack and she fell forward and lay gasping on his chest.

After their breathing had returned to normal, Dawn Flower whispered, "That is how Cheyenne women please their men. Did you like it, Longarm?"

"I sure did, Dawn Flower. I liked it so much I'm ready to do it all over again, if you've a mind to."

"I have a mind to do much more," she said softly. "So that when you go tomorrow you will take with you a long memory of the time when Dawn Flower opened to you in the night."

Chapter 5

With his rifle tucked into the crook of his elbow and his saddlebags slung over one shoulder, Longarm swung off the Katy flyer in the depot at Kansas City and started for the baggage car to pick up his saddle. The sight of a tall, broad-shouldered man wearing a wide-brimmed hat, a long black coat, and skintight cavalry boots and carrying a Winchester and saddlebags drew stares from the passengers waiting on the station platform; the days when rifles and saddlebags were part of almost every railroad passenger's luggage in the depot where the East became the West had ended ten years ago.

Longarm paid no attention to the turning heads he left behind him. He stopped at the open doors of the baggage car long enough for the baggagemaster to hand him the well-worn McClellan saddle and walked on through the station. The big clock on the wall told him it was almost noon, and he hurried to the rank of cabs that stood outside the station door.

"I need to stop off at the federal building for just a few minutes. Then I'll want you to take me to a good hotel," he told the hackman.

Settling back into the seat, Longarm batted his eyes to keep awake while the cab jolted over uneven brick paving and drew up a few minutes later at a slablike three-story greystone building. Longarm left his saddle and Winchester for the hackman to look after and went inside. On the second floor, he entered the door bearing the legend DEPARTMENT OF JUSTICE—U. S. MARSHAL, KANSAS DISTRICT.

Inside, Longarm felt at home at once. The office might have been patterned after the one in Denver. The only difference was that the outer office clerk was not a pink-cheeked young man but a bent and wizened greyhead far past the age of active duty.

"If the chief marshal ain't left for his lunch yet, I'd like to see him for a minute or two," Longarm told the clerk. "Name's Long, outa the Denver office."

38

"Chief Norman's usually ready to leave about this time, but I'll—" The clerk's jaw dropped. He stopped short and tilted his head to get a better look at Longarm through his thick spectacles. In a hushed voice he asked, "Would you be the Denver deputy they call Longarm?"

"Folks call me that sometimes," Longarm admitted.

"Well, you just stand right there. I'll tell the chief you're waiting." The deputy tapped on the door of the inner office, stuck his head inside for a moment, then turned, nodded, and said, "Chief Norman says to come in."

Longarm found Norman a striking contrast to Billy Vail. He was lean, pale, and cadaverous, with a heavy underslung jaw, and his desk was clear except for an inkwell and blotter pad. He did not get up or motion for Longarm to sit down, but stared at him with pursed lips.

"I hope you're going to tell me you just got to town, Long," Norman said. His voice had all the charm of two sheets of coarse sandpaper being rubbed together.

"I did," Longarm replied. "Stepped off the train maybe ten or fifteen minutes ago."

"Very interesting. And I suppose Vail knows you're here?"

"Not yet. Fact is, that's one reason why I stopped here the minute I got off the train. I need to send him a message on the private wire and let him know where I am."

"You said one reason," Norman grated. "What's the other?"

"Why, Rule Eleven, Chief Norman. The last time—"

"Don't remind me of the last time you were here, damn it!" Norman snapped. "You invaded my district without authorization, Long, and you broke every other rule in the book as well! You got the local police so mad they still won't cooperate with us, and you made *me* look like a goddamned fool!"

"Now, hold on a minute, Chief," Longarm said calmly when Norman sputtered to an incoherent stop. "Billy Vail explained to you why I had to do what I done then. Things was just busting too fast. I didn't have time to follow Rule Eleven and tell you I was here! And you got to admit I saved you as much trouble as I made. Them two fellows I had to kill was primed to give you a lot more trouble than I did."

Norman was silent while the flush of anger that had suffused his face faded. Then he said more calmly, "Yes, I'll have to give you that. Judge Claypool goes out of his way now to cooperate with us, and so does the federal attorney. And the

39

local police will stop sulking sooner or later."

"They generally do," Longarm agreed. "It's all right if I send my message to Billy Vail, then?"

"You have my permission, Long." Norman nodded.

"Thanks, Chief Norman," Longarm said. "I won't bother you again unless I got to."

"You're not asking for help on your case?"

"Not now," Longarm replied. "All I got in mind right this minute is to get that telegram off to Billy, then find me a hotel and sleep a while. I spent two days on horseback and a night and a day on the train getting here, so I think I got a nap due me."

As Longarm turned to go, Norman snapped, "Hold on, Long! You still haven't told me what kind of case has brought you into my district this time."

"Steer-swindling," Longarm replied.

Norman frowned. "That could mean a lot of things. Maybe you'd better give me some details."

"Trouble is, I ain't real clear yet myself about what's going on, so there ain't much I can tell you," Longarm said. "About all I got to start with is that it looks like some cattle brokers is mixing in stolen steers with ones they bought, and some of the stolen cattle are sick, but they're passing them off as being healthy."

"That's not a federal crime," Norman snorted. "How in hell did Vail get the marshal's force mixed up in something the local sheriffs ought to be handling?"

"Because some of them cattle's being sold to the Indian Bureau and the Army," Longarm replied evenly, holding back his anger at the criticism of his chief. "Last time I looked, it's a crime to rob or swindle the U. S. government, Chief Norman."

Norman was thoughtfully silent for a moment, pursing his rubbery lips. Then he said, "Well, I suppose that does change things. I guess you're here because of the stockyards, then?"

"That's right." Longarm nodded. "I've got evidence that a shipment of cattle to an Indian reservation over in Colorado was made by a cattle broker here."

"There are twenty or thirty cattle brokers on this side of the river," Norman said thoughtfully. "That many more on the Missouri side. It'll take you some time to check all of them."

"Oh, I figure to be here a while. That's why I need to send

a wire to Billy. If he gets anything fresh, he'll have to know where to reach me."

"You'll find the telegraph room in the basement," Norman said. "But let me tell you something before you get out of my office, Long. If you upset this town the way you did the last time you were here, I'm going to get your badge! Now, go on and send your wire."

With his message to Vail on the way, Longarm got back in the cab without revisiting Norman's office. He asked the driver, "What's a good hotel right close to here?"

"That'd depend on whether you're looking for a place that ain't a fleabag or whether you want to be close to the federal building, here," the man replied. "If it's an A number one hotel you're after, the closest one is the Stockman's House."

"I guess that's where you better take me, then."

When Longarm woke from his nap, there was still enough time left in the day for him to make a start on his case. Flagging a hack in front of the hotel, he started for the stockyards. When the brick pavement over which the hackney carriage rattled at a good clip gave out, and Longarm glanced out its small oval window, he saw that they were passing Rattlebone Hollow.

He'd never seen the place by daylight before, and he gazed at the shanties that sprawled in an unsightly blotch between the road and the riverfront. For a moment he wondered what had happened to Fern, the beautiful mulatto girl he'd saved from one of those shacks. Then the smell of the stockyards came to him on the breeze and he turned his thoughts back to the present case.

Fred Arnold, the stockyard manager, shook his head sadly when Longarm explained his problem. "You've got an impossible job, Marshal Long, if you came here expecting to get a list of all the shipments and the names of the shippers of the cattle that have passed through here in the past three or four months."

"You're bound to keep some kind of records, Mr. Arnold. Don't the cattle brokers and ranchers pay by the head for the herds you handle?"

"Yes, of course. We get paid for making up shipments and if a herd stays in the yards longer than overnight, we charge for pen rent and feed."

"Suppose somebody tries to cheat you on the count?"

Arnold shook his head. "They might get by with cheating once in a while, but not for long. My clerks balance receiving and shipping tallies every day. If they're too far apart, then we do start going out and counting the cattle."

"Well, I can follow you so far. And this is the place where most of the steers pass through, ain't it?"

"Here, or the yards on the Missouri side of the river. They don't handle as many, though. Not even Chicago handles as many cattle as we do."

"Is that a fact?"

"It certainly is. I don't think you realize how big this place is, Marshal Long. Come on with me. I'd like to show you something."

Longarm followed Arnold out of his office, along a short hall, and up a flight of stairs. They passed through a huge room where desks were lined up in solid rows. Men were sitting at them shuffling piles of statements, invoices, and waybills.

"I told you we checked the records carefully," Arnold commented as he led Longarm up a shorter flight of stairs at the end of the room. They emerged on a balustraded walkway on the roof; Arnold moved to one of the railings and waved a hand. "Just take a look, Marshal Long, and you'll get an idea of the size of this operation."

Within a crescent formed by a curve in the wide Missouri River, Longarm gazed out over a sea of stockpens, most of them packed with cattle. Railroad spurs extended between the largest of the pens, allowing cars to be unloaded into them directly. Men on horseback and on foot moved along the paths left between the rows. Around the perimeter of the pen-covered area, small buildings were dotted here and there. The stock-yards covered more ground, Longarm thought, than many towns in the West.

"That's quite a sight," he said to Arnold. "A man don't realize how big this place is till he gets this kind of look at it. How much ground does the yard cover, anyhow?"

"About fifteen square miles. We run along the river five miles, and the yards extend three miles from the bank."

"A fellow could walk himself to death in a place like this," Longarm said thoughtfully. "I see what you was talking about when you said it'd be a big job checking back in your records."

"I think I said impossible," Arnold replied. "Would you

42

like to guess how many head of cattle pass through these yards every day, Marshal Long?"

"I wouldn't have no ideas, but I'd imagine it's a lot."

"A lot is an understatement. More than thirty thousand head a day come in and go out."

Longarm whistled. "That's a right smart amount of beef on the hoof. I guess there's not many drove in from the range any more. Why, that many steers would make a herd fifty miles long!"

"Well, we still get a few driven in, the way herds were handled in the old days, but most of them come in by rail now. And they go out the same way. Those heading for the four biggest slaughterhouses here and across the river aren't even put in pens to be tallied. They stay right in the cattle cars."

"How do you keep tally, then?" Longarm asked.

"Waybills, shipping invoices. You got a look at the size of that job when we passed through the room downstairs."

"It'd help if I knew just how far you check out your shipments, Mr. Arnold," Longarm suggested.

"Very thoroughly, for our purposes. We bill the brokers or the ranchers, whoever owns the carload when it gets here, but as I told you, all our billing is done from the papers, not from counting cattle. And not all the papers show where the shipment actually began. Only the brokers would have that information."

Longarm lighted a cheroot while he debated about asking the question that had come to his mind. He didn't want to throw the stockyard manager into a panic, but Arnold didn't seem to be the panicky type, and he needed the information. He puffed the long, thin cigar into life before saying, "I can see you wouldn't be able to inspect every steer that comes in, but what would happen if there was a bunch of sick cattle hit here? Maybe some that had hoof-and-mouth disease?"

"We'd have no defense at all," Arnold said promptly. "The only thing we could do would be to close down. But that's not likely to happen in this day and age, Marshal. The ranchers and brokers know what a disaster that would be. None of them would be foolish enough or greedy enough to risk wiping out the cattle industry and putting themselves out of business by shipping diseased stock."

"That makes sense." Longarm nodded. "Well, I see why you told me my best bet's the brokers. I'll start with them."

43

"You're on the right track, Marshal Long. They're your best bet to get the information you're after," Arnold said.

"I guess you got a list of 'em I could use?"

"Yes. I can help you that much. We'll pick up a list as we go through the tally room on our way downstairs."

When the stockyard manager handed Longarm the list a clerk took from a file in the tally room, Longarm skimmed through the pages, and shook his head.

"I can see there's going to be more to this job than I figured," he said. "Now, while we're talking about brokers, there's one I'd like to ask you about special. He's the only cattle broker I know the name of."

"Who's that?" Arnold asked.

"His name's McCoy. His first name's Sam, but he calls himself the Real McCoy."

"Oh, sure." Arnold grinned. "Everybody knows the Real McCoy—or at least they know his name. You'll find him on the list I gave you. I suppose you know him, since you're asking about him?"

"Well, I run across him a time or two, a long while back, when I was cowhanding."

"Then you'll know his reputation, at least. Everybody says he's as honest a man as you'll ever hope to meet. He knows the cattle business, too."

"He's got an office someplace close by, I understand."

"Yes, right at the north edge of the yards. It's a little white building. His name's over the door, so you can't miss it."

Passing on Arnold's directions to the hackman, Longarm got to McCoy's office in a quarter of an hour. Telling the hackie to wait, he went into the building that had McCoy's name over the door. He didn't know quite what he'd been expecting, but the cattle broker's office was very much like that of the Indian agent at Sand Creek.

A partition with a door in its center divided the building into two rooms. A counter ran parallel to the wall on one side, and behind it there was an oak filing cabinet. In the space between the counter and the opposite wall there was a desk, but the chair behind it was unoccupied.

"Anybody here?" Longarm called.

When there was no response, he raised his voice and repeated the question. In a moment the door in the partition opened and a woman came in. As she passed through the door, the desk in the back office caught Longarm's eye; it was of fine walnut, ornately carved, with two front compartments which swung open.

He turned his attention to the woman who was coming through the office door. At first glance he decided she was probably the mousiest-looking female he'd ever encountered.

Her hair was a faded brown and in loose wisps from a tiny bun on the crown of her head. She had on large round silver-rimmed spectacles, the glass in them tinted a light green, so that he was unable to determine the color of her eyes. Her face was totally without color, her skin dead white, and her lips so pale that they blended into her skin and became invisible. Her nose was straight, thin, and pinched. She was wearing a tan-colored dress with a high neck. The dress fell from her shoulders to her ankles in a long, unbelted line.

"Yes, sir?" she said in a thin, high-pitched voice that was as colorless as the rest of her. "What can I do for you?"

"I'm looking for McCoy."

"Mr. McCoy isn't in town today. I'm Elsie Mae Glover. When he's not here he leaves me in charge of his office. Maybe I can help you if you want something?" Her voice trailed off into silence before she'd quite finished the question.

"I guess I better find out if I got the right McCoy before I go to plaguing you with questions, miss," Longarm said. "This McCoy you work for—is he the one calls himself the Real McCoy?"

"Yes, he does, but it's a kind of joke, of course."

"His first name's Sam, ain't it?"

She nodded, then almost whispered, "Samuel."

"You look for him to get back any time soon?"

Shaking her head, Elsie Mae said, "I don't know. You see, Mr. McCoy isn't here very often any more. He sends me a wire every week or so to let me know where he is, but he hasn't been in the office for more than a month now."

"Mind telling me where he is now?"

"I had a wire from him early this week from Laramie, that's up in Wyoming Territory—"

"Yes, I know," Longarm interrupted. "He didn't happen to say how long he'd be there, did he? Or where he was stopping?"

"Oh, Mr. McCoy never mentions things like that. I just wire him in care of the station agent. If he has anything special he wants me to do, something he's gotten a letter about, he'll wire

45

back right away. Most of the time he doesn't bother."

"You mean you look after all his business?"

"While he's away, I do. I answer his mail and pay whatever bills have come in. And whatever money's come in, I deposit in the bank."

"I guess you're—" Longarm stopped quickly and changed the phrase that was in his mind. "I guess you're the one I better talk to, then. My name's Long, Custis Long, and I'm a deputy United States marshal outa Denver."

"Oh, Mr. McCoy was there about six weeks ago. It's too bad you didn't see him then."

"Six weeks ago, I didn't know I wanted to see him, Miss— Miss Glover, didn't you say?"

She nodded and said, "Elsie Mae Glover. I hope Mr. McCoy's not in any trouble. I know he does a lot of business with the government, selling cattle to the Indian reservations and to the Army, and to the new prison up at Leavenworth."

"As far as I know now, Miss Glover, Mr. McCoy's not in any trouble at all," Longarm assured her. "Everybody who knows him says he's about as honest a man as there is going."

"You don't know him yourself, then?"

"Oh, I run across him a time or two, but that's been a lot of years ago. I misdoubt I'd recognize him if he was to walk in that door right now."

"Well, there isn't much chance he'll do that," Elsie said, managing a small smile. "You don't mind telling me why you want to see him, do you?"

"Why, it ain't no secret. The reason I'm here is, it seems Mr. McCoy shipped a little bunch of steers over to the Sand Creek Indian Reservation in Colorado three months or so ago. I got a copy of the waybill, if that'll help any."

"What did you want to know, Marshal Long?"

"Mainly, where he got them steers he shipped to Sand Creek."

"Why, it shouldn't be too hard for me to look that up."

"I'll be right obliged if you'll do it, then."

"You said you have the waybill?" Elsie Mae held out her hand. "I'll need it to compare with our file records."

"I've only got this one copy of it, and it ain't in too good shape," Longarm said, taking out the waybill he'd gotten at Sand Creek and showing it to her.

She glanced at the date on the bill and frowned. "This is almost three months old, Marshal. It'll take me a little time to go through my files to get the information you want, and I can't do it in what's left of the day. If you'd like to leave the waybill with me—"

"I usually wouldn't mind at all, but I need to save it if it has to be used in court as evidence. You reckon you could make yourself a copy of it?"

"Of course, Marshal." She took the waybill from Longarm and moved to the desk where she started making a copy of it. She'd written only the date and number when she looked up and said, "I can't help worrying about the reason you're looking for Mr. McCoy, Marshal. From what you said about this being used as evidence—"

"In this business I'm in, that's the way we look at just about everything, Miss Glover. Don't let it bother you."

"Well, if you say so." She handed the waybill back to Longarm. "You'll be stopping in tomorrow, then? I suppose you're staying in town?"

"At the Stockman's House," Longarm replied. "And I'll be back tomorrow for sure. I got to do a lot more more poking around the stockyards before my case gets to the point where I can start making some arrests."

Chapter 6

At the Stockman's House, Longarm dismissed the hack and headed for the bar. He hadn't yet picked up a bottle of rye to take to his room, he'd eaten lunch later than was his habit, and it was still too early for dinner.

At that hour of the evening the bar was busy. Most of the small tables which stood along the walls were unoccupied, but there was a solid line of men at the bar. The two barkeeps on duty were busy filling and refilling glasses and clearing away those left by patrons who'd stopped in for a single drink.

When Longarm finally found a space to step into, he told the barkeep, "Just reach right behind you and pass me that bottle of Tom Moore Maryland rye and a glass. I'll go over and set down at one of them tables and won't bother you till I get ready to go in the dining room and get my supper."

"No chaser?" the barkeep asked as he placed the bottle and a shotglass in front of Longarm.

"You know what they say," Longarm replied. He laid two silver dollars on the polished mahogany. "What's the use of starting a fire if you're going to douse it with water before it gets going good?"

"They do say that," the aproned barkeep agreed. He looked at Longarm closely. "Aren't you stopping here at the hotel?" When Longarm nodded he shoved the cartwheels back to him. "Then your drinks before supper are on the house."

"Well, now, that's right nice," Longarm said. "Thanks."

Picking up the shotglass and the bottle of rye, he moved to one of the empty tables, found one where he could look into the lobby, and lighted a cheroot before pouring his first drink. The well-aged liquor slid down his throat with a pleasant pungency, and as he began to relax his mind turned to what he'd found out during the day.

You sure as hell ain't made much headway, old son, he told himself. *Seems like the cattle business has got to such a size now that nobody knows what anybody else is doing any more. Used to be, a man could read a brand on a steer and know the name of the man that owned the ranch it come from, generally know him, too, but that ain't the way it is any longer.*

Why, just look at that stockyard, his thoughts ran on. *It's so big and sprawled-out and there's so many steers in it a man'd walk himself to death trying to find sick critters in them pens. And that Arnold ain't about to admit there's much chance of having a case of hoof-and-mouth slip by him, even if he ain't watching for it. If he was to think about it too much, he'd be so spooked all the time he couldn't tend to business.*

While thinking about the case, Longarm watched the lobby. It was astir with new arrivals checking in at the desk, men crossing it to come to the bar, men escorting women into the dining room, which opened off the rear of the lobby at right angles to the bar. He saw only one or two family groups that included children, and there had been no unescorted women in the lobby until a stunning blonde passed through.

She was perhaps a year or two under thirty, he thought after he'd watched her for a moment. She wore her golden hair dressed high on top of her head, and her face was a study in creamy ivory and blushing pink. Her eyes were sapphire-blue, her lips full and crimson under a daintily aquiline nose. She wore a dinner dress of watered silk in a sapphire hue a shade deeper than her eyes. The dress was cut low and her ostrich-feather boa did not hide the beginning of the cleft between her swelling breasts. She glided rather than walked, and paid no attention to the admiring looks of the men who turned to watch her.

As he observed her slow, stately progress across the lobby, Longarm frowned. There'd been something about her that stirred a chord in his memory at his first glance, but after watching her for a moment he was positive that if he'd seen her before he would remember where and when.

For a moment, he tagged her as a type he'd seen in other hotels similar to the Stockman's, a high-class prostitute, though it was early for ladies of the evening to be abroad. The way she studiously ignored the frankly inviting looks of several of the unattached men dispelled that notion; she was obviously at home in the lobby of the best hotel in Kansas City, and while her dress was flamboyant, it was not flashy.

Longarm watched her with appreciation, but without recalling her face, until she disappeared into the dining room. Then he lighted a fresh cheroot and refilled his glass. However, his train of thought had been interrupted. His mind was no longer on his case and on the stockyards. He finished the drink he'd poured a few moments earlier and went into the dining room.

Only one of the smaller tables was unoccupied. It stood near the door. The dining-room steward looked at it and said, "If you'd rather wait for a few minutes, I'm sure there'll be a better table I can give you."

"Why, I ain't all that particular," Longarm told him. "I'd as soon have that one as any."

"Very good, sir. I'll have a waiter here to take your order in just a few minutes."

By the time the waiter arrived, Longarm had already found that by moving his chair a short distance around the table he could get a clear view of the blonde at the opposite side of the room. Ignoring the menu, he ordered his favorite dinner: a thin steak cooked well-done and fried potatoes. He discovered that his order included soup, a salad, and coffee, and swallowed a few spoonsful of the soup while waiting for the steak to arrive.

As he sipped the soup, he covertly watched the woman who'd attracted his attention. The longer he looked, the less certain he grew that he'd seen her before. By the time his steak was served he'd dismissed his first impression as being the result of a chance likeness to someone else he'd seen in his travels, someone with whom she shared a resemblance as a type. After he'd reached that somewhat unsatisfactory conclusion, Longarm looked less often at the woman and concentrated on his meal.

He was on his second cup of after-dinner coffee when the woman across the dining room rose to leave. He glanced at her idly, only academically interested now, his mind back on his case and what he'd do tomorrow. She'd almost reached the dining-room door and Longarm was turning away when a tall, bulky man wearing a gambler's checked suit and grey derby hat came in. His scarred face and beetling brows gave him the appearance of a thug. He stopped in front of the woman, barring her way.

"Pearl!" the newcomer exclaimed. "Pearlie Brophy! I never thought I'd run into you here in Kansas City!"

"I'm afraid you've mistaken me for someone else," the woman said coldly.

"Not a chance, Pearl!" the man replied. "Why, you remember me! Frank Grogan! You ain't forgot the good times we had in Dodge City in the old days, have you, Pearl?"

"I've never been to Dodge City, and my name isn't Pearl Brophy," she told him. "Now, please step aside and let me pass."

"No, sir!" Grogan said. "I just blew in and I'm looking for company to spend the evening with. You're just what I need!"

By this time the eyes of everyone in the restaurant had turned toward the pair standing in the door. The woman was looking from one side to the other, her face drawn in fear and distaste. Longarm jumped to his feet and was moving toward them when Grogan grabbed the woman's wrist and started tugging her toward the door.

"You heard the lady say you made a mistake," Longarm said. He spoke just a bit louder than a whisper, but his low-pitched voice held a touch of steel.

"Please—" the woman began.

"Listen, mister, this is between Pearl and me. It's not any business of yours," Grogan told Longarm. "You just butt out and let us settle things between ourselves."

"I'll give you just two seconds to let go of that lady's arm and make yourself scarce," Longarm said coldly.

"Nobody bluffs Frank Grogan! Now do what I told you and butt out!"

Grogan moved his free hand toward the opening of his coat, and before he could complete his move Longarm's Colt was in his hand and Grogan found himself staring into its blue steel muzzle.

For a moment Grogan was silent. Then he said, "Now, hold on here, mister!" He released the woman's hand and spread his arms out. "I'm not moving, see? Just don't get your finger too heavy on the trigger!"

"Please," the woman said to Longarm in a half-whisper. "I'm all right now. Let him go. I don't want anyone hurt or killed."

Longarm's free hand had already disappeared under the lapel of Grogan's coat. He brought it out, holding a stubby .32 tip-barrel revolver.

51

"I wasn't going to shoot!" Grogan said quickly. "Just let me go, now. I won't make any more fuss."

"Do let him go, please!" the woman said. "This is too embarrassing to endure!"

Longarm holstered his Colt. He broke the .32 and upended the barrel to let its cartridges fall from the cylinder into his hand. He gave the pistol to Grogan.

"Now, git!" he said sharply. "If I see you again I'll know you've got a gun, and I won't wait for you to start to draw it. You understand me?"

"Yes, sure!" Grogan was already retreating as he spoke, scurrying across the lobby.

"Please, can we get out of here?" the woman said. "I've never been so embarrassed in my life!"

"All we got to do is step out of the dining room," Longarm told her.

He offered her his arm. She laid her hand on his wrist and they walked out into the lobby, but a group of half a dozen men who'd apparently witnessed the incident through the open double doors of the dining room stood in a half-circle just outside.

Longarm glanced around and saw a chair in the corner between the doors to the dining room and the entrance to the bar. The chair was almost hidden by the low-spreading leaves of a pair of potted palms. He led her to the chair and stood in front of her, his back to the lobby, shielding her from the curious.

"Isn't there anywhere we can go?" the woman asked. "Those people are staring at me, and the ones in the dining room will be coming out soon. I— I just feel uncomfortable, with all those eyes watching me!"

"I'm afraid there ain't anyplace else to go," Longarm said. "You sure wouldn't want to go back in the dining room, and ladies ain't allowed in the bar."

"This is one time I wish we were!" she said fervently. "I'd like nothing better right now than a glass of sherry or a sip of champagne, to settle my nerves."

"I seen you come in through the lobby, so I don't suppose you're staying here at the hotel," Longarm said.

"No, I just came here for dinner. I often do on the evenings when my maid has her day off." She looked up at Longarm and asked, "Are you a guest in the hotel?"

"Well, as a matter of fact, I am, but—"

She didn't let him finish, but burst in to say, "Please. If you wouldn't mind letting me stay in your room until all the fuss out here dies down, I'd be very grateful."

"I didn't ask you, because I didn't want you to think I was acting like that masher who was trying to get fresh with you, but since it's you done the asking, I'd be happy to let you use my room." Longarm fished the key out of his vest pocket. "Here you are. The number's on the tag. I'll just set in the bar and have a drink while you get over being nervous."

She took the key, looked at it for a moment, then looked up and said, "No. I couldn't take advantage of you, Mr.— Mr.—"

"Long, ma'am. Custis Long. From Denver."

"My name is Charlene Hart, Mr. Long, and I'm very grateful to you for saving me from what was beginning to be a very ugly little scene," she told him.

"No thanks needed, Mrs. Hart."

"Miss," she said quickly. "Miss Hart. And I don't feel right about depriving you of your comfort. I imagine you've been travelling, and would like to rest in your room."

"Now, don't you worry about me," Longarm said.

"I'll risk you thinking that I'm forward, Mr. Long. I meant what I said about wanting a sip of something to settle my nerves. If you'd care to join me, I'd like to treat you to a glass of champagne."

"Why, I'd be right proud to sit with you for a while. But I never have let a lady buy my drinks yet, and I don't care all that much for champagne. Now, you take the key and go on up to my room. I'll step into the bar—"

Charlene interrupted him. "No. As you men say, the drinks are on me."

"I ain't listening to you." Longarm smiled. "You go on. I'll give you a few minutes to get your nerves composed, and then I'll bring up our drinks."

A few minutes later, a bottle of Tom Moore protruding from a side pocket of his coat, carrying a bottle of champagne and a stemmed glass in one hand, Longarm tapped discreetly on the door of his room. Charlene Hart opened it at once, and when Longarm was inside the room, she closed and relocked the door.

"You feel better now, Miss Hart?" Longarm asked, placing

53

the champagne and glass on the bureau and taking the bottle of Tom Moore from his pocket.

"Much better." She smiled.

Charlene had taken off her ostrich-feather boa and turned up one of the gaslights that bracketed the bureau. The smooth ivory of her neck and upper chest shone in the soft glow, and from the aroma of perfume that hung heavily in the air, Longarm deduced that she'd also done a bit of primping. He picked up the champagne and began stripping the foil from the cork.

"You better have a glass of this while it's still good and cold," he told Charlene as he untwisted the cage and began working the cork from the bottle. "The barkeep promised he'd have a bellhop set a bucket of ice outside the door, but no telling how long it'll be before he gets here."

"My goodness!" she said, looking at the champagne. "I can't drink that whole bottle by myself, Mr. Long. You'll have to help me."

"There ain't much champagne in a bottle." Longarm smiled as the cork popped from the bottle and a wisp of vapor followed it. "Like I told you, it don't have enough bite for me."

He filled the hollow-stemmed champagne glass and handed it to her, then picked up the bottle of Tom Moore and thudded its base hard on the heel of one hand. The rim of the cork slid up and he clamped his strong teeth on it and yanked the cork free.

"This is what I enjoy," he said, pouring an inch or so of the whiskey into a tumbler he took from the tray on the dresser.

"Now for my toast," Charlene said, raising her glass. "To you, Mr. Long, with all my thanks for coming to my rescue."

After he'd tossed off half his whiskey and Charlene had drained her glass, Longarm said, "I don't take no credit for helping you out, Miss Hart. It's a pretty poor sorta man that won't step up when a lady's in trouble."

"That terrible man!" she said. "And with a gun, too!" She held out her glass and Longarm picked up the champagne bottle to refill it. While he was pouring, she said, "I haven't had a chance to ask you something I'm curious about, Mr. Long. Do all the men in Denver carry guns? Because the men here in Kansas City generally don't."

"Well, I got a reason to," Longarm replied, tilting the bottle of rye to replenish his own drink. "I'm a deputy U. S. marshal."

"Really? And are you here looking for some desperate law-breaker?"

"My case ain't far enough along for me to know who I'm looking for yet," Longarm replied. "So I don't rightly know what kind of man I'm after." He raised his glass. "But you better enjoy your champagne before it gets warm and goes flat."

"It tastes delicious, and it's just what I need," Charlene said, sipping. She went on, "I don't know anything about guns, Marshal Long, but the one you carry looks a lot more dangerous than the little one that man tried to draw. Why is that?"

"It's a real gun. His wasn't much better'n a toy."

"Would you mind letting me look at yours? To tell you the truth, it fascinated me."

Longarm drew his Colt. Charlene ran her fingers along its blued steel barrel and peered curiously at the grey lead noses of the cartridges in the cylinder.

"Could I hold it a minute?" she asked.

"Why, sure. But if you don't know nothing about guns, I'll just play safe and unload it," Longarm replied. He pulled the hammer to half-cock and opened the loading gate, then rotated the cylinder and slid the cartridges out. Closing the gate, he handed her the Colt.

"My, goodness, it's heavy!" she said, almost dropping the weapon. "I don't think I could hold it up and aim it." She lifted the revolver to eye level, but it wobbled in her hand.

"You need to use both hands with a heavy gun like a .44," Longarm said. Charlene tried to grasp the butt with both hands, but the grip was too large for her to close her left hand over the right. He said, "Not like that. Here, wait till I get my coat off so it won't be in the way, and I'll show you."

Sliding his arms from the sleeves, Longarm hung his coat over the back of a chair. His arm brushed against his vest and the derringer in its bottom pocket. Turning his back to Charlene, he took his watch from the opposite pocket and slid it in with the derringer, removed his vest, and hung it over the coat.

Stepping behind Charlene, Longarm placed her left hand on her right wrist, and lifted her arms. She tried to extend them full-length, but he pulled them back, bending her elbows. Then he raised her hands to bring the Colt up to eye level. Each time she moved, a wave of her sensuous perfume swept into Long-

55

arm's nostrils. He ignored the distraction as best he could and got her arms and hands properly positioned.

"Oh, yes," she said. "I see what you mean. This is much better. But how do I aim it?"

"First you got to relax," Longarm told her. "If you try to hold a gun too tight, you'll freeze up and that'll make the muzzle wobbly."

Charlene relaxed so completely when Longarm pulled her wrists back that he suddenly found himself holding her in a close embrace. His hands were still on hers, but his forearms were pressing against the billowing softness of her breasts and her back was pushing against him from shoulders to knees. Her full buttocks were plastered against Longarm's crotch so tightly that he could feel the warmth radiating from them. He felt himself becoming erect.

Longarm followed his instincts. He bent his head and began kissing Charlene in the soft perfumed hollow between her neck and shoulder. She shuddered and sighed and snuggled closer to him. He heard the Colt thud to the floor when she released it and then twisted her wrists out of the grasp of his hands. Longarm felt her hand on his head, pulling his lips down more firmly onto the warm flesh of her shoulder.

"Oh, my!" she whispered. "This is making me giddier than the champagne!"

Longarm wanted to answer, but Charlene's hand was pressing his mouth to her shoulder. His hands were free now, and he cradled her breasts firmly in his palms. Charlene turned his head and guided his lips up her neck. Longarm slid his tongue between his lips and let its tip trail in a moist caress along her soft skin.

Her sighs grew louder, and she started rubbing her buttocks gently over the bulge that was swelling in his crotch. After a moment, the gentle writhing was not enough to satisfy her. She slid her free hand between them and began fingering Longarm's burgeoning erection. He felt her fingers move to the buttons of his fly and open them, and he slipped his hands into the low-cut neck of her dress until his fingers found her breasts' pebbled centers and began caressing them.

Charlene shuddered as he touched the tips that stood firm in the centers of her rosettes. She had succeeded in opening his fly and freeing his erection now. Quickly she lifted her skirt and pulled down the elastic waist of her pantalettes. With frantic haste she guided Longarm between her thighs and pressed them together around his throbbing erection.

Neither of them had spoken since the gun demonstration had escalated into an intimate embrace. Now Charlene whispered, "If you won't say it, I will. Take me to bed, Marshal Long!"

Chapter 7

"Just as soon as we can get our clothes off," Longarm said.

"I'll help you, and you help me," Charlene panted. "Undo the hook-eyes on my dress. You can do that faster than I can."

Longarm's fingers fumbled for a moment with the fasteners at the back of her dress before he found the easiest way to get them apart. Then he quickly undid them down to the waist. Charlene stepped away from him and with a single shrug and push shed her dress, underskirts, and pantalettes. For a moment Longarm looked at her. She was naked from the waist down, clad only in her thin lawn camisole, her skin a shade deeper than the sheer white fabric, the gold of her pubic brush glistening between swelling thighs.

Charlene's eyes were fixed on Longarm as she started to unbutton her camisole. With both arms behind her back as she worked the buttons free, her full breasts strained against the translucent fabric. Their rosettes showed as dark circles accented by the peaks pushing like pointing fingers from the centers.

She watched Longarm lever off his boots and unbutton his shirt and balbriggans. He peeled off his trousers, then shrugged out of the shirt and undersuit, dropping them in a tangled heap on top of the boots. Charlene reached the last button of the camisole and let it fall to the floor. Longarm stepped across the short span that parted them, and she melted into his arms.

They kissed for the first time, their bodies pressed close. Charlene's mouth opened to the thrusting of Longarm's tongue, her voluptuous body soft and warm against him. She slid one hand down his ribs and hips and he felt her fingers close on his jutting shaft. Without breaking their kiss, Longarm lifted her and carried her to the bed.

When he started to put her down, Charlene twisted to land on her back on the bed. She kept her arms locked around Longarm's neck and pulled him down on top of her. Spreading her legs, she raised them high and crossed her ankles, capturing

Longarm's hips between the warm, soft pillars of her thighs. Longarm lunged futilely once or twice before Charlene's arm darted down and her eager hand positioned him.

"Now," she panted. "Now drive in, Marshal Long!"

Longarm drove. Charlene brought up her hips to meet his lunges, and little cries of ecstasy bubbled from her throat. Her hands wandered over Longarm's chest and back, and soon her voluptuous body began writhing, squirming, and tossing as he stroked steadily. Her ecstatic bubbling cries became a single vibrating note that grew higher and higher in pitch until it was a single low-pitched scream. The rhythmic heaving of her body broke and became a series of spasmodic jerks. Her screams faded and she looked up smiling at Longarm.

"That was wonderful," she gasped. "But don't stop! Don't stop even if I beg you to!"

"I ain't about to stop," Longarm promised. "Not for a long time, anyhow."

Charlene's sapphire-blue eyes were closed now, her eyelids squeezed tight. Her lips were twisting as though she was trying to talk, to tell Longarm something, but only inarticulate gasps came from her throat. Longarm lunged harder and faster and her gasps grew shrill once more, then broke and began again, and her hips heaved up in a series of jerks.

She screamed, short piercing bursts of sound, then suddenly she grew limp. Her body sagged, trembling. Longarm eased the vigor of his thrusts and finally stopped moving, holding himself pressed firmly against her, his shaft fully buried. Charleen's climactic shudders seized her at longer intervals, then stopped altogether. At last her face grew calm and she opened her eyes and looked up at him.

"You stopped, even after I asked you not to," she said accusingly.

"Just for a minute, to let you get your breath."

"Don't wait for me to breathe! Go on!" Charlene urged. "I'm feeling better than I've ever felt before!"

Longarm began stroking again, strong, slow lunges that took a long time to complete. Charlene began responding sooner than he'd expected her to. She rolled her hips from side to side for a few moments. Then suddenly she gasped and locked her legs around Longarm's hips again and began writhing and heaving into another climax. This time Longarm did not stop when she reached her spasm, but carried her through it while she

59

shrieked and sobbed and her body went limp.

Even then he did not ease up. He was building to his own climax and drove harder than before. Charlene began sobbing after a few minutes, but her sobs faded as Longarm continued to drive into her with hard, steady thrusts. Suddenly she came to life and for the next few minutes the fierce, rolling heaving of her hips matched the vigor of his pounding.

Longarm waited until the trembling of her body told him she was once more nearing her brink. He no longer held back, but speeded up, and felt his orgasmic urge beginning. Charlene's hips were jerking spastically again, and her face was twisted into a grimace of ecstatic agony when Longarm reached his peak. He held on for a few more lunging thrusts, and when Charlene began shrieking at the uttermost limits of her own spasm, Longarm released himself and jetted while he slowed the tempo of his thrusts, and then stopped when he felt Charlene's tense body relax and grow soft.

"I guess you had to stop sometime," she sighed.

"Most men do."

"You're not like most men, Marshal Long." Charlene frowned and asked, "What did you tell me your first name is? Curtis?"

"It's Custis. But if you'd like to, I got a sorta nickname you can call me by."

"What's that?"

"Longarm."

"Yes. I like that better than Custis."

"So do I." Longarm got off the bed and started for the bureau. "I guess this champagne's still cold, if you want some more. I'm going to finish my drink."

"You did me a lot more good than a whole case of champagne," Charlene said. "And I'm sure you're not through yet."

"That depends on you, Charlene."

"I'll have another glass of champagne while you finish your drink. Will you be ready then to start again?"

"Why, sure I will. I'll be ready whenever you are."

An authoritative knocking on the hotel-room door brought Longarm instantly out of a sound sleep. Sunshine was glowing on the shades of the windows of the wall beside the bed, and Longarm blinked, realizing he'd slept later than usual. The knocking was repeated, more insistently this time. He reached for the butt of his Colt, hanging in its holster from the bedpost where he'd put it last night after reloading the revolver when Charlene had finally left. Naked, he padded across the carpet to the door, and stood against the wall beside it.

"Who is it?" he called.

"Deputy Deal, Long. The chief sent me over with a wire you got from Chief Vail."

Longarm unlocked the door and opened it a crack. "Just slip the message in, Deal. And say thanks to Chief Norman for me."

Unfolding the strip of thin flimsy paper as he walked over to the bureau, he pulled the cork from the bottle of Tom Moore and tilted the bottle to his lips. As he swallowed his morning eye-opener and touched a match to the day's first cheroot, Longarm read the telegram from Vail. It was brief and to the point:

ARMY REPORTS SHIPMENT SICK CATTLE
FT. GIBSON, INDIAN TERRITORY

Longarm read the message a second time, then laid it on the bureau and began assembling his clothing. His balbriggans, shirt and trousers still lay in a heap on top of his boots where he'd dropped them the evening before. He hadn't bothered to pick them up after Charlene had left in the grey of the beginning dawn.

He untangled the garments and dressed, puffing his cheroot to quiet the rumblings of his stomach that were reminding him it was long past his regular breakfast time. While he dressed, Longarm searched his memory, recalling the geography of the Indian Nation and the location of the few outposts the Army still maintained there.

Now, let's see, old son. Fort Gibson, that'd be over in the east part of the Nation, someplace along the Arkansas. It ain't more'n a hop-skip-and-jump from here, the Katy runs down that way now, so it won't be such a much of a trip, couple of hundred miles on the train, give or take a bit. And it'd be a good idea to keep Billy Vail off of your back, and get started just as fast as you can sweep up the corners of what you got going here.

After he'd had his usual ham-and-eggs breakfast at the hotel, Longarm took a hack to the MK&T ticket office and found that he could get a southbound train in the early afternoon. He glanced at the big Railroad Regulator clock on the ticket-office wall, and hurried back to the waiting hack. He reached McCoy's office at the stockyards a half-hour before noon. Elsie Mae Glover looked up from the papers on her desk when he came in.

"Oh, Marshal Long," she said in her small, high-pitched voice. She peered at him through the green-tinted spectacles that made her eyes look totally blank. "I found out about that shipment of steers to Colorado."

"That's fine. Where'd they come from?"

"Why, they were the overage out of two herds Mr. McCoy had just gotten in from Fort Worth. That's in—"

"Texas," he interrupted. "I guess you know the name of whoever it was he bought 'em from?"

"Both the herds he bought came from Texas ranches, and when he had to fill that little order for the Indian reservation, he just took what he needed from both herds."

"That sure ain't much help." Longarm frowned. "I don't guess there'd be any way except the brands to tell which steers come from where, would there?"

Elsie Mae shook her head. "I'm afraid there wouldn't. It was a long time ago, you know."

"Well, you better give me the names of the ranch owners, and maybe I can find out from them. I don't know as that'll help much, but it's more'n I got to go on now. Worse comes to worst, I guess I can check out both of 'em."

"Oh, my!" Elsie Mae exclaimed. "All I have is the brands of the ranches. I don't know who the owners are, or where exactly they are located."

"You oughta have it in your files someplace."

"It's not in the files there." She gestured toward the oak cabinets, frowning, then her face brightened and she said, "I can look in Mr. McCoy's file in his desk. They might be in there. If you want to wait a minute, I'll go in his office and look."

"I'd take it as a favor, Miss Glover."

Longarm took out a cigar and lighted it as Elsie Mae went to the door in the rear wall. He got a quick glimpse of McCoy's office as she opened the door, a passing glance at a massive desk and chair before the door closed.

Elsie Mae returned in a few moments, carrying two or three

62

sheets of paper. As she approached her desk, moving with short mincing steps, the stray wisps of faded brown hair waving, her ankle-length dress falling in a straight line from shoulders to hem, he could not keep from contrasting her with Charlene. He wondered idly what Elsie Mae might look like without the dress and decided he'd be better off not knowing.

"I'm sorry, Marshal," she said. "I didn't find anything in there except the brands of those ranches."

"Well, you better tell me what they are, then," Longarm told her. "I can find out about the ranches, if I need to."

"One is the Rocking Chair and the other one is—well, I guess it's Keyhole. At least, that's what it looks like to me."

Longarm stepped over to look at the sheet of paper she was holding. She handed it to him and he glanced quickly at the pencilled delivery receipt for the herd. It was signed with the initials "H. R." and a crude sketch of a keyhole, drawn with the same blunt pencil lead.

"That's what it is, all right," he nodded. "You sure you ain't got any more ideas about where to find them names I need?"

"My goodness, no!" she said. Her shrill, high voice grated on Longarm's ear, and he returned the receipt to her and stepped away.

"Well, I do thank you for your trouble, Miss Glover," he said. "I don't guess you got any more idea today than you did yesterday about where I can find McCoy?"

"I'm afraid not. I might hear from him before the end of the week, if you'd like to stop by in a few days."

"I ain't going to be here that long," he said. "Matter of fact, I'll be taking a train south in a few hours."

"My goodness, you haven't been here very long! Did you find out all you needed to know?"

"I picked up a lead or two," Longarm replied. "And now I got another one to follow, so I got to head down to the Indian Nation. I still need to talk to your boss, but I'll catch up with him sooner or later."

Dawn was still almost three hours away when Longarm stepped off the train in a misty drizzle at the Fort Gibson siding. Except for the dim lights that spilled from the windows of the passenger coaches and the yellow fanned-out glare of the locomotive headlight several cars ahead, the darkness was total.

63

He dropped his saddle to the ground beside the tracks and tucked his Winchester into the crook of his arm while he looked around, trying to pierce the gloom. All he could see was the glint of light from the coach reflected from the wet rails of a siding that ran parallel to the main line, and when he looked down the siding he could make out the dim shapes of boxcars.

"This is one hell of a place to get off a train at this time of day," Longarm remarked to the conductor who was stooping to pick up the box step that he'd placed for Longarm to use getting off the coach. "I don't see any signs of life close by. My ticket said I'd get off at Fort Gibson."

"You're about two miles or so from the fort," the conductor said.

"Now, that don't make sense. How come the railroad didn't put the line right up to it?"

"Mister, when the Katy got this far into the Nation, the Army'd moved out of Fort Gibson," the conductor said. "They came back a few years later, of course, but the rails had already been laid."

"Seems to me you could've put in a spur," Longarm grumbled. "But I guess I can walk that far, even if I don't want to."

"Unless you want to get a lot wetter than you will in this drizzle, you'd better stay here until the quartermaster's teams get here in a couple of hours."

"I don't follow you." Longarm frowned.

"We didn't lay a spur to the fort because there's a little half-assed river, the Neosho, that you've got to cross to get to it. There's a ford across the river, but no railroad bridge, so we shunt our freight cars off here and the quartermaster wagons come and haul the load the rest of the way."

"What makes you think they won't come to unload these cars until tomorrow, or even a week from now?" Longarm asked.

"Because about once a week we haul in a carload of fresh garden truck for the mess. When the sentry that comes on watch at the fort at daybreak sees cars here that wasn't on the siding the night before, he tells the quartermaster to get the wagons over right away."

"Looks like I'm stuck here a while, then."

"Looks like you are," the conductor agreed. "You can wade the ford, but it's more than knee-deep in the middle, so I'd say your best bet's to get out of this drizzle and wait for the wagons. You can shelter in one of those empty boxcars up the siding. At least you won't be too bad off."

Hunkering down beside the main line, Longarm took out a cheroot and lighted it. By the time he'd smoked it down to a stub the engineer had backed the freight cars at the end of his string onto the siding and a brakie had cut the coupling free. As the train pulled away, the drizzle began to turn into a light rain.

Watching the red lanterns on the last coach fading from sight, Longarm up, ground the cigar stub under his boot heel, and picked up his saddle. He started walking up the siding to find one of the empty boxcars the conductor had mentioned. The first two cars were those left by the train he'd come on. Their doors were sealed. A seal was also on the doors of the next car. He was halfway to the door of the third boxcar when he heard voices.

Longarm's instincts stopped him at once. The chances were that the voices were those of harmless hobos, but criminals on the run also hopped freight trains to avoid the risk of being seen and recognized in a passenger coach. He lowered his saddle quietly to the ground and levered a shell into the chamber of his Winchester. Then he moved on toward the boxcar door, walking as quietly as he could on the crunching gravel of the roadbed. He stood at the edge of the boxcar door for a moment, listening, but the voices had stopped.

That might mean whoever was talking just run outa anything to say, old son, he told himself. *But it might also mean they heard you pussyfooting up on 'em. Looks like you better move first.*

Dropping to a crouch, Longarm swung the Winchester's muzzle to cover the black square of the open boxcar door and called, "You in the boxcar! I'm a United States marshal and I'm holding a rifle on the door of this boxcar! Come on out with your hands up so I can get a look at you!"

A shot from the car's black interior answered him, and a slug tore through the side of the boxcar with a thunk and a splintering of shattered wood. Longarm raised himself to a crouch and fired at the spot where he'd seen the muzzle-flash, but a second shot from inside the car followed the first. He triggered his Winchester again before he dropped, but a third shot, this one from the top of the next boxcar in the short string,

65

kicked up the gravel a foot from his feet.

Longarm dropped flat and rolled under the edge of the car. He waited for a moment, heard no sounds of boots moving across the floor above him, and there were no more shots.

He called into the blackness again, "You in the boxcar! If you got any sense, you'll give up! I got you pinned down, and you know it. If you didn't hear what I said before, my name's Long, and I'm a U. S. marshal. Toss out your guns now and come out with your hands up. I guarantee I won't shoot you on sight!"

Another shot from the top of the boxcar ahead and two from inside the car, fired through the floor this time, replied to Longarm's offer. Like the earlier shots, they were ineffective, but their message was clear.

Longarm decided to give it one more try. He raised his voice again. "If you got any sense, you'll surrender now before the soldiers get here! The sentries at the fort's heard the shooting from over here by now. There'll be a squad or so of cavalry riding this way in about five more minutes! You better quit while you still got some room to talk in!"

This time no shots answered Longarm's words. There was silence for several moments, then a voice called from inside the boxcar, "A minute ago you said your name, Long. Are you the one they call Longarm?"

"That's me," Longarm replied.

"Do not shoot, Longarm. We must talk."

"Talk away. I'm listening," Longarm replied.

"Standing Bear!" the man inside the car called. "You have heard? This Longarm is the man Jessibee Vann told us of. We can trust him to keep his word, maybe to help us!"

"I remember what Jessibee said of him," the man atop the boxcar replied. "I will do what you and the others decide!"

"Wait a minute while we talk," tbe man in the boxcar called back. "Longarm, we have a truce. Be patient!"

"Go ahead and palaver," Longarm answered. "I'm waiting."

Although he'd been surprised to hear her name mentioned, Longarm remembered Jessibee Vann very well indeed. She was the beautiful Cherokee girl he'd met while he was posing as an outlaw in Belle Starr's hideout at the southern edge of the Indian Nation. In fact, Longarm recalled, Jessibee's family was kin to the halfbreed Sam Starr, who'd been the Bandit Queen's husband at that time.

Longarm's wait was not a long one. Only a few minutes went by before the man in the boxcar spoke again. "Standing Bear! We have decided to talk with Longarm. Do you agree?"

"I told you I would!" Standing Bear replied.

"You have heard, too, Longarm!" the voice from the boxcar said. "We come out in peace! We will not bring our guns!"

"I won't shoot unless you got some trick up your sleeve," Longarm replied. "Just come on out with your hands in the air!"

Chapter 8

While he waited for the Indians to come out of the boxcar, Longarm took the precautions that years of experience had taught him were wise if he wanted to survive. He stepped to one side of the boxcar door to prevent any of the men inside from leaping out in a surprise attack that could carry him to the ground. He leaned his Winchester against his saddle and stood with the toe of his boot touching the butt, so he'd know without groping in the darkness exactly where to reach for the rifle. Finally, he shrugged his shoulders to adjust the set of his coat in case he was forced to draw his Colt quickly.

His preparations required little time. He'd been standing in his changed position for only a few seconds when the first of the men came from the boxcar. He was followed by two more, and in a moment a fourth man came around the far end of the car and joined the group.

Longarm could not see the faces of the four clearly in the dense darkness, but he'd known from the beginning of their conversation that they were young Indians. He still wasn't sure of their tribe, but here in the eastern half of the Indian Nation they would probably belong to one of the Five Civilized Tribes. Judging from their voices and easy use of English, he'd decided they were young, probably in their early twenties, perhaps even younger. While this meant that they'd undoubtedly attended a white-taught school, tribal customs were still maintained, so to gain face, he wanted to force them to speak first.

When the Indians realized that Longarm was ready to wait as long as necessary for them to begin the conversation, the first man who'd come from the boxcar said, "I am Hungry Wolf, Longarm. My friends are Standing Bear, Running Fox, and Soaring Eagle."

"You know who I am," Longarm said. "You mentioned knowing Jessibee Vann, so I figure you're Cherokees."

"We are Creek," Hungry Wolf replied. "This is Creek land on which we stand. Jessibee lives at Talequah. It is not far from here. Jessibee's people are our friends."

"Where do you live, Hungry Wolf?" Longarm asked.

"At Tahola. It is to the west, almost a day's ride."

"I don't see your horses. You'd have 'em hid, I'd guess?"

"Yes. A half-mile from here, in a little gully."

"What I want to know is how come you tried to bushwhack me," Longarm said. "You're bound to be up to some kind of mischief here, or you would'nt've fired first."

"I am to blame for that," Running Fox volunteered. "I was nervous. I have not been a thief before."

"It was a child's thing you did," Hungry Wolf told his companion angrily. "The soldiers could have heard your shots!"

His words might have been a cue, for just as he finished speaking the notes of a bugle sounded in the distance.

"I'd guess the soldiers *did* hear them shots," Longarm said calmly. "Maybe we better go take a look."

Picking up his rifle, he led them to the gap between the boxcars. They looked toward the fort. Lanterns were moving about between the buildings, and they could see the dark forms of the soldiers moving around.

Longarm said, "They heard the shots, all right. There'll be a squad riding over here soon as they can get saddled up."

"You knew they would come!" Running Fox said angrily. "Now they will arrest us! You have tricked us!"

"Now hold on," Longarm snapped. The authority in his voice held the Creeks silent. "I didn't think about them shots being heard at Fort Gibson, even if I should've. But if they do come, I'll see you don't get arrested."

"How can we trust you?" Soaring Eagle asked suspiciously.

"I don't see that you can do anything else," Longarm told him. "But this ain't on government land, and I got as much right to hold you as the Army has. I'll rig up a story that'll satisfy the Army you ain't done anything wrong."

"But we attacked you!" Hungry Wolf protested. Then, his voice showing his shock, he asked, "Would you lie to your own people? Jessibee said—"

"I didn't say I'd lie," Longarm broke in. "All four of you are under arrest right now, in protective custody." Before any of them could speak, he added, "Which don't mean I'm going to put you in jail. You know what protective custody means?"

"No," Hungry Wolf said. "But it sounds like it means you have arrested us to protect us."

69

"That's exactly right," Longarm replied. "But before I could cart you off to jail, I'd have to arrest you and tell you why I was doing it."

Hungry Wolf turned to his companions. "I am sure we can trust Longarm. Jessibee Vann says he is a good man. Remember, when the Army comes, we must say we are in his protection."

"Well, now that we got that straight, you better tell me the whole story," Longarm told the Creeks. "There'll be time to work things out between us before the Army detail gets here."

"What are we to tell them?" Hungry Wolf asked.

"You don't say a word, none of you. I'll do the talking, but I want my story to be straight," Longarm said sternly. "Now start out by telling me what you come here for. Was you going to steal something? From the railroad, maybe, or the Army?"

"From neither one," Hungry Wolf replied. "We came because there is a beef shipment due and many of our people are hungry."

"What happened?" Longarm asked. "Your folks get shorted on the last shipment?"

"All Creeks were cheated," Soaring Eagle answered angrily. "The steers we got were sick. The agent kept the best ones for himself, and to sell in No Man's Land. Our people have no meat."

Longarm's ears pricked up when Soaring Eagle mentioned sick cattle. He asked, "Where'd the sick steers come from?"

"We did not steal them," Hungry Wolf broke in quickly. "We got the steers in our regular beef allotment from the agency."

"When was that?" Longarm asked.

"Three weeks ago, almost a month," Hungry Wolf answered. He seemed to be the leader of the group.

Longarm had his next question ready. "Were all the steers you got sick?"

"No, Longarm. Half of those we got were healthy. We ate them first. We thought the rest would get better if they had water and feed, but they got worse. Some died before we could slaughter them."

"How many head of cattle are you talking about, Hungry Wolf?" Longarm asked.

"Our regular allotment. Fifteen. It was twenty before the Indian Bureau made it smaller several months ago."

"How many families is the allotment supposed to feed?"

"Thirty."

Standing Bear said quickly, "It is not enough for so many, but the agent says the government does not have enough money to buy more."

"For all I know, he might be telling the truth. The government money's all spent outa Washington, and they might not know how things is, this far away," Longarm suggested. "Do you get the same amount of other food you used to?"

"No. But Mr. Meecham will sell us flour and lard."

"Meecham—that's the agent's name?"

"Yes," Hungry Wolf replied.

"How long's he been agent at Tahola?"

"Not long. Not yet a year."

"Your people get along with him all right?" Longarm asked.

"He is worse than the agent before him, or the one before that one."

"Meaning that the others saw your folks got enough to eat?"

"I mean more than that. Those before him were honest. They did not steal our food," Hungry Wolf said sullenly.

"And this fellow Meecham does?"

"When we buy flour, it is the same kind the government sends with our allotments. And the same kind of lard. The bags and the pails have the same names and designs on them."

"You figure he's been stealing from your allotments?"

Hungry Wolf shrugged. "Every Indian on every reservation in the Nation knows most of the agents steal from us."

Longarm had no answer to this. He'd handled enough cases in the Indian Nation to know that many of the agents were crooked. He'd made reports of widespread theft and cheating by the agents, and twice he'd persuaded Billy Vail to request that an investigation be made of the agents' activities. Both requests had been denied by Washington.

"Let's get back to these sick cattle that were in your last allotment," he said to Hungry Wolf. "Are any of 'em left?"

"No. They have all died."

"What'd you do with the meat?"

"We ate it. Bad as it was, it was meat."

"I guess the hides are gone, too?"

"They are being tanned now."

"That means they been soaked and all the hair scraped off?"

"Of course. We do not tan steer hides with the hair on."

71

"I don't guess you noticed the brands on the critters?"

"No. But even after they are tanned, you might be able to see the brands. On some hides you can do this."

Distant hoofbeats could be heard now. Longarm said, "It sounds like the Army's on the way. You men keep quiet while I'm talking to whoever's in command. Whatever I say, don't you butt into it."

"Why are you doing this, Longarm?" Hungry Wolf asked. "You owe us nothing. We attacked you, and now you defend us. I do not understand this."

"I got pretty good reasons," Longarm told him. "You'll see what they are before the day's over, if things work out the way I think they will."

Sounds of splashing water reached their ears as the riders from Fort Gibson crossed the Neosho. The little group at the railroad tracks stood silent, listening to the soldiers approach.

One of the cavalrymen said, "Hadn't we better spread out, Lieutenant? Dark as it is, there might be a hundred redskins hid behind them boxcars, and we'd never see 'em till too late."

"Ease your nerves down, Corporal," the lieutenant replied. "There wasn't all that much shooting. My guess is that it was a handful of Indians settling some kind of fuss between themselves. But keep your carbines handy just in case."

"It don't seem to me like there's nobody around," the corporal said. "I'd give a lot if it was daylight."

Longarm decided it was time for him to take a hand. He went across the tracks and called, "Lieutenant! Tell your men they aren't going to be jumped! I'm a deputy U. S. marshal, and I've got some prisoners here, but they're not going to cause trouble!"

"'Tachment! Halt!" the lieutenant sang out. The hoofbeats trickled off to silence except for the snuffling of a horse. The lieutenant called, "Identify yourself, if you're a federal officer!"

"My name's Long. I work outa Denver. If you want to see my badge, you're welcome to. Come on up here and take a look."

A slow thunking of the hoofbeats of a walking horse came from the darkness and then the figure of the horse and rider loomed as lighter forms through the gloom. The lieutenant's face was a shapeless white blob. Longarm took out the wallet containing his badge and walked to the horse. He had a match ready and flicked it into flame with his horny thumbnail. He passed the wallet to the lieutenant and while he held the match up, took out a cheroot.

"Looks like you're who you say you are," the lieutenant said, handing the wallet back to Longarm. "Glad to meet you, Marshal Long. My name's Cleghorn, by the way."

In the flickering flame his face showed him to be young, and not yet tanned like veterans of the service. Longarm puffed his cheroot into life and flicked out the match.

"I got four young Creeks over there. I arrested 'em right after they done a little shooting and roused you up," he told Cleghorn. "They're material witnesses in the case I'm here on."

"What was the shooting about?" the lieutenant asked.

"Just a little misunderstanding. It's all cleared up now."

"Will you need any help handling the prisoners, Marshal?"

"No." Longarm held up his Winchester and puffed hard on the cheroot so that Cleghorn could see the rifle's barrel. "I got the guns, they ain't. But I'd appreciate your help on something else, all the same."

"What's that?"

"When I got off the train here, I didn't figure it'd be such a job to get to the fort, and I need a horse, so I'll have to go across and requisition a remount."

"That's won't be any problem. We're not short of horses."

"There's a little bit more," Longarm said. "If I recall rightly, you got a telegraph line to Fort Supply, and their line connects to a civilian wire. I got to send a message to my chief in Denver."

"Since it's government business, I'm sure Colonel Brent will give you permission," Cleghorn replied. "Anything else?"

"What I'd like to do is put these men in one of the empty boxcars," Longarm went on. "Then I'd appreciate it if you'll stay here with your detachment and keep an eye on 'em while I borrow a horse from one of your troopers and ride over with the corporal to the fort to take care of my official business."

"I don't see any reason why we can't accommodate you, Marshal Long," Cleghorn said after a moment's thought.

"Then the sooner I start, the faster I'll be back," Longarm said. "So if you'll just give your men their orders, I'll be on my way."

73

• • •

An hour past sunset, Longarm and the four young Creeks rode into Tahola. The settlement was located on the south bank of the Arkansas River's North Fork, where the river swept in one of its hundreds of serpentine bends. Longarm found it to be a less ramshackle version of the Sand Creek Reservation. There were more houses, better kept, a larger Indian Bureau building, and a substantially larger population.

Since midafternoon the road had taken them through rolling bottomland and past dozens of small farms, families in the fields bringing in the corn crop or hoeing in smaller green garden patches. Houses dotted the farmland, most of them neatly painted, and even those with bare board walls looked well-kept.

"Looks to me like you wouldn't have to depend too much on agency rations," Longarm had commented as they drew closer to town, the setting sun in their eyes.

"There was a time when we did not," Hungry Wolf replied. "Our fathers had farms twice as big as these, and we needed no rations or allotments then."

"That'd be when the Indian Nation all belonged to the Five Civilized Tribes, I guess?" Longarm asked him.

"Yes. But when the men in Washington took away their lands from the Cheyennes and Comanches and Kiowas and Pawnees and Tonkawas and Seminoles and sent them to live in the Nation, we had to give back much of the land that once had belonged to us. So did the Cherokees and Osages and Chickasaws and Choctaws."

"And that was when the allotments started?"

Hungry Wolf nodded. "I do not remember the good old times, but my father has told me how it was. There was no agent to rob us then, or cheat us of our allotments."

"Like I told you, I'll do what I can to settle Meecham's hash while I'm here, Hungry Wolf," Longarm said. "But you got to remember the reason I come here is them sick steers."

"We understand that, Longarm," the young Creek replied. "But the agent is truly a bad man. He has made my people suffer a great deal."

Even if he has not been forewarned about Pleas Meecham, Longarm would have disliked the agent on sight. He'd gone to the agency headquarters at once, in spite of the late hour,

74

after leaving the young Creeks at the edge of town to go to their own homes.

As he'd expected, the agency headquarters was part office, part residence. The office section occupied the front of the building, contained the usual counter, filing cases, desk, and a small pot-bellied stove, cold now in late summer. Pleas Meecham, the agent, was a far cry from Jack Lawson at Sand Creek. The few Creeks on the street in Tahola looked away from the agency when they passed by. Longarm introduced himself to Meecham, who listened with an expressionless face as he outlined the case that was being investigated.

Meecham was a lardy man. His eyes were pale blue and were embedded in surplus flesh pushed up around them by his chubby cheeks. His mouth was a crooked and almost lipless gash above a nubbin of a chin that rested on a shelf of his fat neck. His body matched his face.

"You mean you've come all the way to Denver to ask about a bunch of sick steers?" he asked.

"It ain't only the sick steers," Longarm explained. "It's a ring of steer-swindlers robbing folks that buy beef."

"What the hell, Long!" Meecham exclaimed. "Far as I'm concerned a steer's a steer. I don't go out and take the temperature of every damned critter shipped in for these redskins."

"Seems to me you'd've been able to tell good animals from bad ones if you looked at 'em at all," Longarm said mildly.

"Well, maybe there was a few puny ones in the last shipment we got," the agent admitted. "But that's no fault of mine. All we do is take what's sent us."

"I don't guess you've got any of the last allotment left?"

"Not likely. Hell, the day the allotment herd comes in, I divide 'em up and the Creeks take 'em away. What they do after they leave here's no concern of mine."

"You get papers with all your shipments, I'd imagine? Waybills, requisition, vouchers, something like that?"

"Oh, hell, yes! I don't imagine it's any different from the department you work for, Long. There's ten pen pushers back East for every one of us out here."

"We got our share," Longarm admitted.

"I'll just bet you do. And if they don't have enough, the pen pushers in Washington make up a lot more, just so they'll look busy and not lose their jobs."

75

During the years he'd spent as a lawman, Longarm had become an expert at recognizing diversionary tactics. He pushed Meecham back to the subject of their conversation by asking, "When's your next cattle shipment due, Meecham?"

"Why, I don't rightly know, Long," the agent replied. "They never tell me anything in advance."

"I noticed when I rode in that the Creeks don't seem to have any steers on their land, and your stock pen out there in back is empty, too."

"Well, I can't guarantee anything, but the allotment herd ought to be getting here pretty soon."

"In a few days, I expect?" Longarm persisted.

"Might be a few days, might be a week or a month. They just deliver 'em when they feel like it. I don't have any say about when fresh beef comes in."

"I'll be around when it does, I expect," Longarm said. "While I'm waiting, I'll be going over the records of your last three or four shipments."

"What for?"

"I need to find out where the sick steers are coming from."

"I ain't sure that'll be on any papers I've got." Meecham frowned. "But I'll dig 'em out tomorrow or next day. It's getting to be bedtime, now. I guess you'll be staying here? I got a spare room for government visitors. It ain't much, but you're welcome to use it."

"I'll take you up on that, Meecham," Longarm replied. "I ain't in that big a hurry to go through your papers. I'll be around a while. Right now, I've had a long day, and I'm about ready to go to bed. The way I feel, it'll take a cannon going off to wake me up before sunrise."

In the small bedroom off the agency's main office, Longarm threw back the bedclothes and blew out the lamp, then crawled into bed fully clothed and pulled the coverlet up to his chin. He had in his saddlebag the almost full bottle of Tom Moore that he'd bought in Kansas City, but he left it untouched. Nor did he smoke his usual before-bedtime cigar.

He'd lain on the bed, fighting sleep, for what seemed to be an interminable time before the creaking of floorboards from the office alerted him. He waited until he heard the doorknob squeak before closing his eyes, and lay motionless until the hinges creaked a second time. Then he got up and cautiously

76

cracked the door open a fraction of an inch.

Meecham was standing in front of the stove, stuffing papers into it. The file cases behind the counter were open, the edges of their contents showing above the rim of the drawer. Longarm waited until Meecham took a match from his pocket and scratched it across the stove top. Then he drew his Colt and threw the door wide.

"Blow out the match, Meecham!" he commanded harshly. "I figure you'd burn the important papers first, and I got a pretty fair idea I can make a good case against you from what you've stuffed in that stove!"

Chapter 9

Meecham was standing half turned away from Longarm, facing the stove. He obeyed the command to freeze, but turned his head to look toward the bedroom door. He stared fixedly for a moment, his pudgy face set in an expression of surprise. The match in his right hand was still burning, getting shorter every second.

"I don't guess you'd shoot me if I let go of this match, would you?" he asked. "It'll be scorching my fingers in another minute or so."

"Let it drop, then," Longarm told him.

Instead of letting the match fall, Meecham twitched his hand as though he was about to flip it at Longarm and at the same time swivelled around. Longarm's eyes followed the flickering match flame for the wink of an eyelid. During that split second of time Meecham moved with surprising speed for such a fat man. He flicked the match into the stove and at the same time let his body sag to the floor. He clawed for his revolver as he dropped.

Longarm was too old a hand to be tricked by such a feeble effort. He fired as Meecham flipped the match. The slug caught the agent's right upper arm. Its impact sent him toppling sideways, and Longarm's second shot took him in the shoulder. Then Meecham hit the floor writhing in pain and flames began shooting out of the door of the pot-bellied stove as the papers ignited.

With three huge strides Longarm crossed the room. He glanced at Meecham as he passed him, saw the blood spreading from the two bullet wounds, and decided the agent would be immobilized for the next few minutes.

Bending over the stove, Longarm tried to reach in and pull out the mass of burning papers, but the dying match had done its intended job only too well. The papers were flaming furiously and the heat was too great. Longarm pulled his hand back and thrust his booted foot into the stove, trampling out the flames. In a moment the papers nearest the front which had caught fire first were no longer burning, but they were mashed into charred, brittle ashes. Only then did Longarm give his attention to the agent.

When Longarm turned away from the stove, he saw that Meecham had passed through the period of impact shock caused by the two bullets. The Indian agent was sprawled on the floor, his left hand clamped over the wound in his right shoulder. Inches below, the bullet hole in his biceps was still bleeding badly, and from the way the arm was lying inert and twisted Longarm was sure that the lead slug which had torn into it had shattered the bone.

"You're a damned fool, Meecham," he said coldly. "I told you not to move."

"In my book I'd've been a bigger damned fool not to get rid of those papers before you got your hands on them," Meecham gritted. "I figured you'd be too tired tonight to keep watch."

"Oh, I'm tired all right, but not that tired. I ain't too tired to wrap up them bullet holes, either, if you'll tell me where you got something I can use for a bandage."

"In my room in the back," Meecham said, squeezing out the words between the contractions of pain that were wracking him. "There's a sack of rags that'll do."

A lamp was burning on the bureau in the room in which the agent apparently lived. In addition to the bed and bureau the room contained a kitchen range, table, and chairs. Longarm found a gunny sack stuffed with rags and pulled out a piece of an old bedsheet. He started back to the office and had almost reached the door when he heard the shot.

Standing beside the pot-bellied stove, looking down at the dead agent's body, Longarm deduced what must have taken place. Meecham's right arm lay at right angles to his body now. His left hand was still clamped around the butt of his revolver, the barrel in his mouth. His face was puffed out grotesquely from the muzzle blast and the back of his head had been blown away.

He was getting ready to kill you, old son, Longarm told himself as he studied the corpse. *He tried to draw and found out his arm was ruined so bad it'd likely have had to come off. Knew damned well that what's in them papers he was fixing to burn would've put him behind bars for a long stretch.*

79

Couldn't kill me, couldn't face losing his arm and going to the pen, so he went out like a lot of other cowards before him. And likely there's not anybody that'll feel like crying over his grave.

Longarm handed Lieutenant Cleghorn the reins of the remount horse he'd borrowed less than a week earlier. The two men were standing beside the Katy tracks. The phase of the moon had changed to full, and the big silver orb rode high in the sky, the landscape almost as bright as day. The lantern that stood at their feet was not for illumination, but to flag the train.

"Well, Lieutenant, I got to say you and Colonel Brent really went outa your way to give me a boost on in getting things settled over at Tahola," he told the lieutenant. "If it wasn't for what you and him done, I'd be stuck here butting into something that ain't really my affair instead of heading for Fort Worth to get on with my real case."

"Oh, the Army's not all bad, Marshal." Cleghorn smiled. "I think you did as much for us as we did for you. If you hadn't caught on to how much of the Creeks' allotment Meecham had been stealing, we'd probably have had a dirty little local Indian war on our hands inside of the next month or two."

"There ain't much chance of that happening now. With that quartermaster sergeant the colonel set to helping Hungry Wolf and his daddy to run the agency till the new man from the Indian Bureau gets here, things oughta settle down."

"I don't suppose you'll be getting back this way?"

Longarm shook his head. "Not likely, but it's hard to say. Them papers I got out of the stove at the agency give me the lead I was looking for. Now I've found out most of them sick steers has been passing through the Fort Worth stockyards, I got a place to start from. Not much way of knowing where I'll head from there."

Up the tracks to the north the headlight of the southbound Katy train appeared, and grew steadily larger. Longarm picked up the lantern and began waving it. The train's whistle sounded as the engineer acknowledged the signal with a double toot. In a few minutes more it was stopping with a squeal of iron brakeshoes on steel wheels.

Longarm handed the lantern to Cleghorn, tossed his saddle up to the vestibule, and swung aboard. The conductor squeezed past him and leaned out to highball the engineer and the train

80

began to move again. The conductor pulled himself back up the steps and joined Longarm, who'd stopped on the vestibule platform.

"Heading for Fort Worth, mister?" he asked.

"You guessed it. When are you due there?"

"It's a good twelve-hour run from here. We'll pull in at eleven tomorrow morning, if we don't have any trouble."

"I guess you'll make a breakfast stop someplace along the line?" Longarm asked.

"We won't be stopping, but there'll be a butcher boy come on at Durant. He'll have a pot of coffee and sandwiches, if you can hold out that long."

"I'll manage, long as you got a seat for me in the smoker, where I can light up a cigar now and then."

"Sure. The smoker's the next car back, and there's plenty of seats. I'll get the porter to carry your saddle up to the baggage car."

"That'll be fine," Longarm said. "I'm travelling on a government voucher, so whenever you feel like it, stop by and I'll fill it out for you."

Settled on the prickly plush seat in the smoker, Longarm lighted a cheroot and took out his wallet. He dug out a voucher to be ready when the conductor stopped, and then took out the flimsy tissue the lieutenant had brought him from the fort's telegrapher. He'd glanced at the message before, and knew what it said, but he unfolded it now to read it again. The wire was from Billy Vail. It read:

LARAMIE CITY MARSHAL REPORTS McCOY
LEFT YESTERDAY ENROUTE FORT WORTH

Looks like you're pulling all them loose ends together, old son, Longarm told himself as he refolded the flimsy and put it back in the wallet. *There wasn't no way to tell from them papers in the agency office whether or not McCoy's mixed up in that steer-swindling ring, but if he ain't he'll sure be able to point you to the ones that are. Once you catch up with him, you oughta be able to close this blame case and get back to Denver in time to settle in before the snow flies.*

"Sam McCoy? The fellow that calls himself the Real McCoy?" asked Joe Franks, manager of the Fort Worth stock-

81

yards. He shook his head. "He doesn't have an office here. Hasn't had one since I've been managing the place."

"He's been shipping a lot of cattle through here. Mostly to Kansas City, some direct to agencies in the Indian Nation, some to the Army."

"Marshal Long, a lot of brokers ship cattle through here," Franks said patiently. "But even if this yard's small compared to the one in Kansas City, I don't know all the brokers we do business with."

"You know McCoy, though, don't you?" Longarm persisted.

"I've met him," Franks replied. "That was five or six years ago. Maybe I'd recognize him if I saw him again, maybe I wouldn't."

"All right, let's forget about McCoy for a minute," Longarm said. "The main reason I want to talk to him is because his name keeps popping up when I start asking about sick steers."

"Wait a minute," Franks said thoughtfully. "Now that you mention sick steers, one of the brokers who has an office here at the yard was complaining he'd been stuck with a bunch of bad ones about a month ago."

"Did he mention who he'd bought 'em from?"

"Not that I remember."

"You had any more complaints like that?"

Franks shook his head. "I wouldn't, though, unless it was a really bad shipment. Usually the shippers expect to lose a few animals from a herd, so they throw in a few head over the tally."

"This broker you said was griping about sick steers—I don't guess he said what ranches they come from?"

"No. But he'd blame the broker he bought them from, not the ranches. Chances are he wouldn't even know what brands were on the steers in a mixed herd."

Longarm took out the sheaf of invoices and waybills he'd saved from Meecham's stove and laid them on Franks's desk. "A lot of these give the brand on herds that's been sold. And most of 'em come through your yards, Franks."

Franks started riffling through the papers. He stopped and looked carefully at one of them. "Wait a minute! This invoice didn't come out of my office, Marshal Long."

"It's printed right across the top that it did."

"I can't help that," Franks replied. "We don't use a form

82

like this, and never have since I've been the manager here."

"You recognize the ranch brands that it shows the herd come from?" Longarm asked.

Franks looked at the invoice again more carefully. "I know the Fiddle brand, it's down in the Cross Timbers country. And the Half-Moon is along the Pedernales, up above Austin. Where'd you get these, Marshal? It looks like somebody tried to burn them."

"Somebody did," Longarm said. "Only he's dead now, and I can't ask him anything about 'em. Go on through that stack, Mr. Franks. See if you find any more that don't look right."

Franks thumbed through the charred papers and separated a half-dozen other invoices or waybills he identified as being forgeries.

"Correct me if I'm wrong, Marshal Long," he said. "You asked about the Real McCoy when you first came in. Do you think he's involved in this?"

"I wish I could say yes or no. From what I've heard about McCoy, he's supposed to be one of the squarest men around."

"He is, or always has been. I've never heard anybody say anything about him that wasn't good."

"That's what I've heard, too," Longarm agreed.

"Even if we don't generally list brands on our waybills or invoices, I can understand rustlers doing it. They'd be trying to pass off stolen cattle as being from a legitimate source."

Longarm said, "I never did run into rustlers that done any forgery, unless you can call altering a brand with a running iron a forgery."

"Well, I'd say you've got a mystery on your hands, Marshal."

"Maybe not," Longrm replied. "I'm beginning to get an idea why them papers was forged, but I still don't know who."

"I'd be interested in knowing your idea," Franks said.

"I'd say it was done to let somebody mix in a bunch of infected steers with a herd of healthy cattle."

"Infected?"

"Hoof-and-mouth disease, Mr. Franks."

"That's impossible, Marshal! Since that infestation from Canada in Seventy-one, every rancher in the West has been careful about importing steers from there or from Mexico. The Department of Agriculture banned imports from Mexico about two years ago when a few cases showed up in some steers from there, and the border's still closed to Mexican cattle."

"Wait a minute now!" Longarm said. "I heard about cattle from Canada being banned in Seventy-one, but nobody's said a word about cutting off shipments from Mexico."

"Well, that's understandable," Franks said. "Most of the Mexican cattle that used to be brought into the country came in across the Rio Grande south of the Big Bend. Texas would be the only state really affected by a quarantine."

"Wouldn't it be the same if they was shipping infected steers across now?" Longarm asked. "What'd happen if somebody was to put a Texas ranch brand on a herd of sick steers and drive 'em across the Rio Grande at night? Or even in daytime, at a place where nobody'd be likely to spot 'em?"

"There's not much we could do about that," Franks admitted. "But the border patrol keeps things pretty tight along the Rio Grande. They might miss the first herd that was smuggled across, but I doubt they'd let a second one get by them."

"Well, I'll just keep pecking away at it till I find out." Longarm stood up. "A minute ago you said there was one cattle broker here in the stockyards who had been griping about getting a run of sick steers. Mind telling me his name?"

"Of course not. Lin Pebbles. He's got an office over on the east edge of the yard. Tell him you've been talking with me; that might make it easier to get him to open up."

Lin Pebbles was a brawny man, as big as Longarm, and he exploded into an angry fit of desk-pounding the minute he heard the name McCoy.

"If you know where that son of a bitch is, I'd sure like you to tell me!" he roared. "I'd always figured him to be at least half as honest as folks said he was, but he sure as hell swindled me."

"I don't know where he is right now, Mr. Pebbles. Fact is, I'm trying to run him down myself. Suppose you tell me about him swindling you," Longarm suggested.

"Sold me a herd of steers that had epizootic, that's what he did!" Pebbles snapped. "Sickliest bunch of critters I ever seen! I was going by McCoy's reputation and didn't check the herd before I bought it. Like a damn fool, didn't check it before I paid the waybill, either."

"How long ago was that, Mr. Pebbles?"

"Three, four months. Hell, Marshal, I buy and sell cattle every day. How d'you expect me to remember when I bought

84

one herd that turned out to be a swindle?"

"Because it *was* a swindle," Longarm replied. "Things like that got a way of sticking in a man's mind."

"Now, by God! That's the first sensible answer I ever got from anybody that works for the damned federal government!" the cattle broker snorted. "Sit down, Long. You sound like a man I can talk to."

Longarm sat down in the chair Pebbles indicated. He lighted a cheroot and waited patiently for the broker to continue.

"Well?" Pebbles asked after a few moments. "Ain't you going to ask me a bunch of fool questions?"

"I might later on, after you tell me what happened between you and McCoy. How you come to buy the steers from him, who you sold 'em to, things like that."

"You know anything about the cattle business, Long?"

"Not much. I cowhanded a little while, but that was a fair time back."

"You know how cattle are graded?"

"Good, bad, and indifferent, I'd imagine."

"That's near enough. Better than the trade terms. Well, I won a bid on some government contracts a while back, beef on the hoof for the Army and for the reservations up in the Nation. The stockyard pens didn't have much except Grade A Prime in 'em right then, and I wanted B Utility, so—"

"Just a minute," Longarm broke in. "You always buy Grade B for the government?"

"Why, hell, yes! So do all the other brokers." He waited for Longarm to ask another question, and when none was forthcoming, went on, "Well, I put out the word I was in the market. Got a wire from McCoy in San Antonio. He'd been buying down in that part of Texas and had some steers for sale. Made me a decent price, I bought FOB the yards here. When the steers got in I paid the waybill, went down to look at 'em in the pens, and saw I'd been had."

"They wasn't any good?"

"Maybe a third wouldn't made B Utility. Half the others was C and the rest was sickly culls. I'd paid, so I was stuck. I culled out the worst, sold 'em for hides, replaced what I'd lost with B Utility from some tag bunches I had on hand, and filled my orders."

"You recall anything about them steers you culled out?"

"Texas brands, mostly from Mexican longhorn stock. You

85

know Texas ranchers castrates when the bulls are calves and in Mexico they wait till the critters are grown. Texas steers got bigger horns and weigh in maybe a hundred pounds heavier on the hoof."

"So you took a loss on the culls," Longarm said.

"You're damned right I did. Close to two thousand dollars."

"You try to get your money back from McCoy?"

"If I ever catch up with the swindling son of a bitch, I'll get my money back—or a piece of his hide! But I can wait for that, Long."

"You wouldn't happen to know where he is now, would you?"

"You're after him, too?" Pebbles asked.

"I'd like to talk to him," Longarm replied.

"So would I. But there's no way of telling where he might be. You know a broker big as him is out buying most of the time. If I got an order to put in, I'll wire their office, and usually hear from 'em in a day or so."

"You ain't wired him lately, I guess?"

"You're damned right I ain't! And won't!"

"Let me ask you a question about them sick steers you culled out of the herd you bought from McCoy. Seems to me you moved mighty quick to get rid of 'em."

"Let me tell you something, Long. You move quick in this business or you go broke quicker."

"Did it occur to you them culls you sold for hides might've had hoof-and-mouth disease?"

Pebbles did not reply for a moment. Then he said, "I don't lie to anybody, Long, so I won't answer that question."

Longarm looked at the broker a moment, then said, "I don't guess you need to, Mr. Pebbles. You just gave me your answer."

"Take it any way you like," the broker grunted.

Both men sat silent for a moment, exchanging stares. Longarm finally said, "You in a swapping mood, Mr. Pebbles?"

"That depends on what you want to swap for."

"If you was to send a wire to McCoy asking about buying a herd of cattle, he'd wire back right away, wouldn't he?"

"I imagine. He's got somebody in his office who knows how to get hold of him, like all us brokers do when we take a trip."

"Tell you what. I'll forget I asked you about them culls if

86

you'll wire McCoy. And when you get your answer, tell me where he's located."

Pebbles hesitated for only a moment. Then he said, "You can't pin him down, is that it?" When Longarm nodded, he went on, "I'll take your swap, Long. Come back here tomorrow about noon. I'll damned near guarantee to tell you where McCoy's at."

Chapter 10

"Well, I found out where you can catch up with McCoy," Lin Pebbles announced without the preamble of a formal "good morning" when Longarm walked into his office shortly before noon the following day.

"You sure done a lot better'n I did," Longarm said.

"Well, now, Long, you been looking for McCoy to make trouble for him. He figures I'm looking for him to make him some money. Stands to reason he'd dodge you and be glad to hear from me."

"That follows," Longarm agreed. "Well, where's he at?"

"Miles City. That's up in Montana. It used to be called Milestown."

"I know where it is, I been up along the Yellowstone a time or two. McCoy gets around pretty good. Last time I had him pinpointed he was in Wyoming Territory, at Laramie."

"That ain't too far from Miles City, and they're both in cattle country." Pebbles frowned. "My guess is he's out buying."

"Just to ease my curiosity, did you find out about him the way you said you figured you could yesterday?"

"Yep. It worked just like I told you it would. Soon as you walked out yesterday, I went over to the telegraph in the stockyards office and sent a wire to McCoy's office in Kansas City. Got my answer about an hour ago. His clerk must've known right where his boss was."

"That clerk's name wouldn't be Glover, would it?"

Pebbles glanced at the flimsy on his battered desk. "Sure is. E. M. Glover. Why?"

"I've met his clerk. That E. M. stands for Elsie Mae."

"Maybe that's what's wrong with McCoy," Pebbles said, shaking his head sadly. "I'd say he's gone soft in the head, taking a job away from a man that needs the work and hiring some damn flibbertygibbet female. I tell you, Long, it just ain't natural for women to work in offices."

"Well, it looks like we'll see more of it instead of less," Longarm said. "I guess it's progress. That wire didn't say whereabouts in Miles City a man can find McCoy, did it?"

"Nope. But it ain't all that big of a place any more, now the gold rush is over and the range freed up for ranching again. You won't have no trouble finding him. I guess that's what you're aiming to do, ain't it? Go up there after him?"

"I'll head north before the day's out," Longarm replied. "This is the first time I've been able to find out exactly where McCoy is since I been looking for him."

"If McCoy's got a U. S. marshal after him, I take it I ain't the only one the son of a bitch has swindled, then?"

"You're right, Mr. Pebbles. That ain't the half of it, though. Them sick steers might be a lot worse than the swindle."

"If they've got something to do with that remark you made yesterday about the hoof-and-mouth sickness, I don't aim to do any more talking to you, Long," Pebbles said firmly.

"I've said all I got in mind to about that, Mr. Pebbles. I won't be around to talk to, anyhow. I thank you for your help, but I got to leave right now and find out about train connections to Miles City."

Longarm alighted from a Great Northern train in Miles City four days after he'd learned McCoy's whereabouts from Pebbles. His destination in the southeastern corner of Montana was one of the few areas of the West where railroad growth far outstripped population. The Black Hills gold rush five years earlier had set off a railroad-building rush as well. Rails had been pushed into the area hurriedly, not only by such well-established roads as the Northern Pacific, the Rock Island, Burlington, and Great Northern, but by half a dozen smaller lines which started with nothing and went nowhere.

Most of the inexperienced, under-financed newcomers had failed when the gold boom ended. The steel tracks they'd built had for the most part stayed intact. They'd been bought, usually through bankruptcy court sales, by the larger, better financed lines. The short stretches of track had by now been connected to the main lines of the large roads to form a railroad network as complete and flexible as those in Eastern metropolitan areas.

Miles City had withered when the prospectors departed, Longarm found as he carried his saddle gear and rifle up the wide unpaved main street from the Northern Pacific depot.

Beyond the town, he could see soldiers moving around the two-story barracks at Fort Keough, but the town itself was ghostly quiet. There were only four or five people and a single wagon abroad, and the surface of Main Street was smooth now, not cut into ruts by the heavy wagons hauling mining equipment, military supplies, and loads of rails and ties as well as hordes of eager prospectors.

Half the clapboard buildings that lined the street were shuttered or had their windows and doors boarded up, and on some of them the false fronts had sagged. The three brick buildings that had been erected at the height of the gold rush were still in good shape, though one was boarded up. The Cosmopolitan Saloon was also boarded up, but Goldwater & Russell's trading post was doing business as usual across the street. The Western Territory Telegraph Company had moved into one corner of the post office, but Longarm's favorite hangout, the Cottage Saloon, was still open, as was Mrs. Mason's Rooming House next door.

Crossing the street, Longarm pushed through the batwings of the saloon, dropped his saddle and saddlebags just inside the door, and leaned his rifle on them. There were no customers at the bar or at the tables. Besides himself, the only occupant was the barkeep, who stood polishing glasses on his apron. He put aside the glass he was working on and came up to the bar.

"Morning, friend. What'll it be?" he asked.

"Maryland rye. Tom Moore, if you got it." Longarm tossed a half-dollar on the mahogany and looked around. When the barkeep returned with the bottle and a glass, he said, "I don't see Jimmy Coleman. He still runs this place, don't he?"

"Oh, sure. You a friend of his?"

"I got acquainted with him when I was here before. Not that I stayed long—it was more like I was passing through."

"If you want to see Jimmy, you'll have to stick around until tomorrow. The reason he's not here today, he's gone to the funeral, along with just about all the other old-timers."

"I didn't see no crowd at the church when I come in."

"Well, the funeral's not here, it's down at Stonestown."

"It must be somebody important, if the whole town's gone to it, and I heard Lou Stone cashed down there a year or so ago."

"If you was around here during the rush, I'd imagine you'd know Katie Arneson. She's the one that died."

90

"Why sure, I knew Katie," Longarm nodded, draining his glass. "She's the madam that used to run the girls at the Cosmopolitan's dance hall back then."

Extending his hand across the bar, the barkeep said, "I'd like to shake your hand, friend."

Mystified, Longarm shook hands with the man. "You mind telling me why?" he asked.

"You said straight out that you knew Katie instead of just hearing about her. Have this one on the house." The barkeep picked up the bottle of Tom Moore and as he poured he went on, "You and the boss and the fellow that paid for Katie's funeral was about the only ones that come right out and said they knew her. The others claimed they'd just heard about her."

"I've found people change," Longarm observed. "Some fellow that starts out as a twenty-dollar cowhand and hits a streak of luck and gets respectable don't like to look back to the kind of man he used to be."

"Well, the old boy that paid for Katie's funeral wasn't one bit ashamed to say he started out being a hand on the Diamond R and pulled hisself up by his bootstraps. I guess he done pretty good, too. He sure cut a wide furrow while he was in town. If you was here before the rush, you might've run into him. His name's McCoy."

Longarm almost choked on his second swallow of whiskey. He cleared his throat and asked, "Was he a big fellow, sorta wide nose that'd been bashed in, light-colored hair, blue eyes?"

"Nope." The barkeep shook his head. "Must've been another McCoy you knew, friend. This fellow was a little feisty runt, wore a big white Stetson pushed back on his head, had a stickpin made like a steer's head only it had diamond eyes."

"That don't sound like the McCoy I know." Longarm frowned. "Did he say what kind of business he's in now?"

"He said he come up here to buy cattle. Carried a bankroll that'd choke an ox and didn't mind spreading it around. First night he was here he dropped more'n a thousand dollars in a poker game. Next night he won it back and three thousand more."

"That don't sound like the McCoy I used to know," Longarm said thoughtfully. "I'd like to get to look at him, though, just to make sure. Did he say he'd be coming back here?"

"Well, he didn't say he wasn't."

"Is there a way I can get to Stonestown in time for Katie's funeral? How'd the bunch that went down there travel?"

"Unless you go horseback, there's not much way to get there from here except to take the NP to the O'Fallon Creek junction where the Chicago & Milwaukee crosses it. Then you switch to the C&M to go down to Stonestown. The bunch that went from here had the NP make up a special train for 'em."

"Too bad I wasn't here to join 'em," Longarm said. "If it wasn't such a long ways, I'd get a livery horse and go anyhow, except I'd get there too late. As I recall where Stonestown is, it takes two days to get there on horseback."

"About that. But they'll be leaving right after the funeral to come home. They oughta get here sometime around midnight."

"Best thing I can do is wait for 'em, then. Is Mrs. Mason still running the rooming house next door?"

"She's gone," the barkeep replied. "Sold out a year so ago. Miz Forbes is the landlady now, and from what I hear she's doing about the same as Miz Mason did. Keeps things clean, changes the sheets every week, ain't stingy with the towels."

"That sounds all right. I'll go see if she's got a room for me after I have another drink. You care to join me?"

"No, thanks." Then, as Longarm had been sure he would, the barkeep went on, "But if it's all the same to you, I'll have a cigar. You want me to send the swampy over to tell you when that special train gets back?"

"Oh, I'll likely drop in again after I've had a nap and some supper. No use bothering. It'll do me good just to stretch out and rest a few minutes."

Longarm did not stop to rest immediately. After renting a room, he left his saddle gear and rifle in it and walked down Main Street to the Western Territories Telegraph office. The operator was leaning back in his chair asleep, the telegraph key close to his ear. Longarm tapped gently on the counter, and the clerk quickly came to life.

"Yes, sir. You want to send a wire?"

"Not right this minute," Longarm replied. "What I'm interested in is looking at your charge sheet, the records of some of the telegrams you've sent outa here for the past week or so."

"Why, I can't let you do that, mister! It'd be worth my job if I did! We don't show our records or copies to anybody!"

92

Taking out his wallet, Longarm flipped it open to show the badge pinned to its inner flap. "This makes a difference, I'd say. I'm on official business here in Miles City."

"Well, I guess that does make it all right," the operator agreed. "You'll find everything in order, Marshal." He produced a spindle file and a buckram-bound ledger. "This file's got the ones the customers wrote when they sent a wire, the book's got my log of the messages that I've took down—where they're from and when they got here and who signed for delivery of 'em."

"Now, that's just what I wanted," Longarm said. "I won't take away none of your records. All I wanta do for now is look."

Longarm started at the back of the book and worked forward. He did not have to go further than the page covering the previous day before he ran into McCoy's name. Yesterday the cattle broker had received three telegrams from Texas—one from Amarillo and two from San Antonio—as well as three from Kansas City, one from Denver, and one from Vaughn, New Mexico.

"I don't reckon you'd have copies of the messages you get in and deliver, would you?" he asked the operator.

"No, sir. Some of the big companies back East do, but ours doesn't."

"You wouldn't remember what any of 'em said, I guess?"

"Did you ever punch a key, Marshal?"

"A little bit. Still do, when I can't get out of it."

"I guess you've tried to remember messages you've taken, after you wrote 'em down?"

"A few times," Longarm replied, smiling. "I know just what you're about to say, son. A man on the receiving end can't remember a message he wrote down five minutes ago, much less one that come in two or three days ago. I just thought I'd ask."

Longarm went through the pages of the ledger until he found the last entry for McCoy, then turned his attention to the copies individuals sending the telegrams had written. Here his search was more fruitful. He hit the pay dirt he'd been hoping for on the first message he looked at. It was addressed to E. M. Glover at the Kansas City office, and dated that morning. Longarm realized instantly that it must be the last message McCoy had sent before getting on the special train for Stonestown.

93

"Leaving MC," the message ran. "Hold wires four days then send Vaughn, New Mexico."

Longarm got the significance of the message at once. It was obvious that the cattle broker was heading for Vaughn and did not intend to return to Miles City. Though his first inclination was to go to the Northern Pacific office at once and check on the schedules of trains out of town, Longarm went through the file of earlier telegrams.

After seeing the first one, those remaining were interesting but anticlimactic. For five consecutive days, McCoy had sent at least two telegrams daily to his Kansas City office; all except one of these concerned orders for cattle or instructions to buy herds. Longarm deduced they must have been written in response to the incoming messages of which he had no copies. As nearly as he could tell, all the transactions were normal and routine, the messages a cattle broker might be expected to send. He put the spindled sheets in order and handed them back to the operator.

"I guess this McCoy fellow must've been in and outa here a lot, judging by the number of wires he sent," he said to the man. "You'd know how he looks, I reckon?"

"Oh, sure. I'd remember him even if I'd only seen him one time, because he tipped me every time he came in. He was a real friendly gentleman. He wasn't very big, and he always had on a pair of fancy handmade boots and a big white Stetson and had a fancy steerhead stickpin with some diamonds in it."

"Anybody ever come in with him?"

After a moment's thought the operator shook his head. "No, sir. Far as I remember, he was always by himself."

"Well, you been a real help, son, and I thank you," Longarm said. As an afterthought he added, "I'll ask you not to mention to anybody that I come in and looked at them wires and your book. Not that it's secret, but the fewer knows, the better."

"You can depend on me, Marshal. In this office, you learn how to keep secrets."

After a bit more walking, to the Northern Pacific depot, Longarm learned there'd be no train until five o'clock the next morning that would allow him to make connections to the south.

"But if it's New Mexico you're heading for," the ticket agent said, "I'll tell you what I told the other gentleman. If you take the nine o'clock eastbound you can make connections at North Platte with a Union Pacific flyer to Denver. Once

94

you're there, you can get the D&RG out and connect with the Santa Fe at Trinidad. That'll get you to Albuquerque, which is about as near as you'll get to Vaughn on a train."

"What other gentleman was it you told that?" Longarm asked.

"Why, the big cattleman who's been cutting such a broad swathe through town. He was asking the same question yesterday."

"Is that the way he decided to go?"

"No. Seems he had to go by way of Kansas City."

"How long's it going to take him to get to Vaughn?"

"Well, if he doesn't stop over in Kansas City too long, he ought to be there in four days."

"I'll be stopping back for my ticket after I make up my mind which way I want to go," Longarm said. "Thanks for the advice."

Back in his room, Longarm shed his coat and vest and hung his holstered Colt over the headpost of the bed. He dug out his bottle of Tom Moore from the saddlebag, yanked the cork with his teeth, and took a satisfying swallow.

Carrying the bottle with him, he sat on the side of the bed, dug a cheroot from his pocket, and laid the bottle beside him while he fumbled for a match. Suddenly he realized that for three nights he'd had nothing but catnaps snatched while sitting upright on a hard plush seat in a swaying train. He lay down on the bed without bothering to take off his boots and was asleep before his head touched the pillow.

Longarm awoke suddenly. His room was dark and something hard was digging into his ribs. His hand was halfway to the butt of his Colt before he realized that the hard round object prodding his ribs was the neck of the whiskey bottle. Sheepishly, he sat up and took a small drink. When the rye hit bottom his stomach responded with a rumble, reminding him that he'd had no supper. His eyes had adjusted to the darkness by this time. He put on his coat and hat and went in search of a restaurant.

A half-hour later, having eased his protesting stomach with a steak and fried potatoes, Longarm pushed through the batwings of the Cottage Saloon. In contrast to its barren appearance of the afternoon, the bar was packed three deep. Dredging up the face of Jimmy Coleman from his capacious memory, Longarm spotted the saloon proprietor standing at the end of the bar. He circled around the drinkers, came up behind Coleman, and quietly stood beside him. After a moment the saloonkeeper glanced up. He looked idly at Longarm and started to turn away; then his eyes widened and his head swivelled back.

"I'll be damned!" Coleman exclaimed. "What rock did you crawl out from under, Longarm?"

"Oh, I heard you was getting outa hand, so I stopped by to see if I could straighten you out," Longarm replied straight-faced. "You hardcases need to be rousted now and again."

"Well, it's damned good to see you!" Coleman said. "Just let me get a bottle of . . ." he hesitated, then went on, "Maryland rye. Then we'll go over and sit down and chin."

After a few minutes swapping recollections of the past, Longarm appraoched the point. He asked Coleman, "How about the funeral, Jimmy? You laid Katie away nice, I bet."

"Just like she'd've wanted," Coleman nodded. "Good bunch of fellows there. Of course, a lot of 'em are dead, now."

"How about this McCoy fellow that footed the bill? Do you recall him from when he was at the Diamond R?"

Coleman shook his head. "No, but it's not unusual. There was so many hands on that spread before the gold rush pinched it down that a man can't remember all of 'em."

"I'd like to have a look at him. Did he come back here with you on the special?"

"Matter of fact, he didn't," Coleman said. "He had to go down to Texas someplace, so he went on to pick up a south-bound train on the Chicago & Milwaukee."

"You mean the UP," Longarm said, frowning.

"No, he was planning to take the UP, but he found out if he got to Belle Forche he could get there faster on the Milwaukee line than by going all the way to North Platte to get a southbound connection."

"It's too bad I missed him, but I guess I'll run into him someplace else sometime. Now, if you'll tip that bottle over my glass again, I got a yarn to tell you that I don't suppose you've heard before."

It was late when Longarm left the Cottage Saloon. Walking next door to his room he told himself thoughtfully, *Old son, whover that fellow might be, he sure as hell ain't the Real McCoy. But he's smart, give him that much. And he's making a sorta pattern, the way he jumps around, just like them sick steers is popping up in a pattern, too. Now what you got to do is figure out the patterns for both of' em. If you can do that, you'll be one jump ahead of this McCoy, and pretty soon you'll know where he's going soon enough so you'll be waiting for him when he gets there.*

Chapter 11

Until he'd discovered that he had a four-hour wait between trains in Denver, Longarm had not planned to report to Billy Vail as he passed through on his way from Miles City to Vaughn. The long period between trains changed his mind. Getting into a hack at the Union Depot, he told the driver to take him to the Federal Building.

"I've been sitting here for a month, wondering what you've been getting into," Vail said without any preamble when Longarm came into his office. "I suppose you've got your case wrapped up and we can put out some arrest warrants in a day or two?"

"I'm a long way from getting that far, Billy. I been going around and around like a little puppy chasing his tail, sorta staying in the same place."

"From the travel vouchers that have come back here to be sent on to the accounting office, I'd say it's more like you've been chasing yourself all over the country."

"Oh, I'll grant you I've covered a little bit of ground, but there's more angles to this case than you can shake a stick at."

Vail extended his hand and said, "Well, I'll get all that from your report."

"Now, Billy, you know I don't ever file a report on a case until I've got it closed."

"I hope it's not going to take you another month to close it. Remember, we're short-handed right now."

"And right now I'm sorta out on the end of a limb, Billy. Don't look for me to start sawing it off between me and the tree. If I'm lucky, I'll only have one more trip to make, now that I've found out where I can catch up with this fellow that's passing himself off as the Real McCoy, but—"

"Wait a minute," Vail interrupted. "Are you telling me the McCoy you've been chasing's not the *real* one?"

"That's how it looks to me right now."

"Who is he, then?"

"I'd give a pretty to know that myself," Longarm admitted.

"If he's not the Real McCoy, what happened to the real one?"

"That's another thing I got to find out."

"What about the steers with hoof-and-mouth? Can you connect them with the fake McCoy?"

"I'm pretty close to doing just that, Billy."

"Have you found out where the sick steers are coming from?"

"It looks like most of 'em comes from Texas."

"That's impossible!" Vail snorted. "From what Jim Fraser says, the ranchers down there jumped on the hoof-and-mouth in time to keep it from spreading. The Mexican border's closed, and that's where the hoof-and-mouth seems to have started."

"Now, Billy, you was along that border when you was a Texas Ranger. How many places would you guess there are where a herd of cattle could be sneaked across?"

Vail thought for a moment, then nodded. "It'd run into the hundreds. Most of the Rio Grande's pretty shallow."

"And how many Rangers are there?"

"Sixty-five, the last I heard. Yes, you're right, Long. There's a lot of border to patrol, and damned few men to do it with. And while we're talking about the Texas Rangers, I hope you manage not to get crossways of them when you get down there on this case."

"Why, I'm not heading for Texas, Billy. I'm on my way to Vaughn."

"Now, that doesn't make sense! Vaughn's in New Mexico!"

"Unless somebody's moved it, it is. And when you figure that New Mexico's got a few hundred miles of border with Old Mexico, and it's even easier to cross than a river, it makes sense." Vail started to say something, but without waiting to see whether his chief agreed or disagreed, Longarm ignored him and went on. "Besides that, New Mexico borders on Texas and Colorado, and *them* borders sure ain't being watched."

"When you put it that way, it makes sense, I guess," Vail admitted.

"Besides all that," Longarm added, "as best I can find out, that's where the fake McCoy's heading."

"Where'd you find that out? And how?"

"Well, I missed the fake McCoy by a day in Miles City—"

"Montana?" Vail asked. "What the devil took you there?"

"Copies of telegrams that passed between McCoy and his office in Kansas City. The same thing that give me the clue to look for him next in Vaughn."

"You know, Long, you could've saved us both a lot of time and breath if you'd just filed a report covering all that," Vail said a bit wistfully. "All right, go on to Vaughn. When are you leaving?"

"I got a four-hour layover here between trains, Billy." Longarm took out his watch and glanced at it. "I've used up one hour already. By the time I get a shave and go out to my rooming house and pick up some fresh duds, it'll be just about time for my train to pull out."

"Go ahead, then. I won't hold you up any longer," Vail told him. "Just let me know where you are every now and then." His voice took on a thin edge of half-serious sarcasm as he added, "If it's not too much trouble, that is."

Dusk was creeping over Denver by the time Longarm left George Masters' barbershop and headed for his room. Leaving his rifle and saddle in the hack and telling the driver to wait, he took his saddlebags and climbed the stairs in the dimly lighted hallway and entered his room. With his time growing short, he did not bother to close the door.

As he'd expected, a small heap of freshly laundered clothing lay on the bed. He emptied his saddlebags on the end of the bed and separated the clothing from the rest of his gear. Tossing aside the shirts and balbriggans that needed laundering, he made several trips from the bureau to the bed, putting into his saddlebags extra shells for his pistol, derringer, and rifle to replenish the relatively small stock he'd carried on his earlier trip. He put the half-empty bottle of Tom Moore in the saddlebags, cushioning it with jerky and a bag of parched corn, and tossed in a handful of cigars.

His bedroll lay on the floor beside the bed, and as he knew that where he was heading he might not always find a hotel or rooming house, he unrolled his blankets and spread fresh shirts and balbriggans on the blankets, then rolled the bedding and started to cinch its straps tight. By this time, the room was almost as dark as the hall, and the holes for the buckles of the straps were hard to find. Stepping to the windows, Longarm raised the shades of both of them, then went back to the bed.

As he leaned forward, his outstretched hand reaching for

the bedroll straps, a rifle barked outside. The glass in one of the windows tinkled as it shattered and the rifle bullet whistled inches above his head and thunked into the wall across the room.

Longarm's lightning-fast reflexes saved him. He hit the floor before the second rifle shot rang out and another bullet cut the air where he'd been standing a fraction of a second earlier.

Rolling to the broken window, drawing his Colt as he moved, Longarm peered cautiously around the windowsill. He saw the sniper on the roof of the house next door, a black form outlined against the darkening sky. Swearing at himself for being so careless as to leave his rifle in the cab, Longarm sharpened his aim and triggered the Colt.

Its report rang out just as the sniper got off a third shot. The slug ripped through the windowsill, deflected, and emerged a few inches from his cheek. Longarm's shot missed. The range was too great for accurate shooting with the Colt. The slug from the revolver was close enough to spook the sniper, though. He turned and started to retreat.

Resting his forearm on the windowsill, Longarm aimed carefully, but the sniper was already starting to slide down on the opposite side of the ridge where he'd been perched when he squeezed off his second shot. He saw the man on the roof flinch, but before he could fire again the bushwhacker had disappeared below the ridgeline.

Free now of any need to be careful, Longarm leaped up and dashed for the door. Stretching his long legs to their utmost, he took the stairs three steps at a time as he went down. By the time he'd reached the door leading to the street, Longarm was moving in response to the keen reflexes that had been born of too many brushes with the lawless to count.

He stopped inside the door and pulled it back until he could get his arm through the crack. Shielding his body behind the wall, Longarm stretched his gun hand through the crack and pushed the screen door open.

Another rifle shot split the quiet dusky evening air, and the slug sailed through the partly opened screen door. It hit the wooden door and slammed it back against the wall. Longarm went to his knees and pushed the screen door wide with a shoulder and plunged through it.

He dropped flat on his belly as he hit the porch floor and lay prone, his eyes straining into the gaslit glows streaming through the windows and door lights of the houses across the street. For a moment he lay motionless, trying to pierce the dimness between the houses, but he could see no signs of movement anywhere. He stood up, but did not holster his Colt.

"Hey, mister!" the cabman called, crawling out from beneath the hackney when he saw Longarm starting down the porch steps. "If you ain't ready to go, I'm pulling out! This place is too damn dangerous!"

"You stay right where you are!" Longarm commanded as he reached the bottom of the steps and started for the house from which the first ambusher had fired. "It was me them fellows was after, not you. I don't suppose you got a look at 'em, did you?"

"I didn't stop to look at nothing!" the cabman exclaimed. "I hit the street when that first shot went off, and rolled under my hack. I couldn't've seen much, even if I'd been trying, but I sure ain't of a mind to stay here no longer! It's too damn dangerous!"

"I'm a deputy U.S. marshal, and I'm not asking you to stay, I'm ordering you to!" Longarm snapped over his shoulder without stopping. "And you'll wait if you know what's good for you!"

"Order or not, if I hear another shot, I'm leaving!" the hackie replied, but he made no move to get back on the seat of his cab.

Ignoring the curious glances of the people who'd come out of their houses when they heard the shooting, Longarm went past the dark front of the next-door house. He saw the ladder leaning against the eaves, but there was no still form huddled at its foot. He reached the ladder, and by looking closely could see smears of blood on its rungs, which told him that the shot which had found a mark in one of the gunmen had not inflicted a wound serious enough to prevent the man's escape.

Give it up, old son, Longarm advised himself silently. He holstered his Colt and started back to his rooming house. *There ain't no way you're going to catch them two bushwhackers now. At least they didn't get off without a scratch, and if they keep on going around shooting at lawmen, they ain't long for this world.*

He found half a dozen men gathered around the waiting cab when he reached it. Two or three of them knew Longarm by

102

sight and one of these asked, "Anything we can do to help you, Marshal Long?"

"Not a thing, thanks," he replied. "Whoever them fellows was, they got away clean as a whistle."

"You're not hurt, are you?" another asked.

"No. I was lucky—they missed me. Now, the best thing you men can do is go on home and just forget about all this."

"What's your landlady going to say when she gets home?" the first man asked. "She'll see the bullet holes."

"I reckon. Well, tell her I'll make it right with her when I get back. Now, if you fellows don't mind, I'm in a sorta hurry to catch my train." The little group began scattering. Longarm turned to the cabbie and said, "Thanks for waiting. If you'll just sit tight a minute longer while I go upstairs and get my saddlebags, then we'll head for Union Depot."

Knowing the delay in talking to the neighbors and the cabbie had cost him precious time, Longarm moved as fast as he could. He buckled the straps of his saddlebag's flaps and those around the bedroll, tossed the saddlebags over his shoulder, picked up the bedroll, and hurried out of the room.

He clattered down the stairs, took one long step from the porch to the walk, and hurried to the hackney. While he'd been finishing his interrupted packing, the cabman had lighted the bracket lamps on each side of the vehicle. Longarm was instantly aware of the easy target he made against their glow, and he dived into the cab quickly.

"Now, let's get going to the station," he told the driver.

After the hackman had wheeled the cab around and headed the vehicle back toward town on Cherry Street he slid open the panel between his seat and the passenger compartment and asked Longarm, "Are you figuring to catch the southbound D&RG?"

"I sure am."

"Well, I'll whip my nag up fast as I can, but I'm afraid that train's pulling out of the station right about now."

Taking the whip from its socket, the cabbie flicked the horse's rump. The animal moved a bit faster, but just as the cab turned off First Street into Lincoln, Longarm looked across the sparsely settled strip of land that lay between the street and the tracks and saw Denver & Rio Grande train he'd planned to catch making smoke on its way south.

"Looks like you was right," he told the hackman. "I've missed it, all right."

"Sorry, Marshal. It wasn't my fault, though," the man said. "You want to go on into town, or go back?"

"I don't guess I got much choice," Longarm replied. "There ain't another—" He stopped short and said, "Hold on a minute! Get me over to the D&RG freight yards. You know where it is, I guess."

"Sure. I'd imagine you're still in a hurry, so I'll zigzag over to it and miss the supper traffic downtown."

Longarm had time to think about his next moves as he took cartridges from his coat pocket and reloaded his Colt while the cab rolled to the freight yards. He didn't try too hard to guess who had been behind the attempt to kill him. He'd given any number of desperate criminals plenty of reason to seek revenge, but at the moment the fact that it had been made was more important than the identity of the criminals who'd carried it out.

You got careless, old son, he told himself. *You forgot telegrams travel a lot faster than trains. There's been plenty of time for somebody McCoy's paying to keep an eye on things in Miles City to've passed the word you taken out after him, if that's the way it was. But them bushwhackers hightailed it fast, and likely figured you'd hole up for a while instead of sticking around to see what you'd really do. If you make the right moves, chances are you can get a leg up on 'em now.*

He dug a cartwheel out of his pocket and passed it through the panel to the driver.

"Here's your fare and a little something extra for waiting," he said. "Now, I want you to put out your riding lights before we get to the yards, and rein in when we get alongside the yard super's shanty. Don't stop, just slow enough so I can jump out."

Without questioning the instructions, the hackie carried them out. When Longarm saw the window of the shanty gleaming against the red and green dots made by the switchlamps he swung his saddlebags over his shoulder. Opening the cab door, he tossed out his saddle and bedroll, got a firm grip on his rifle and saddlebags, and jumped from the slowly moving cab. He landed running and skidded to a halt. After picking up his saddle and blankets he headed for the shanty.

"I missed getting on the southbound passenger," Longarm

explained to the night yard superintendent after showing the man his badge. "But it seems to me I recall you got a freight moving south that'll get me to Trinidad in time to connect up with the Santa Fe passenger train that'll be passing through there for Albuquerque."

"You've got a good memory, Marshal," the superintendent replied. "That drag will be pulling out in about ten minutes, and if you want to ride the caboose, you're more than welcome."

"I don't think I'll take you up on the caboose," Longarm said. "There's an outside chance somebody might be watching, and they'd see me in there. If you'll show me a freight car that's manifested all the way to Trinidad, that'll suit me just fine."

Ten minutes later, Longarm heard the highball whistle as the freight started, and the clanking of couplers as the engineer took up slack in his string. The freight car to which the yard superintendent had taken him rolled slowly ahead.

Longarm stood just inside the sliding door, watching until he saw the last of the yard switches in the near distance. He decided it was safe for him to relax then. Pulling his gear to the back end of the freight car, he pushed the saddle and bags against the wall and sat down, using his bedroll as a cushion. He laid down his rifle and took a cheroot from his vest pocket. He was just about to strike a match when a dark form appeared in the light of the open door, and a shadowy figure tumbled into the coach.

Longarm let the match fall, tucked the cheroot away, and drew his Colt. Raising his voice to make himself heard above the rumbling wheels, he said sharply, "Stop right where you are and put your hands up, or you'll get yourself a bullet in the belly!"

Chapter 12

"Don't shoot!" the newcomer said quickly.

Judging from the high-pitched, youthful tone of the new arrival's voice, Longarm decided the speaker must be a boy in his middle teens.

"I ain't about to unless you move," Longarm said, starting to jackknife to his feet, but keeping his pistol ready.

"I haven't got any money or a gun, and I'm not interested in hurting anybody," the newcomer protested. "All I care about is getting to Trinidad."

Still keeping his voice harsh, Longarm replied, "You ain't got anything to worry about, if you're telling the truth. Stand still and keep your hands up while I make sure you ain't got a gun tucked away someplace."

As Longarm started forward the train entered the curve that led from the yards to the main line. The boxcar swung around and moonlight flooded into the open door, lighting a rectangle where the new arrival stood. Longarm could see that he'd been right in his deductions. Though the pulled-down bill of a cloth cap threw the upper half of the young freight-hopper's face into deep shadow, there were no signs of beard or stubble on the chin and jaw that the bright moonlight revealed, not even fuzz on the youngster's upper lip.

He was dressed in an over-large coat and baggy trousers, and from the way the garments hung and sagged, it was apparent that below the badly fitting clothing his frame was small. After a cursory look, Longarm felt the pockets of the coat and pants and ran an experienced hand lightly around the newcomer's slim waist, feeling for a pistol butt and finding none. He nodded.

"All right," he said. "You don't seem to be carrying a gun of any kind. You can let your hands down."

"Thanks." The youth let his arms fall. "You scared me for a minute there. I thought I was going to get killed."

106

"If I had an itchy trigger finger like some do, you might've been," Longarm said. "But seeing as we'll be riding together a good part of the night, we might as well be sociable."

"That depends on what you mean, mister," the youth said with a question in his tone.

"I didn't mean a thing except that we might as well sit down close enough so we can talk," Longarm answered. He gestured toward the back of the car. "I fixed up a place where I could settle down and get a little bit of comfort. It ain't exactly a feather sofa, but it's better'n the bare boards."

He walked to the rear of the boxcar. After a momentary hesitation, the youth followed. Longarm picked up his saddlebags and placed them against the rear wall a short distance from his saddle and rifle.

"You can use my bedroll for a cushion," he said. "I'll sit on my saddle. Neither one of 'em's much good, but they're softer than the floorboards."

After they'd settled down, Longarm took out the cigar he'd been holding when the youth boarded the boxcar and clamped it between his teeth. "I got enough of these to spare you one, if you want it," he told his companion. "Unless you got makings, or chew."

"I don't use tobacco, thanks."

"Guess I'd be better off if I swore off the weed, too," Longarm remarked as he flicked his thumbnail across the head of the match and puffed the cheroot to life. "I get a notion to do that every now and again, but so far I never have got around to it." In the darkness of the boxcar the cigar glowed like a beacon while he puffed it until it was drawing properly. In the light radiating from the cigar's glowing tip the pale face of his companion looked even younger than Longarm had taken the youth to be. His voice showing his surprise, Longarm said, "Why, you ain't much more'n a youngster."

"I'm old enough to take care of myself," the youth said stiffly.

"My name's Long, but I answer better to a sorta nickname folks has given me. Call me by it, if you want to. It's Longarm."

"Glad to meet you, Longarm."

"You got a name, I suppose," Longarm ventured after a few moments of silence passed.

"Mine's—" The youth stopped abruptly, then went on, "Pat. Just call me Pat."

107

"I guess that's good enough," Longarm replied. "You come from these parts?"

"No. I'm from Wisconsin."

"I see," Longarm nodded. "Back East."

"Well, we don't think of it as east, but I guess it would be, here in Colorado."

They sat silently, Longarm puffing on his cheroot, while the freight train rumbled and rattled onward through the night. Longarm finished his cigar and stepped to the car door to toss away the butt. The full moon was high in the sky, and outside the low peaks along the west side of the tracks that marked the landscape between Denver and Colorado Springs were almost as clearly defined as they would be at high noon. Ahead he could see Pike's Peak thrusting above all the others, a black cone against the clear night sky.

"Mighty pretty country out there," he remarked to Pat, who had not moved. "You oughta take a look, if you ain't from around here. I don't imagine it's much like Wisconsin."

"I'm just too tired to move," Pat said. "This is the first chance I've had to rest since I walked all the way across Denver from the Union Pacific yards. I don't know whether I'm sleepier than I am hungry, but all I want to do is just sit here."

"If you're hungry, I can give you a bite to eat. It won't be much, just some jerky and parched corn, but it'll sure keep the sides of your belly from touching."

"I can't eat your food, Longarm," Pat protested. "You'll need it for yourself."

"If you eat all of it, which ain't likely, I can always get more," Longarm said. He pulled the saddlebag to his side and rummaged in it until he found the packet of jerky and the sack of parched corn, and passed them to his companion. "Here. Get some of these inside you and you'll feel better."

There was enough moonlight flooding into the open door for him to see Pat examining the sticks of jerky as though they were something new and strange.

"Ain't you had jerky before?" he asked.

"I'm afraid I haven't. What on earth is it? It feels just like leather."

"It's beef that's been dried in the sun," Longarm explained. "Just take a bite off of one end of a strip of it and start chewing. You'll have to work awhile till it gets soft, but it'll sure stop your belly from growling."

Longarm watched while Pat gnawed at the end of the strip for several minutes before managing to bite off a chunk. Then the youth began chewing, with difficulty at first, then more easily, frowning all the while at the strange flavor.

"Eat a bite of parched corn with it," Longarm advised. "I don't know why, but it's easier to chew that way."

Pat nodded and added a few grains of corn to the jerky. At last the bite could be swallowed. "It's funny, but good," Pat said, starting on another bite.

Longarm lighted a fresh cheroot and puffed patiently while his young companion devoured bite after bite until the entire stick of jerky was consumed. For a moment they sat in silence, then Pat said, "I guess I needed some food to quiet my stomach down. But now it's not bothering me any more, and I'm getting sleepier than ever."

"Well, I'd say the thing to do is go to sleep, then," Longarm observed. "I could use a little shuteye, myself. Suppose I just spread out my bedroll, and we snooze a while."

"I—" Pat began, then stopped for a moment, and finally finished, "Why, sure, Longarm. That'll be just fine."

Longarm unrolled the blankets. He took out the bottle of Tom Moore. He said, "Seeing as you don't smoke, I don't suppose you'd want a nightcap?"

"No. Thanks all the same."

Longarm tilted the bottle and took a healthy swallow of the smoothly sharp rye. He tucked the bottle in his saddlebags and laid his hat aside, took off his coat, and folded it to make a pillow. He unbuckled his gunbelt and laid it where his hand would fall on it naturally, and stretched out on the blankets. Pat had been sitting on the other side of the improvised bed watching Longarm's unhurried preparations. He sat quietly for a moment, then shed the oversized coat and folded it as Longarm had folded his, and lay down quietly. Except for the click of the wheels on the rails and the rush of wind through the open door the boxcar grew quiet.

How long he'd been asleep before he was suddenly roused by Pat's high-pitched screaming, Longarm didn't know. He sat up on the blankets and had his Colt in his hand before he identified the source of the loud screams. He glanced at Pat, saw that the youth was sitting erect, head thrown back, mouth agape, throat throbbing with wildly ringing cries.

Letting his Colt drop from his hand, Longarm rolled over,

109

his arm going out, reaching for Pat's shoulder. Pat pulled away from his touch, leaped up, and started running toward the square of moonlight that marked the boxcar's open door. Longarm rolled to his feet in one swift fluid move and overtook the youth just before he launched himself from the moving train.

Pat's screams grew louder. He raised his hands and began to pummel Longarm's chest. Longarm could feel the youth's slender body trembling convulsively, and shook his shoulders hard, trying to break the grip of the nightmare. Pat's eyes opened, and the shapeless cap fell off, freeing a cascade of long blonde hair. Longarm stopped shaking his companion and stared.

"Well, I'll be damned!" he gasped. "I knew there was something about you that didn't jibe, but I figured you was just a sissified kinda boy! It never struck me you was a girl!"

For a moment, Pat did not answer. She stared with glazed eyes at Longarm, her mouth still gaping in an interrupted scream. Her body continued quivering, her chest rising and falling, and now that she did not have on the oversized coat, Longarm could see a pair of small, dainty breasts pushing against the fabric of her shirt. Gradually, her convulsive breathing became normal.

"Oh, God!" she panted. "I had another nightmare!"

"You mean you've done like this before?" Longarm asked.

"Yes. Quite a number of times."

"What you need's something to quiet you down," Longarm told her. He led the trembling girl back to the blankets and helped her sit down, then picked up the bottle of Tom Moore and pulled the cork. Handing her the whiskey, he said sternly, "Now take a big swallow. This ain't whiskey. It's medicine."

Like an obedient child, Pat gulped down the whiskey. She crimped up her eyelids and coughed, her lips turned down, but in a few moments the potent rye did its work, and the quivering that had been shaking her body quieted and stopped. Longarm let her sit quietly for a moment, then closed his big hand over her small one and the bottle and lifted it to her mouth.

"Take another swallow, now," he said. "Go ahead."

Obediently, she drank. Longarm took the bottle from her unresisting hand, corked it, and set it aside. He pushed her shoulders gently back until she lay on the bed, then folded his legs and sat down beside her. She lay quietly, her eyes big in the reflected moonlight, staring up at him.

"You're running away from something, ain't you?" he asked.

For a moment, she did not reply. Then she nodded and said quietly, "Yes. My husband."

"I don't aim to pry into your private affairs, Pat," Longarm began. He paused and went on, "Is that your right name?"

"Yes, only it's short for Patricia instead of Patrick. And almost everybody calls me Patty."

"I didn't tell you before," Longarm continued, "but just in case you been wondering if I'm some kinda desperado, carrying a rifle and a pistol and hopping freights, I ain't. I'm a deputy United States marshal, and the only way I could get to Trinidad in time to pick up a southbound Santa Fe train was to get on this freight. I'm going south on a case."

"Well, I'll admit I wondered about you," Patty said with a sigh of relief. "I was even a little bit scared. But one thing I've learned since I started out from home, when you're traveling like a hobo, you don't ask anybody you meet any questions."

Longarm went on, "Like I started to say, what's between you and your husband ain't no affair of mine, but sometimes it helps if you can talk a thing like that outa your system."

"I—I don't know whether I can talk about it or not."

"I don't aim to prod you," Longarm told her. "If you feel like it, I'm a pretty good listener, but if you don't, I sure ain't going to try and persuade you."

Patty sat silently for several minutes. Longarm said nothing, realizing she needed time to think. He studied her face in the dimness, and wondered how he could have been deceived, for with her long blonde hair loose and framing her face she did not look at all boyish. At last she turned and looked at him, her expression very sober.

"I suppose you've seen just about every kind of trouble there is," Patty said thoughtfully.

"Just about," Longarm agreed soberly.

"Maybe it would help if I told you about mine. I haven't had anybody I could talk to about it before."

"Like I said, I don't mean to prod you into saying anything you don't feel like talking about."

"It's been weighting me down, Longarm. That's why I'm running—to get away from it."

"It might be you're carrying your trouble with you," he suggested, his voice gentle.

111

"I think I must be, or I wouldn't still have nightmares. If you hadn't caught me in time a minute ago, I'd've jumped off the train and probably killed myself. And I haven't thanked you for saving me," Patty said, "but I do. You see, I want to talk to you, but I can't think of a place to start."

"Don't be in any rush," Longarm advised her. "If you need a little Dutch courage, take another sip of that rye whiskey. If you don't want another swallow, I do, so when you've decided, pass me the bottle."

Longarm took out a fresh cheroot and lighted it. In the flare of the match, he looked at Patty. She was staring at him, her eyes troubled. He held the match a moment, long enough to see her lift the bottle to her mouth, then flicked it out. She passed him the whiskey and he tilted it and drank. They sat in silence for a few moments before Patty began to speak.

"It's not easy to talk about what happened to me, Longarm," she began. "I guess it's happened to other women, but I'm not sure. All I know is, it happened to me. And I don't know how to start telling you."

"Usually the beginning's a good place," Longarm said.

"Well, the beginning goes back to when I met Todd, I guess," Patty said thoughtfully. "He was a preacher. Older than me by almost twenty years. That was six years ago, when I was fourteen. He didn't notice me for a while. Then he did, and he started to look at me. Funny looks. I didn't understand what they meant then, and maybe I still don't. But—well, after a while he was looking at me so funny that I couldn't help noticing him. Then he began coming to visit us. He'd pat me on the head, only it wasn't just patting all the time. It was more stroking, like I was a kitten."

Patty stopped. Longarm didn't want to interrupt her now that she'd begun to talk. He took another sip of rye and held the bottle out to her. Absently, as though she wasn't aware of what she was doing, Patty took another swallow, coughed, and gave a little shiver as the liquor went down her throat. After a moment, she began talking again.

"Todd started asking me to do little things for him at the church after a while," she said. "Like dusting in his office, and helping him look up passages in the Bible that he wanted to use in his sermons. And he'd come stand over me where I was sitting in a chair, and stroke my head. Then after while, he

112

didn't just stop at my head. He began rubbing my neck and shoulders and cheeks. And then he went on past that."

Again, Patty stopped talking. Longarm said nothing. Even in the dimness of the freight car he could see that her eyes were fixed beyond him, as though she was looking at something hanging in the air. He waited patiently for her to go back to her story.

"I knew it wasn't right for Todd to be feeling of me the way he got to doing," she said, bringing up her hands to indicate her breasts. "Only I didn't know how to stop him. And, if you want to know the truth, I kind of liked it. But then one day I was standing by his desk and Todd came up in back of me and began feeling of me and the first thing I knew he'd pushed me down over the desk and was pulling off my pantalettes. Then he was hurting me, really hurting me." She brought her hands down to her crotch. "Here. I guess you know what I'm saying, Longarm."

"Yes, I know." Longarm thought it was safe for him to talk to her now that she'd gone past what must have been the hardest part of her story. "It's happened to girls before, Patty."

"I didn't know that then," she replied. "I don't really know much about it now. But Todd hurt me a while, then he quit. I was bleeding—not bad, but some. And he took his handkerchief and helped me clean up. I was scared to death, but he told me to lie to my folks if they asked me anything. I didn't know what to think, a preacher telling me to lie, but as it turned out, I didn't have to. Todd came over to our house the next day and told my folks he wanted to marry me. They didn't like the idea much, but he was a good talker, so finally they said all right. So we got married, and then the really bad times started."

"I'd've thought getting married would've straightened things out between you and him," Longarm suggested when Patty stopped talking and sat silently once more.

"It didn't, though. I don't know what it was, but something happened to Todd. He never could—" Patty stopped and Longarm could see she was struggling to find words, but feared that if he broke in, she'd freeze up. She went on at last, "He couldn't do anything in bed, Longarm. He tried, and he made me feel of him and hold him and squeeze him and things like that, and he'd feel of me with his fingers and all, but nothing did any

113

good. He even got me to bend over his desk again, and pull up my skirt, and take my pantalettes off, but nothing happened."

Patty stopped, and to keep her story moving, Longarm asked, "And that went on for all those years?"

She shook her head. "No. He stopped trying after—oh, I guess almost a year. Then he turned mean. He'd slap me and poke me and bite at me, and pinch me. Then he began poking things in me. I don't want to talk about it, if it's all the same to you."

"You don't need to," Longarm assured her, his voice soft. "I guess I know the rest of it. You stood for it as long as you could, then you ran away."

"Yes. My folks were dead. Both of them died close together about a year ago. Todd got worse than ever after that. He wasn't a good preacher any more, and folks stopped coming to the church, all but a few, so there wasn't any money. I just took one of Todd's old suits and a shirt and left."

Patty fell silent. Longarm could almost feel her relaxing after the strain of telling her story. He said, "There ain't much I can say to you, Patty, except that you done the best thing you could do when you left."

"You really mean that?" she asked eagerly.

"If we was better acquainted, you'd know I don't say things I don't mean. You'll do fine now you've broke away. After a while you'll forget all the bad things that happened and start fresh."

"Maybe you're right," Patty said hopefully. "I know I feel better right now, just having somebody to listen to me. And all of a sudden, I'm sleepy again."

"Then go back to sleep," Longarm told her.

Obediently, Patty stretched out on the blanket. Longarm took a final sip of Tom Moore and lay down on his side of their improvised bed, careful not to get too close to her. He'd been lying there for several minutes and was drifting off to sleep when Patty sat up.

"Longarm," she said softly, "I thought I wanted to go to sleep, but I don't. Longarm, show me how it is when a real man is with a woman."

114

Chapter 13

For a moment Longarm did not reply. Then he said, "I ain't sure you know what you'd be getting into, Patty."

"I know what I'm asking you to do," she replied. "Don't you see? I never can be a real woman until I know. I'm not sure of anything now. After all those years with Todd, I still don't have any idea what it's like to be a woman with a man."

When Longarm still didn't answer her, Patty leaned down and pressed against him. Through the thin cloth of her shirt he felt her breasts rubbing against his chest. She stroked his cheek with her soft hand and he felt her fingers brushing along his moustache.

After a few moments, when Longarm did not object or make a move to push her away, Patty grew bolder. Her hand crept to his crotch and she began to stroke and feel him through the cloth of his trousers. Then she brought her lips down on his, and Longarm embraced her. He thrust his tongue between her lips. Patty did not respond for a moment, then with a smothered gasp she joined her tongue with his.

Longarm needed no further urging. He knew it was not the time for talk. His hands found her breasts. They were small, but fully rounded, and softly yielding. He began rubbing their rosettes with his hardened fingertips, feeling them pebble under his caresses. Patty quickly unbuttoned her shirt and flung it aside. She wore nothing under the shirt, and Longarm began to caress her bare breasts with his mouth instead of his hands, while her hands returned to Longarm's crotch.

He felt her fumble at the buttons of his fly for a moment, then it was open and Patty was fondling him with her warm, soft hands. When Longarm felt her busy fingers close on his shaft, his earlier doubts vanished. He did not try to hold himself limp, but began swelling to an erection.

"You're awfully big," she murmured. "I didn't know how big a man could get. And you're getting bigger all the time!"

"If you got any doubt about what you're getting into—"

Patty did not let him finish. "I don't. Please don't try to talk me out of it, Longarm."

"I ain't trying to do that, Patty," he said. "I just want to be sure you're sure."

"I'm sure," she replied firmly. "And if the way I feel now is any sign, all I can think about is going on."

Longarm levered his boots off and slid out of his pants, then his fingers found the waistband of Patty's loose trousers and slipped them below her hips.

"Hurry, Longarm!" she gasped, kicking her legs free of the trousers. "I don't know what's happening to me, but I've got feelings that I've never had before!"

"This ain't the time to hurry," Longarm said. He ran his hands along Patty's slim body, gently caressing her soft skin from her ribs to her thighs. "Let's just take our time and be sure you ain't going to be scared or hurt."

"I don't want to take my time," Patty protested. "I'm not a bit scared. And after what Todd did to me, I don't think that you'll hurt me a bit."

Longarm moved away from her long enough to shed his shirt and balbriggans. Patty sat up, watching him, her hand still closed around his burgeoning erection. Then she pressed her breasts into the coarse curls of his chest and began rubbing against him.

"I've never felt this way before!" she gasped breathlessly in the moment before Longarm's lips sought hers again. "I'm burning up inside! Put out my fire, Longarm! Don't make me wait any longer!"

Patty had parted her thighs now, and was pressing the dark gold curls of her brush against Longarm's erection. He did as she was asking, and went into her very gently, shallowly, holding himself away from her, still hesitant about penetrating fully. Patty sighed and pushed her hips toward him, trying to bring him into her more fully. Longarm cupped one big hand around her slim buttocks and lifted her, moving above her as he helped her to lie prone on the blankets.

"Now, Longarm, now!" she whispered urgently. "Stop holding back! I'm aching to feel all of you in me!"

Longarm felt Patty locking her legs around his hips. He let her clasp them firmly, then slowly lowered himself until he was fully buried in her. For a few moments he did not move. Then he started stroking, gently at first, but as her writhing

116

became frantic, he plunged faster, lunging without restraint as Patty came to sudden frenzied life beneath him.

He did not stop when Patty began keening, a high-pitched cry of ecstasy that rose to a peak and stopped abruptly, then began again and tapered off to breathless little whimpers. He felt her relax and held himself pressed firmly against her while the tremors that had shaken her small slim body rippled in receding waves until she lay quiet.

After a few minutes Patty opened her eyes and looked up at him through the gloomy darkness. "Is that what it's supposed to be like?" she asked.

"Pretty much. There's more to it than that, of course."

"Show me what else there is then."

After the brief respite he'd had, Longarm was ready. He began stroking again, but now he was neither slow nor gentle. He lengthened his lunges and speeded them up until he was driving into Patty with the speed and force of a triphammer.

She began responding at once. Her legs grasped his hips as she pulled herself up to meet his strokes, and almost at once her breathing grew faster, her movements more frenzied, until Longarm stopped suddenly and held her pressed beneath him while she panted and wriggled and tried to move, but could not.

"Why did you stop, Longarm?" she gasped. "Go on, please! I know something tremendous is going to happen to me any minute!"

"It'll be a lot better if it don't happen for a while."

"I don't understand," Patty said, uncertainty in her voice.

"You will," Longarm promised. "Just be patient and wait."

Longarm started stroking again, slowly once more, then increasing the tempo and force of his driving thrusts, letting himself build now as Patty's cries rose, louder than before, and she began trembling, approaching her climax.

When Longarm felt her final spasm begin he pounded into her full-length with each long stroke, reaching his own peak as he drove. Patty's shrieks filled his ears and her hips rose and fell in a frenzied rhythm. Longarm let himself go and began to jet as Patty began twisting in her climax. Her lips parted in a final keening moan that rose and fell and faded to a long deep sigh while Longarm pressed against her. Then they lay still.

After a while, Patty said softly, "You were right, Longarm.

There was more to it than I thought, a lot more than I could ever have imagined."

"You don't feel bad about it, then?"

"Of course not! Why should I? I'm not mad at anybody except Todd, for having cheated me all those years."

"Don't feel that way, Patty. It'll make you sour. Maybe he tried but couldn't help himself."

"I'd like to think that," she said. "Maybe I'll be able to some day." She was silent for a moment, then sighed, "I'm really sleepy now, Longarm. Hold me, will you, while I sleep?"

Longarm took her in his arms. She murmured something in a tangled whisper that he could not understand, and in a moment was breathing deeply, a serene smile on her face. Longarm watched her for a short time, then he went to sleep, too.

"I still wish you'd let me get you a ticket to someplace you want to go to," Longarm told Patty. "It's dangerous for a lone woman to be hopping freights and riding in boxcars."

They were standing outside the station at Trinidad, waiting for the switching crew to put on the helper engine that the southbound Santa Fe train would need for the tricky run over Raton Pass.

"I've told you, I don't know where I want to go," she said. "Except not back to Wisconsin. And I've got to find my own way to wherever it is, don't you see?"

"Well, you remember what I told you, now. If you need help any time, send me a wire to Denver."

"I'll remember what you've told me, and what you've showed me, for a long time, Longarm. But I don't think I'll ever have to ask anybody for help again."

"It's best that way," Longarm nodded, as the twin blasts of the engine sounded in the "all aboard" signal.

Longarm swung his saddle and saddlebags onto the vestibule and followed them up the steps. He waited as the train began to move, returning Patty's waves. Then the car entered the first of many curves that lay ahead on the winding roadbed, and she was out of his sight.

Through most of the morning, as the train rolled across the eastward-sloping prairie at the edge of the Sangre de Cristo Mountains, then humped hooklike into the foothills, Longarm dozed. The plush cushions of his chair car seat were softer than the boxcar floor where he'd spent a largely sleepless night.

118

He got off to stretch his legs at Lamy, where the passengers bound for Santa Fe left the train. Between dusk and daylight, he got off again, this time at Albuquerque, to eat an early supper in the big red-tiled reverberating dining room of the Harvey House while waiting for the bobtail accommodation train that would carry him and half a dozen other passengers to Vaughn.

In the rosy sunrise of the next morning, Longarm dropped off the train at Vaughn and looked around at the straggling new one-street town that had become the Santa Fe's railhead in its challenge to the rival Southern Pacific. Both roads were pushing rails as fast as the gandydancers could move, competing for the cattle shipments now going east to Kansas City's stockyards from the ranches which for more than a decade had been creeping over the shortgrass prairie from the overgrazed Texas Panhandle.

That Vaughn had become an important cattle-shipping point for both the Santa Fe and the Southern Pacific was obvious at a glance. Both rail lines had their depots at the edge of town, only a scant quarter of a mile separating them. Filling the gap between the two small stations and extending for a mile on both sides of both main-line tracks there were stockpens. Longarm felt that he was looking at a miniature Kansas City or Fort Worth as he gazed at the backs of the penned steers. Marking them for later investigation, he turned his attention to the town itself.

Looking at Vaughn from the station platform at its edge, Longarm found it very little different from the other brand-new cowtowns he'd seen wherever there was enough dependable water and decent grass.

It was a town of raw, unpainted, yellowing boards or red-painted one-story board-and-batten buildings and houses. The only difference he could see between them was that the commercial buildings were bigger, and almost all of them had story-and-a-half false fronts designed to make them look more imposing than they were. There were two genuine two-story structures facing the street, and Longarm headed for them, certain that one would be the town's biggest saloon and the other a hotel.

At that hour of a weekday morning the streets were bare of people. Not even the hitch rails of the hotel or the saloon had any horses or buggies or wagons standing in front of them.

119

Vaughn was obviously still asleep, and Longarm had no intention of being the one to wake it up.

Since he'd had an eye-opener on the train a short time before it stopped at end-of-rail, and there was still an inch or so of Tom Moore left in the bottle to provide a drink or two, Longarm passed by the saloon and headed for the hotel. His eyes smarting from the cindery smoke that for a day and a night had assaulted them through the day coach's windows, he scrawled "C. Long" on the hotel register and went upstairs. The bed looked too inviting to pass up. Longarm downed a swallow of Tom Moore, washed the coal dust off his face and hands, and dropped on the bed. Before he had time to think about lighting a cheroot, he was asleep.

When he woke after his nap, Longarm was ravenously hungry. He lighted a cigar while he stepped into his boots, drained the bottle of Tom Moore after he'd adjusted the set of his Colt's holster, and stopped in front of the mirror to put a final upward twist to his moustache and reset the angle of his wide-brimmed snuff-brown hat. He went down the short flight of uncarpeted stairs to the tiny lobby and stopped at the desk.

"I guess I'm about to ask you what everybody else does his first time here," he told the clerk. "What's the best place in town to get a decent meal?"

"If you can stand Chinee food, there's the Oriental," the clerk replied. "If you want meat and potatoes, walk down to the Santa Fe tracks and try the Wrangler's Restaurant."

"I'm a steak man myself," Longarm said. "So I guess you've answered my question. But I got one thing more to ask you. Has a man named McCoy signed in yet?"

"McCoy." The clerk frowned. He turned the register ledger around and looked at it for a moment. "No. He's not registered, Mr. Long, but the name's familiar. Of course!" He turned to the narrow line of pigeonholes behind the desk and indicated one that held several fat envelopes, their edges protruding. "We're holding some mail for Mr. McCoy, that's why I recognized the name. He's not here yet, because even if he'd failed to sign the register, he'd certainly have picked up his mail."

"Thanks," Longarm said. "I guess I got here just in time."

"Do you want me to tell him you're here, if he comes in while you're at the restaurant?" the clerk asked.

"No, don't bother to do that. Matter of fact, I'd sorta like

120

to surprise him. He ain't expecting me to be here yet, so if you'll just forget about mc asking, I'd be right obliged."

Outside the hotel, Longarm found that while he'd slept Vaughn had come to life. There were horses crowded together at almost every hitch rail now, and ranch wagons in front of many of the stores. In front of the Plainsman's Saloon a crowd of cowhands were idling, and from inside the tinkle of a honky-tonk piano carried its jingling melodies into the street.

Well, old son, Longarm congratulated himself silently as he walked along the street looking for the cafe, *seems like you're finally going to meet up with that McCoy you been after all these weeks. And it's going to do you a lot of good to see his face when he finds out this is one time when you've jumped a step or two ahead of him.*

With his mind at rest, Longarm ate a combined breakfast and lunch at the Wrangler's Restaurant, sat over coffee while he thought out his next moves, and finally left the place as a crowd of hungry ranch hands came in looking for a noon meal. Longarm looked up the street toward the hotel, decided he had no reason to hurry back, and started for the stockpens to take the look he'd promised himself earlier.

Longarm had almost reached the pens when a Southern Pacific engine with a long drag of cattle cars pulled off the main line into the long curve that led to the service siding which ran close to the pens and had loading chutes spaced along it at intervals. There were perhaps twenty cars in the drag, all loaded; Longarm could see steers milling around in them as he got closer to the pens. Brakemen stood on top of several of the cars, ready to open their doors when the train stopped at the loading chutes.

Now here's a prime chance for you to get a good close look at a fresh bunch of range-run steers without having to bust your britches bending around to try and see their hooves or mouths or brands in a jam-packed stockpen, old son, he told himself.

Walking a bit faster, he threaded his way through the alleys that separated the pens, heading for the siding. He'd reached the last line of pens and was almost to the rails when he heard a loud crack of metal breaking. It came from somewhere down the siding beyond the pens, and Longarm stepped on a rail of the nearest loading chute to determine its source.

He looked back along the track just in time to see one of

the cattle cars in the center of the string leaning dangerously toward the interior arc of the tracks' curve. As he watched, the car teetered, balanced at a precarious angle for a moment, then toppled on its side with a crash.

Like dominoes in a closely spaced line, the cars on either end of the fallen car were tilted by the unyielding coupler. They balanced momentarily, just as the first car had, then fell in the same fashion. Their couplers levered the next two cars over, and if the brakemen riding the tops of the cars had not leaped to the ground and disengaged the couplings the whole train might have gone over.

Already the area around the toppled cars was a scene of pandemonium. The slats on most of the fallen cars had not survived the crash. They splintered like matchsticks. The cars quite literally burst apart, and the air was filled with the blatting of the panicked steers and the shouts of the brakemen as well as the continuing splintering of wood slats as the cattle fought their way out of the shattered cars.

By now men were heading for the wreck from the stockpens. Only a few of them were on horseback, far too few to control the number of cattle that were now running around on the prairie beyond the tracks, blatting as they exhausted their mindless frenzy. One of the riders came down the path between the loading chutes and the track. He saw Longarm and reined in.

"What the hell're you standing there for?" he called to Longarm. "Half of my hands is in town, and I need every man that can fork a horse to get them steers bunched up before they kill theirselves running!"

"Mister, I ain't a cowhand, and even if I was, I ain't got a horse," Longarm replied.

"There's a horse tethered down at that next chute," the man shot back, pointing. "And I ain't asking who you are or what! You got on boots and a wide hat, so in my book you're a cowhand."

Before Longarm could reply, the rider whipped out his gun and Longarm found himself staring into the muzzle of the pistol.

"Now, git!" the rider snapped. "Walk on ahead of me and take that horse and do what you can to help!"

Longarm had no doubt that the angry, excited rancher would shoot if he refused or even protested further. He dropped to the ground, and with the gun at his back preceded the rider to the tethered horse. He swung into the saddle.

"Ride on ahead of me!" the man with the gun commanded. "I can tell the way you forked that hoss that you know what you're about. Now, let's get after them loose steers!"

Longarm did not argue. He toed the cow pony into motion and rode toward the end of the pens, then turned his mount and headed for the prairie where the milling steers were running wild.

Chapter 14

Before the last of the panicked steers had been rounded up and driven to the stockpens, the sky in the east had darkened and its deeper blue hue was creeping toward the sun, which now hung in the west, its bottom rim just above the low, ragged lumps of the Monzanos.

Longarm had kept working even after word of the derailment reached the ranch hands who were in town, and they'd arrived to help. Even with the reinforcements the job of rounding up the scattered cattle had gone slowly. Not only did the loose steers have to be ridden down and hazed back to the railroad tracks, but once there they had to be driven the length of the train, around the last car on the tracks, then back over the lane between the tracks and the stockpens.

Fresh from the open range, the steers were cantankerous and wild. Until they'd been rounded up for shipping their lives had been virtually undisturbed, but now their systems had been thrown out of kilter by the hazing they'd gotten during the roundup and by their long trip in the crowded cattle cars. The derailment had brought out their dormant wildness, and many of them had to be lassoed and dragged to the stockpens.

Quite a few years had passed since Longarm had worked as a cowhand, and he'd had some problems adjusting to the quick moves, sudden spurts, and quick stops required to control the scattered animals. Like all special skills, deftness in roping is lost if not practiced, and after trying to rope a few he'd coiled up the lariat and retied it to the saddle strings of the strange horse. In spite of everything, though, he'd stuck with the job until the more skillful range-wise hands had arrived from town. Then he had let them take over the work on the prairie and joined the men who were hazing the cattle that had been rounded up down the lanes and into the stockpens.

Penning the cattle was slower work and not a great deal easier than running them down on the prairie. The steers were too wild to be driven in large numbers. They arrived at the lanes leading to the pens singly or in bunches of three or four, and Longarm had all the time he needed to check their condtion and examine their brands. He'd noticed immediately that there were wide differences in many of the animals as well as in the brands they bore.

Though all the steers were longhorns, he estimated that roughly half of them had the smaller configuration and shorter horns characteristic of Mexican stock. In nine cases out of ten, the Cross W brand marks on the Mexican-bred steers did not have the clean, sharp-edged lines left by a blacksmith-forged branding iron. The brand marks on the smaller steers were wavering and thin, a sure sign that they had been drawn free-hand on the animals' rumps with a running iron.

Yep, them's Mexican steers, old son, Longarm told himself as he drove a pair of the smaller animals down the lane to the nearest pen. *Even if it wasn't for them wavy brands, the horns is a dead giveaway. And they won't make the weight of them other critters by a couple of hundred pounds.*

While the steers Longarm identified as Mexican-bred showed no signs of apthos fever now, he knew that the disease could lie dormant for months, even years, then suddenly appear without any preliminary indications of its presence and sweep through a herd in a few days. Some of the Mexican steers were scrawny as well as undersized, and Longarm wondered if their weight loss was the result of shipping or whether it was a preliminary indication that the animals might be infected.

A grizzled old cowhand with a gimpy leg was handling the gates of one of the pens. He looked like the veteran he was, and Longarm stopped to light a cheroot after he'd delivered a pair of steers to the pen the old man was tending.

"It's a slow job," he commented as the oldster closed the gate and used the bandana around his neck to wipe off the sweat that was dripping from his stubbled chin.

"It is that," the old-timer agreed. He looked at Longarm. "You don't hand at none of the spreads hereabouts, not with them citified duds on. How in hell did you git roped in on this?"

"I just happened to be here looking around when the train derailed," Longarm replied. "Before I knew what was going on, I was on a horse and out there on the prairie trying to round up the critters that had busted loose."

"Old Clay Barnhart's lucky, at that," the old man said. "If

125

that damn train had busted up where there wasn't no help to hand, he'd be out a good-sized bunch of steers right now."

"Barnhart owns the Cross W, I take it?"

"Yup. Boughten it off of McSween's boy a few years back."

"A lot of them steers looks like they come up from Mexico not too long ago," Longarm commented casually.

"I wouldn't know," the veteran said.

"You've been around long enough to tell a Mexican-bred steer when you see one," Longarm persisted. He pointed to one of the small animals just inside the gate. "Wouldn't you say that one there come across the border someplace down south of here?"

"Who in hell are you, mister? Some kind of range detective or an Association snooper?" the old man asked suspiciously.

Longarm shook his head. "I'm no range detective and I don't work for the Cattlemen's Association. Just curious."

"Well, I wouldn't be asking too many questions, was I you," the grizzled veteran warned. "There's some thin-skinned folks hereabouts might take things the wrong way."

Longarm kept his voice carefully neutral as he said, "No offense meant."

He looked around. There were very few cattle still running loose, and by now there were enough men to handle them. Around the derailed cars a crew of railroad workers was already busy clearing away the debris of the wreck. Along the tracks and beyond the train and around the end of the pens, spectators drawn from town by the derailment were watching the repair crew and the cowhands who were rounding up the remaining steers. Swinging off the horse, Longarm handed the reins to the old cowhand.

"I don't guess they need a green hand like me any longer," he said. "I'll be obliged if you'll see that this horse gets back to whoever it belongs to. I got some business in town I need to tend to."

Without looking back at the grizzled cowhand, he walked slowly down the lane to the end of the pens and started toward Main Street. While the sun hadn't yet dropped out of sight, dusk was creeping over the town, and the lights spilled from the stores and shone around the batwings of the saloon. Longarm headed for the batwings and pushed through them. The place was deserted except for the barkeep. Longarm walked

126

up to the bar and looked at the rows of bottles that flanked the narrow mirror.

"I hope one of them bottles has got Tom Moore's name on it," he said to the barkeep.

"I'm afraid not, friend," the aproned man replied. "But if it's rye you're looking for, we sure can fix you up."

"Maryland rye." Longarm nodded. "That whiskey they make up in Pennsylvania don't have the true bite."

"How about Joe Gideon?" the barkeep asked, placing a shotglass and a bottle on the bar in front of Longarm. "It's from Kentucky, but that's about as close as I can get to Maryland."

"That'll do me fine," Longarm replied, filling the glass.

"Looks to me like you got mixed up in that wreck out on the siding," the barkeep remarked, indicating Longarm's dusty clothing. "It sure emptied this place out in a hurry."

"I done what I could to help," Longarm said, refilling his glass. "It's been a while since I cowhanded, though." He tossed a pair of cartwheels on the bar. "You better let me have a bottle of that Joe Gideon. I feel like I'd been sent for and couldn't go. It'll take me a while to get cleaned up when I get back to the hotel, and I'll want another sip before I go get my supper."

Tucking the bottle into his elbow, Longarm walked on to the hotel. As he passed the desk he glanced at the pigeonholes on the wall behind it and his eyes widened. The thick sheaf of fat envelopes which had protruded from one of them earlier was gone.

Stepping up to the desk, Longarm tapped the clerk's call bell. Its tinkle did not bring out the clerk to whom Longarm had talked earlier. This time a husky man with a moustache that had a span and sweep which almost matched Longarm's came through the door behind the desk. He looked at Longarm inquiringly.

"Oh, Mr. Long," he said. "What can I do for you?"

"You was holding some mail there—" Longarm pointed to the empty pigeonhole—"for a man named McCoy. I see the letters are gone, so I reckon he's got here now."

For a moment the man gazed at Longarm. Then he said, "No, Mr. McCoy's not here."

"You mind telling me what happened to his letters?"

"I don't like to discuss my guests' business, Mr. Long. Not

unless I have a very good reason to."

Longarm thought for a moment, then said, "From the way you talk, I reckon you own this place?"

"Yes. My name's Darby, by the way. If you can give me a good reason—"

A bit impatiently, Longarm broke in, "I got the best reason in the world, Mr. Darby." Taking out his wallet, he opened it to show his badge. "I work outa the Denver office, and I'm trying to run down this McCoy fellow."

Darby smiled for the first time. "That's all the reason I need, Marshal Long. What do you want to know?"

"Was McCoy here today? I got caught up out at the derailment, they needed some help, so I didn't get back to be here in case McCoy showed up. Didn't know that he'd show up at all, as a matter of fact. Now it looks like I missed him."

"I wasn't here myself when he came in, but my clerk told me about it when I relieved him for supper. It struck me then as being odd. It seems that Mr. McCoy was about to sign the register when the clerk handed him the mail we've been holding. He put down the pen to take the letters, the clerk bent down to get a room key for him—we keep the keys on a board under the desk, here—and when he straightened up, McCoy had—well, he'd just disappeared."

"And he ain't been back since, I guess?"

Darby shook his head. "No. But he'd started to sign his name when the clerk bent down to get the key. Look here." Darby opened the register ledger and turned it around for Longarm to see. He pointed to a single downstroke of a pen. "That's as far as he got in signing. I can't explain why he disappeared the way he did. Perhaps you can?"

Longarm did not reply. His eyes were fixed on the ledger page. Three lines above the single pen stroke McCoy had made, his own signature, "C. Long," leaped out at him. A name strange to him was on the line below, but on the next line, immediately above McCoy's short, bold pen stroke, was another familiar name: "Miss Charlene Hart," inscribed in flowing script.

Darby repeated his question. "Do you know of any reason why McCoy should behave as he did, Marshal?"

Longarm said wryly, "I sure do. He run because I pulled a damn fool stunt when I ought've known better." He turned the ledger back around and pointed to his own name above the line

128

on which McCoy had started to sign. "I guess I had my brains down in my boots when I put my own name there. I ought've been smart enough to know McCoy'd see it."

"You're looking for him to arrest him, then?"

"I imagine I'd be reaching for my handcuffs after I talked to him a few minutes, unless he could show me a real good reason why he's been acting like he has."

Darby said, "It's really not my affair, Marshal Long, so I won't ask you any more questions."

"I got to ask you a few more, though, Mr. Darby. Does McCoy stop here regular?"

"I don't remember that he's been here at all until now. I do know him by reputation, of course. I've heard some of the cattlemen and ranchers who stop here mention him. Isn't he the cattle broker who calls himself the Real McCoy?"

"Well, I ain't real sure whether he is or he ain't. All I got to go by is his description. He's a little fellow, talks fast, always wears a stickpin, a gold steerhead with diamond eyes."

Darby frowned. "I recall the stickpin, Marshal, but I can't remember anything about the man wearing it. Of course, there might be more than one stickpin like that in this part of the country."

"Yes. I thought of that myself." Longarm lighted a cigar, then said, "There's another name on your register I'm curious about. This Miss Hart—did she come in with McCoy?"

"I really couldn't say," Darby replied, looking at the signature. "My clerk would know, though. He'll be back soon, when he's finished his supper."

"I don't guess I need to talk to him," Longarm said. "I got a pretty good hunch I know the answer myself. Well, thanks for your help, Mr. Darby. I don't imagine you'll see McCoy again, but if he does show up I'd sure like to know."

"I'll see that you're told at once, if he does come back," the hotel man said as Longarm turned toward the stairs. "And if there's anything I can do to help, Marshal, please let me know. I don't want my hotel to get the reputation of being a place that welcomes shady characters."

Longarm mounted the stairs and walked down the hall to his room. He passed the door of the room the register entry had told him was occupied by Charlene Hart, but passed by it without stopping. In his own room he sponged off hurriedly, shook as much of the afternoon's dust as possible out of his clothing, and walked back down the hall. At the door of Charlene Hart's room he stopped and knocked.

"Who is it?" called the contralto voice he remembered quite well from their encounter in Kansas City.

"Custis Long," he replied.

In a moment the door was opened and Charlene stood in front of him, smiling broadly. "Why, Longarm!" she said. "What a pleasant surprise!"

Longarm did not reply at once. He was looking at her as she stood silhouetted against the light of her room. Even though her face was shadowed, Longarm could refresh his memory of her blonde upswept hair, vividly red lips, sapphire-blue eyes, creamy skin, and regal figure. He said, "I was sorta surprised to find you here, too. This is a long way from Kansas City."

"How did you find out I was here?" she asked.

"I just happened to see your name on the register when I was checking it over," Longarm replied. "And I figured maybe we could have supper together, even if there ain't anyplace here in Vaughn that's as fancy as the Stockman's House."

"Well, I wouldn't expect there to be." Charlene smiled. "But I'll be delighted to have dinner with you, Longarm. I was getting ready to go look for a cafe myself." Her smile grew wider as she added, "And there'll be time for us to have a nice long visit after we've eaten, if you'd like to."

"Now, you know there ain't a thing I'd enjoy more," Longarm said. "Suppose I wait downstairs till you're ready."

"There's no reason for you to wait. All I need to do is get my scarf and we can go right on."

Leaving the door open, Charlene stepped back into the room. In the mirror of the bureau Longarm could see her pick up a cream-colored silk scarf. When she moved to the bureau to drape the scarf over her head she saw Longarm's reflection, and smiled at him in the glass. Then she lifted her handbag from the bureau and came to the door to join him.

"There's a restaurant right down the street," he said as they left the hotel and started down the dark street. Its only light was that spilled from the store doors. "It ain't such a much for fancy, but I ate there at noon, and the grub ain't killed me yet."

"I wouldn't expect a deluxe cafe in a town the size of Vaughn," she said. "I'll settle for edible food."

"That's what we'll get, and not much else," Longarm told

130

her as they entered the restaurant. He looked around. There was only one unoccupied table, in front of a window and near the door. He said, "Well, I guess we ain't got much choice where we sit. Is that table all right?"

"Since it's the only one vacant, I'm sure it must be."

After they were seated, Longarm reminded her, "You still ain't told me what brings you to Vaughn."

"Oh, it's a matter of some family land that's close by," she replied, dismissing the subject with a flick of her hand. "I don't want to bore you with a long story that isn't really very interesting. I suppose you're here on some kind of case?"

"One I been working on quite a while," he told her. "It looks like I'm getting right close to the man I'm after."

"And I'm sure you don't want to talk about it any more than I do about my family's land." She smiled.

"Oh, we can find something else to talk about, I bet."

"I'm sure we can," Charlene replied as the waiter came to take their orders. Both of them ordered steak, and after the waiter had left she said, "I've thought about you quite a bit since we met, Longarm. I wondered if you'd go back there again, and while I was wondering that, I remembered that even if you came back you wouldn't know how to find me."

Her words gave Longarm the opening he'd been waiting for and solved the question he'd been debating with himself. Since he'd seen Charlene's name on the hotel register, Longarm had been trying to decide how to question her. That they should meet by accident in Vaughn was a coincidence too great for Longarm to accept, even if he'd believed in coincidences. Until she spoke he hadn't decided how to handle their meeting, whether to use a brutally swift frontal attack or approach her indirectly.

"I don't imagine I'd have much trouble finding you, even in a place as big as Kansas City," he said, fixing her sapphire eyes with his own gunmetal-blue ones. "That's a part of my business, Charlene—finding people that're trying to hide from the law."

"Of course," she said. Her voice betrayed her uneasiness, though she tried to mask it with a dazzling smile. "I suppose I hadn't thought of that."

"Oh, I'm sure you thought about it," Longarm replied. "I got a hunch you been thinking about it ever since you started out from Kansas City."

131

"I don't understand, Longarm," she said. Uneasiness had crept into her eyes now, as well as into her voice.

"A minute ago you said something about me not wanting to talk about the case I'm here on," Longarm reminded her. "Well, I don't. But I got some questions I want to ask you about it."

"Is this a joke you're trying to play?" she asked. "If it is, I don't think I like it."

"I didn't suppose you would." Longarm's voice was hard now. He went on, "But I ain't joking. The first question I want an answer to is, did McCoy put you to spy on me there in the Stockman's House? And be careful what you say, because I'm real sure I know what the answer is."

"I—I don't know what you're talking about!" Charlene said quickly. Her voice betrayed her fully now.

"Sure you do. You and that fellow was putting on a show for me. You was the bait McCoy was dangling," Longarm told her. "I bit once, but I don't take the same bait twice."

"Longarm, I swear that—"

"Don't do no false swearing!" Longarm broke in, his voice harsh. "I ain't sure you know what you've let yourself in for, working that steer swindle McCoy's got going. I ain't caught up with McCoy yet, but I'm close behind him. And when I do, he's going to spend a lot of years in the pen. You'll go to prison, too, likely for ten or fifteen years. You look at yourself in the mirror a lot, I guess. Now just think what you're going to be looking at in that mirror when you'd get out. A penitentiary ain't no place for a woman to keep her looks."

"Longarm, I—"

"Keep quiet and listen!" Longarm snapped. "You tell me all you know about that steer swindle McCoy's pulling and I can get you off with maybe a few months in jail. Now, are you ready to start talking?"

"Yes!" she said, an eager plea in her voice. "Yes, if you can keep me out of jail, I'll tell you—"

But before Charlene could finish, a pistol barked from the next table. Charlene's body jerked with the impact of the slug. She toppled out of her chair and fell in a heap on the floor.

Chapter 15

Longarm's finely honed reaction to the unexpected attack saved his own life. While the sound of the shot that struck Charlene was still echoing, before she had toppled limply and begun to fall, his Colt was in his hand and a bullet was on its way. The slug cut down the man at the next table while he was swinging his pistol to get Longarm in its sights. The dying gunman's reflex action triggered the revolver, but the bullet from his sagging weapon missed Longarm. It plowed a furrow in the tabletop and shattered the window while the gunman, still seated in his chair, was crashing to the floor.

For an instant following the three shots the interior of the restaurant was totally silent. Then it exploded into a babble of excited voices as the other patrons leaped from their seats and started toward the two bodies lying on the floor. Longarm stepped over Charlene's prone form and spread his arms wide.

"All you men keep back!" he commanded. The authority in his voice stopped the headlong rush. Taking out his wallet, Longarm unfolded it and held it up to show his badge. He said, "I'm a U.S. marshal, and this shooting's connected with the case I'm working on. Now, everybody stand back outa my way for a few minutes. I'll talk to all of you later."

Slowly the men backed away, moved as much by the authority in Longarm's voice as they were by the Colt which he still held in his right hand.

Longarm glanced at the dead man, but did not recognize him. He could have been any cowhand who'd come in from a ranch for a badly needed shave and a day in town. Turning away from the man's body, Longarm bent over Charlene. She lay in the shadow cast by the table at which the gunhand had been sitting, but even in the dim light he could see bright arterial blood spurting from the bullet hole high on her right breast.

"One of you men go get a doctor, quick!" Longarm called. "She's still alive!"

Charlene's soft cream-colored scarf was still around her

neck, the ends crossed on her chest. Longarm reached for the scarf, folded one end, and pressed it over the bullet hole. The soft fabric soaked up instantly and he tugged at the scarf.

Slight as his pull was, it caused Charlene's head to roll to one side. Longarm's jaw dropped as her upswept blonde hair rolled away from her head and revealed a thin covering of mousy brown hair pulled tightly over her scalp. He looked back at her face and found that it had undergone a sudden transformation with the blonde wig removed.

Longarm was no longer looking at Charlene Hart. The woman on the floor was Elsie Mae Glover.

While he was still absorbing the shock of his discovery, Elsie Mae opened her sapphire-blue eyes and looked up at him.

"I wish I hadn't—" she began.

"Hush, now!" Longarm commanded. "There's a doctor coming. He'll fix you up."

"No. I know what's happening to me, Longarm. McCoy gets rid of anyone he doesn't trust any more," she gasped. Her voice was a thin thread, the high voice of Elsie Mae, not the rich contralto of Charlene. "I told him you're too smart to let him set you up."

Longarm had accepted the inevitable as soon as he'd realized the nature of Elsie Mae's wound. He asked her, "Where is he now, Elsie Mae? Where'd McCoy go?"

"Office," she gasped, her words a faint whisper. "Special drawer—in—"

Her eyes rolled upward and for a moment Longarm thought the end had come. Then she opened them again, and the clear sapphire of her pupils grown clouded as she tried to look at him.

"Elsie Mae!" Longarm's tone was urgent. "Hang on till the doctor gets here!"

"Call me...Charlene," she whispered. "I always...liked her better...than Elsie Mae."

"Charlene, then," Longarm replied, but even as he was repeating the name, he saw that the woman was beyond hearing him.

Lowering her lifeless body gently to the floor, Longarm stood up. The men bunched at the rear of the restaurant stared at him. Their earlier excitement had been stopped by the lifeless bodies on the floor, mute evidence of the swiftness of death. They waited silently for Longarm to speak.

134

"I guess all of you got a good look at this fellow on the floor," he said. "Any of you see him before?"

"He don't belong in Vaughn, Marshal," one of the spectators volunteered. "I'm the barber here, and I don't guess there's a ranch hand inside of a long day's ride that ain't been in my shop one time or other."

Another man spoke up. "Slim's right. That man don't come from anyplace hereabouts."

"And the woman don't, neither," a third man said. "I was at the depot and seen her get off the train. A man'd have to be blind not to look at her. But that's the first and only time I set eyes on her till you and her walked in here a while ago."

Longarm's questioning was interrupted by the arrival of the doctor and the man who'd been sent to get him. The doctor took one look at the two bodies and turned to the men standing at the rear of the cafe. "All right," he announced. "You can go on about your business now. I know all of you. If I want to ask you any questions, I'll know where to find you."

Within a few minutes, as the spectators left, Longarm, the doctor, and the proprietor were alone in the cafe. "I got a lot of work to do in the kitchen," the proprietor announced. "If it's all right, I'll get to it."

Bending over each of the corpses in turn, the doctor made a quick examination, then stood up and told Longarm, "I don't suppose I need to tell you anything much, Marshal. The man was hit in the heart and died instantly. The woman . . . well, it appears to me that the bullet severed her aorta and she bled to death internally. You've probably figured that out yourself. In your line of work I imagine you see as many bodies as I do."

"I seen my share." Longarm nodded. "Well, settling things up is a case for your local law. Can you take care of it?"

"Very quickly," the doctor replied. "I'm also the coroner, and I now pronounce them both dead of gunshot wounds. I'll have the undertaker come and do the rest of it."

"Even if it's your case now, I'll need to see what they've got on 'em," Longarm told the doctor. "I don't guess you mind?"

"Go ahead. If you need me as a witness, I'll watch."

From the dead man's pockets Longarm took a bandana, a Barlow knife, a sack of tobacco and cigarette papers, and ten mint-fresh double eagles. He spread the items on the nearest table.

"That's a lot of money for a saddle tramp to be carrying," the doctor commented, indicating the gold coins. "Close to a year's wages for a good hand in these parts."

"He wasn't no saddle tramp," Longarm said. "More likely the money's what he got paid by the man that hired him to gun down me and Elsie Mae. I'd figure it to be a hundred dollars apiece."

He picked up Elsie Mae's beaded purse and opened it. The aroma of musk and patchouli wafted upward as he upended the purse and let its contents spill out on the table. There was a vial of perfume, a powder puff, a coin purse, a filmy handkerchief, two keys, and a leather folder that contained a sheaf of cashier's checks. He emptied the coin purse on the table. The gold and silver coins that fell out totalled just less than fifty dollars.

"At least they both had enough to pay for their funerals," the doctor remarked. "The town won't be out anything."

Longarm nodded absently. He was riffling through the sheaf of cashier's checks. They'd been issued by the Midland Bank of Kansas City, and there were nineteen of them, each for a hundred dollars. As he fanned them out a stub fluttered free and dropped on the table. He picked it up, glanced at it, and saw that it had come from the twentieth check. He started to slip it in with the uncashed checks when a notation on the back caught his eye.

Giving the brief inscription a closer look, he recognized Elsie Mae's neat writing. The note read: "La Junta, 2 weeks." Turning the stub over, Longarm found that the check had been cashed three days earlier at the Missouri Kansas & Texas railroad ticket office in Kansas City.

Returning the checks and the stub to their folder, Longarm told the doctor, "These checks and them two keys is all I see that I might need for evidence, so I guess I better hang on to them." He tucked the folder and both keys into his wallet and returned the wallet to his pocket, then said, "Well, I guess the rest of it's up to you. I had a real busy day, so I'm going to the hotel and make up on my shuteye."

Back in his room, Longarm uncorked the bottle of Joe Gideon and took a healthy swallow. He made his bedtime preparations with extra care, aware that a partner of the dead gunman might be lurking in the background. Before blowing out the lamp he went to the bureau for a final sip of rye. Standing with

136

the bottle in his hand, Longarm addressed his image in the mirror.

Looks like you finally hit a hot trail, old son. Whatever it is that's going to happen in La Junta won't be for two weeks, so you got all the time you need to try and pick up McCoy's tracks after you go see what Elsie Mae or Charlene or whatever her real name was told you to look for in that office in Kansas City. And it might just be you'll find something in that office that'll put you on his trail before then. But even if you don't, you got your best chance yet to get off of the zigzag trail you been on, and get this damn case closed up.

Longarm stepped up onto the narrow porch of McCoy's office at the Kansas City stockyards. He had both the keys in his hand. The first one didn't fit the lock, but the second one did. The office looked as though a hurricane had passed through it. Desk drawers were open, their contents spilling out, and the oak file cabinets were in much the same condition. For a moment, Longarm stood in the doorway, looking at the disordered office.

Looks like somebody got here first, old son, he told himself as he stepped inside and closed the door. *But now you're here, you might as well take a look. You might turn up something that whoever done this overlooked.*

There was no doubt in Longarm's mind that McCoy had paid a hurried visit to the place to find and remove anything that might help prove a case against him. That in itself encouraged Longarm as he began going through the ransacked office, for if the elusive cattle broker was worried badly enough to destroy his files, it meant that Longarm was getting close to catching up with him. It also meant that McCoy was indeed guilty and that he had evidence of guilt which needed to be destroyed.

Methodically, Longarm began examining the papers straggling from the desk Elsie Mae had used. There were several dozen of these sheets, and after he'd collected them and smoothed them out, he sat at the desk while he studied them. Most of them were railroad waybills, and as Longarm went through them and noted the dates and destinations of the shipments, a pattern gradually took shape.

There were many waybills showing shipments of cattle north from points along the Mexican border in both Texas and New

Mexico, and all these were to Vaughn. There were also waybills covering shipments of cattle to Vaughn, shipments moving west from Texas and south from Colorado, as well as a disproportionately large number of steers being shipped from Vaughn to La Junta. Waybills dated a week or ten days later showed a large shipment of steers had been made from Vaughn or La Junta to the stockyards in Kansas City or Fort Worth.

What you got here, old son, is two ends without no middle to join 'em up, Longarm mused as he made neat stacks of the crumpled waybills. *Now there ain't no reason but one to ship steers to Vaughn from Texas or from Colorado either. And there ain't no reason to ship Colorado cattle from way up by Fort Morgan or from Colorado Springs to Vaughn and then turn around and ship 'em right back to La Junta. If they was going to market clean and healthy, like they come off the range, they'd go direct to the stockyards here or at Fort Worth.*

And there ain't enough steers in New Mexico to make up these here shipments from Vaughn to the stockyards, so it just stands to reason Vaughn's the place where good U.S. beef cattle is being mixed up with scrawny and maybe sick steers from Mexico. And it's a good bet the same thing's happening at La Junta. Them steers is shipped on to the stockyards with the whole herd graded as good U.S. steers and what the poor sucker that buys it gets is a few good-grade steers, but mostly he's paying his good money for sickly cattle and runts.

But just figuring all that out don't help a lot. You got to have the middle part to tie it all together. And that's what McCoy taken when he cleaned this place out.

Looking for more evidence to back up his deductions, Longarm went to the file cabinets. He went through several of the deep paper-stuffed drawers and found nothing he could connect to the material salvaged from the desk. After he'd checked a dozen of the files in each cabinet, he concluded the papers they held covered the purchase or sale of cattle in what he assumed must be legitimate transactions, since they'd been left untouched. Most of the drawers seemed to have been undisturbed, and everything he'd looked at concerned nothing except aboveboard and routine business such as might be carried on by an honest broker.

His eyes aching from the thousands of words of often only half-legible writing he'd deciphered, Longarm stopped to light a cheroot. The door to McCoy's private office stood a few inches ajar, and remembering how Elsie Mae had been so careful to keep him from seeing its interior when she went into it on his first visit, Longarm pushed the door wide and went in.

Though the smaller back office had been gone through just as thoroughly as the outer room, and showed the same evidence of a hasty search, it was in a much less dishevelled state. The back room was smaller, and it contained no filing cabinets. In fact, it had only two pieces of furniture in it, the desk and chair he'd glimpsed on his earlier visit. The chair was extraordinary in its carving, but it did not attract Longarm's attention in the way the desk did. His first glimpse of it had struck him with a sense of familiarity, and he frowned as he tried to remember where he'd seen a similar desk before.

Although its upper section was curved, the desk was not a roll top desk of plain golden oak. As he stared at it, Longarm realized that he'd identified it so readily as a desk only because of the almost identical one he'd seen somewhere else—he couldn't quite recall where.

It stood almost as tall as Longarm himself. Its top was level with his eyes, and he had to tilt his head back to examine the details of the deeply carved pediment that ornamented the center of the rear panel that rose several inches above the flat top. Its front and sides were deeply panelled in dark burl that had been smoothed to a satiny finish before they were varnished.

On the side of the desk that was visible Longarm could see the butts of dark japanned hinges, but the molding down the center of its face concealed its opening. A keyhole in a brass plate a few inches below the curve of its top led Longarm to try the second key he'd found in Charlene Hart's purse. He was not too surprised when the key turned smoothly. He tugged at the ornately chased brass pulls that at first glance seemed to be mere ornaments, and the sides swung apart, moving smoothly on oversized casters.

A brass nameplate set in the edge of one side caught his eye and he bent to read it: "Wooten Desk Manf. Co., Indianapolis, Ind., W. S. Wooten's Patent Oct. 4, 1874." Only then did Longarm remember where he'd seen the desk's twin. Silver Dollar Tabor had shown him a desk in his mansion in Leadville which was a twin to the one at which he was now looking.

He recalled Tabor's remark that a desk of that sort was an

expensive luxury which only a rich man could afford, and the thought flashed through his mind that cattle-swindling must bring in a lot of money for McCoy to be able to afford a desk that a man as rich as Tabor had described as being expensive.

Longarm resumed his examination of the desk. On each of the movable sides there were what seemed to him to be an endless number of small drawers and pigeonholes. The pigeonholes were all empty, but there so many that he did not even try to count them; not only did the drawers fill both of the swung-out sides, but there were even several shallow drawers below the recess at the top, from which a flap had been released as the sides swung open to form a writing compartment.

Longarm began opening the drawers. As he pulled them open, one after another, and saw only the green felt linings, his frustration mounted. Finally he reached the last drawer, and when he saw it was empty, too, he stepped back and stared with compressed lips at the fancy desk.

You let McCoy get the jump on you again, old son, he told himself angrily. *He's just about the slipperiest son of a bitch you been after for a long time. Now McCoy ain't that smart and you ain't that stupid. Buckle down and use the brain God give you the way you was intended to.*

Standing in front of the desk, Longarm again compared it, this time without really being aware he was doing so, with the similar one he'd been shown by Tabor in Leadville. Tabor, he recalled, had called the desk by name, as though it had a personality not usually found in an inanimate object such as a piece of furniture. Walking around the desk, he looked at its back. It was as carefully carved and finished as the front. Only then did he remember something else.

Old Tabor said there's a secret drawer in all the desks that Wooten fellow makes, old son. You better find where it is, because if McCoy left anything worth a plugged penny behind him, that's where it'd be.

Stepping away from the desk, Longarm studied it with fresh eyes, trying to recall the area of the desk to which Tabor had pointed on that day. As best he could remember, the silver king had indicated one of the back corners. Bending close to the corner nearest to him, Longarm began examining the corners and joints between the panels with his keen eyes. He was not at all sure exactly what he was looking for, but trusted that

140

his hunter's instinct would signal him when he saw it.

He found the clue at last, a hairline crack so thin it was almost invisible in the joint between the side and the back. At first he thought the tiny crevice was nothing more than a place where two pieces of wood had been inexpertly butted together, but as he examined the crack more carefully he found that it ran all around the panel, though in places it fitted so closely as to be almost invisible.

There's got to be a latch of some kind to hold that piece shut, he told himself. *And a latch has got to be inside someplace where a man can get to it. Now, there's drawers all down the inside, and if you was to push one of 'em, or maybe take one out, chances are it'd trip that latch.*

Still not certain he'd found what he'd been seeking, Longarm moved to the front of the desk and began pushing the drawers that lined the inner side in front of the latch. He found the right one on the third try. He heard a thunk from the back of the desk and hurried around to look.

A panel, the same rectangle that the hairline crack had outlined, had dropped down on concealed hinges. The cavity revealed by its opening was lined with green felt, like the drawers. From Longarm's standpoint, only one flaw marred his success in finding the secret compartment. The cubicle that had been hidden behind the panel was completely empty.

Chapter 16

For a moment Longarm stared at the felt-lined hollow in the back of the desk. His fingers moved almost of their own accord as he took out a cheroot and lighted it. He looked at the side of the desk opposite the opened compartment and bent close to examine it, but on that side there was no telltale crack.

Well, old son, he told himself philosophically, *I guess you can't win all the time, but even if you come up a dud on the desk, you found enough to put McCoy behind bars. All you got to do now is catch up with him, and your best bet's in La Junta. So that's where you better cut a shuck for now.*

However, it was not La Junta, but Denver, that Longarm chose as his next destination after he'd given the matter a bit of thought. He still had more than a week before whatever event the cryptic notation on the check stub indicated was supposed to happen in La Junta.

Longarm reasoned that his time might as well be spent where he could sleep in his own bed, be sure of having a clean shirt when he needed one, sit in on a poker game or two with his friends at the Windsor Hotel, and get the clicking of wheels on steel rails out of his ears. Perhaps the main reason he decided to return, however, was that his supply of travel and expense vouchers was running low and he needed more.

"Don't tell me you've closed out that steer-swindling case!" Vail exclaimed when Longarm walked into his office the morning after he'd arrived in Denver.

"It ain't closed yet, Billy. But give me another week or two and I'll have it all finished."

"It's not like you to take so much time on a case, Long. You've been chasing the Real McCoy for almost three months now. Since you don't bother to send me reports the way the other deputies do, I'm curious to know whether you've even gotten near McCoy yet."

"Oh, a time or two I got close enough to him to've reached

142

out and grabbed him," Longarm said. He added hurriedly, "And before you ask me why I didn't, I'll tell you."

"Do, by all means," Vail said. "What's his secret? Does he just go up in smoke when he gets close to a lawman's badge?"

"Sometimes I feel like he does just that, Billy. But it taken me a month before I could even get a decent description of him to go by, and another couple of weeks till I figured out some kind of pattern to the way he was zigzagging all over hell and gone. Now I figure to head him off."

"Where's this all going to take place?"

"If my luck holds good, it'll be at La Junta," Longarm said.

"La Junta?" Vail frowned. "That's not ranch country any more. It's mostly farmland now."

"Why, that's where the Santa Fe Railroad splits, you know. They'd pushed their rails up close to Denver before they settled their fight with the Denver & Rio Grande over Raton Pass. Then after they got the pass away from the D&RG, they built a new line into Raton. Later on, they put down the line they use now, at the edge of the foothills through Pueblo and Colorado Springs and on in direct to Denver."

"Yes, yes, I know that. But there aren't any cattle ranches left around La Junta, at least none of any size."

"You're right about that, Billy. But the Santa Fe's still using that line from La Junta into Raton. And did you know they'd built a bunch of stockpens at La Junta? Them stockpens are still there, Billy."

"I didn't even know they'd built any. But what's that got to do with your case?" Vail frowned.

"Well, when the cattle range was cut up into farms, and La Junta got started as a town, it wasn't close to the stockpens. But they're still there. I stopped in and asked at the Santa Fe's district office when I pulled into town yesterday, and it turns out that about a year and a half ago, the railroad signed a five-year lease on them stockpens."

"What's so interesting about that?"

"That lease was made to an outfit called the Hart Land and Cattle Company, outa Kansas City."

"I still don't see what difference it makes," Vail said a bit impatiently.

"There was a girl named Elsie Mae Glover worked for the Real McCoy, or the fellow that calls himself that now, in his office at Kansas City."

"Damn it, Long! Quit beating around the bush and give me the whole story without making me guess what you're driving at!" Vail said, not bothering to hide his impatience now.

"Elsie Mae Glover got shot and killed in Vaughn. I was with her at the time. Only she wasn't going by that name. She was decked out in a blonde wig and called herself Charlene Hart, like she did when I met her the first time in Kansas City, three or four weeks earlier."

This time, Vail said nothing when Longarm stopped talking. He sat with a furrow deepening in his brow until he looked at Longarm and said, "In other words, the Real McCoy, whoever he is now, owns the stockpens at La Junta."

"That's what I been trying to tell you. Now, there's two things that makes La Junta and Vaughn like each other, Billy. They're both a long ways from anyplace, and there's a lot of cattle passes through both of 'em," Longarm said. "Places like them is just made to order for them steer-swindlers I'm after."

"Is that all you're going by?" Vail asked.

"Not quite. I got some waybills outa McCoy's office when I went there after the girl was killed. A whole lot of 'em are for shipping cattle McCoy's bought someplace else."

"Why do they bother to ship them all over the country?" Vail frowned. "I don't see the need for it."

"Oh, they need both of them places. They buy cattle here in Colorado, or up in Wyoming and Montana. Now, that's good stock they can grade, heavy U. S. steers. So they ship 'em to Vaughn or to La Junta, and mix in sick critters and runts from Mexico and ship 'em out to the stockyards without changing the grading."

"I suppose you're sure about that, Long?"

"I got chapter and verse on both ends of the swindle, Billy. It's the middle I'm working on now. I can't connect up the ends and make my case till I catch up with McCoy and get him and his gang behind bars."

Vail was looking thoughtful. He said, "I wonder why Jim Fraser and his bunch of range detectives haven't caught on to that swindle yet? If La Junta's one of the places where McCoy's crooks are operating, the swindle's being pulled off right under their noses."

"I don't think the gang's been doing a lot at La Junta, Billy. It'd be easy for Fraser's range detectives to overlook the little bit of steer-switching that's been done there. The big swindles are all set up at Vaughn."

"Speaking of Fraser, have you run into any hoof-and-mouth disease?" Vail asked. "If you remember, that seemed to bother him more than the steer-swindling."

"I ain't found out much about the hoof-and-mouth, Billy, except it's a disease that's hard to spot until it's pretty far along. I'm right sure I run into a little bit of it down on the Sand Creek Reservation when I first started out. Trouble was, they'd already killed the sick steers, so there wasn't any way for me to be sure, let alone proving anything."

"Since you're going to be in Denver a few days without much of anything to do, suppose you stop by and check with Jim about the hoof-and-mouth," Vail suggested.

"I sorta had it in mind to do just that, Billy. You want to go along with me? He's your friend more'n mine."

"You know I don't like to mix into cases my deputies are working on unless they need help. Is that what you're asking for in this one?"

"I wouldn't exactly call it asking," Longarm replied. "I just figured you might feel like sitting in because you know Fraser. Seeing as you don't want to, I'll go by myself."

Although the Chaffee Building was one of Denver's oldest commercial structures, and its brownstone front showed signs of its age, the third-floor offices of the Colorado Cattlemen's Association would have done credit to the lobby of the Brown Palace Hotel. Longarm's boot soles sank into deep-piled carpeting as he approached the polished mahogany reception desk where a pink-checked youth who might have been a twin to Henry in the marshal's office waited to greet him.

"Mr. Fraser? Yes, of course," the young man said, looking at Longarm's battered boots, snuff-colored hat, long black coat, and tightly fitting twill trousers. "You're one of our members, I suppose?"

"No, I ain't, sonny," Longarm replied. "I'm a deputy U. S. marshal, and I want to talk to Mr. Fraser on official business."

"I'm sure he'll see you right away, Marshal. Shall I tell him your name?"

"Long. He'll know who I am and why I'm here."

145

Longarm's wait, in one of the most uncomfortably low and soft chairs he'd ever sat in, was very brief. Fraser bustled into the office, as immaculately dressed and polished as he'd been at their first meeting.

"Marshal Long!" the manager exclaimed with a broad smile on his deeply bronzed face. "I hope you've got good news for me?"

"Well, it ain't all that good, Mr. Fraser, but it ain't all that bad, neither."

"Let's go into my private office," Fraser said, pointing to the panelled walnut door from which he'd just come. "We can talk in there without being interrupted."

Fraser's office was a striking example of austere elegance. It had a Turkey carpet on the floor, two or three comfortable-looking chairs covered in natural cowhide spaced casually in front of the large mahogany conference table that occupied the center of the room. An opened cellarette with a decanter and glasses stood in one corner. Behind the table there was a high-backed leather-upholstered thronelike chair. In back of the chair stood a desk which might have been a twin to the ones Longarm had seen at Silver Dollar Tabor's mansion and at the deserted office of the Real McCoy in Kansas City.

Fraser waved at one of the calfskin chairs. Longarm sat down and put his hat on the floor beside him. Fraser moved on to the cellarette. He turned to asked Longarm, "What'll you drink, Marshal?"

"Why, if you got some Maryland rye there, I'd enjoy a sip of it."

Longarm stared at the desk while Fraser poured the drinks. The Association manager came up to Longarm, a glass in each hand, and held out one of them. Longarm took his eyes off the desk and sat down, the glass in his hand.

As Fraser walked around the table to the big thronelike chair, he said, "I see my Wooten desk has caught your eye."

"It sure has. It's just like one I seen . . ." Longarm hesitated for a fraction of a second, reluctant as always to share with anyone even the most inconsequential bit of information about a current case. Then he went on, "Silver Dollar Tabor's got one that might be a twin to it in his house over at Leadville."

"If it's another piece of Wooten's work, I'm sure it would come close to being a twin to mine." Fraser nodded. "I wasn't aware you were acquainted with Tabor," he went on.

146

"Oh, we ain't close friends or anything like that," Longarm replied. "The only reason I know him is because I got the job of keeping an eye on President Grant when he come to Colorado to visit the Tabors some time back. I had to stay at the Tabors' house while the General was there."

"You do cover a lot of ground, Marshal Long," Fraser said, smiling. "I hope you're covering as much in your investigation of the case we're interested in."

"I been doing some work on it."

"Have you made progress in uncovering any cases of apthos fever?"

"Not many. There was some over in the southeast corner of the state, I'm pretty sure, but the cattle had all been butchered before I got there."

"There's not a lot of cattle range left to the southeast." Fraser frowned. "That used to be rangeland, but it's farmland now. Our range detectives don't even bother to go down there any more. What about the northeast and the central foothills around Colorado Springs?"

"I'm going to look there, too. I don't intend to give up, Mr. Fraser. Have you heard about hoof-and-mouth being in them parts lately?"

"No. But the disease spreads so fast that we're all very much concerned about it. I hope you'll keep me informed of what you find out." Then, as though it had just occurred to him, Fraser added, "And about the steer-swindle that we suspect is going on, too."

"Oh, sure, I'll do that." Longarm paused while he lighted a cigar. When it was drawing properly he went on, "I don't recall that we had any names to work on in the steer-swindle case when we talked in Billy Vail's office a while back."

"No, we didn't. Do you have some now?"

"A few. I guess you know a cattle broker, one that calls himself the Real McCoy?"

"I met him casually a number of years ago. But I know his reputation quite well, of course. He's supposed to be one of the most honest and trustworthy brokers in the business."

"So I've heard. There's a fellow calling himself the Real McCoy that's mixed up in the steer-swindle, though."

"You say he 'calls himself the Real McCoy.'" Fraser frowned. "Does that mean you think someone else is posing as McCoy?"

"That's what I figure. Trouble is, I can't seem to catch up to him. Every place I find out he's heading for, he's already been there and gone by the time I get there."

"Your luck will change sooner or later, I'm sure," Fraser said. "I'll see if I can find out anything about him."

"Now, I'd appreciate that, Mr. Fraser," Longarm told the Association manager. "The fellow I'm looking for is little, and about all I know is he wears a steerhead stickpin with diamonds in the steer's eyes. Does that ring any bells for you?"

Fraser frowned thoughtfully, then shook his head. "No, I can't say that it does. But I'll pass the word to our range detectives. They cover a lot more ground than I do. Most of my work's done in this office, you understand."

"Oh, sure. I can see how that'd be." Longarm reached for his hat and stood up. "I know you're busy, Mr. Fraser, so I better be getting along. Thanks for the drink and your help."

"You'll keep me informed of whatever progress you're making, I hope?" Fraser asked. "You know the Association's interested."

"That's sorta hard for me to do, Mr. Fraser. Since I been on this case, I ain't stopped travelling. Even Billy Vail don't know where I am half the time. I'm just in Denver for a day or two before I go down to La Junta."

"That's the second time you've mentioned the southeast part of the state," Fraser said, swivelling his chair around to face Longarm. "What's taking you there?"

"Why, I don't give away things that I got planned, Mr. Fraser. I might make a damned fool of myself if I did, because things don't always work out the way I plan 'em to."

"I'm not pressing you to give me any confidential information, of course," Fraser said quickly.

"I understand that, Mr. Fraser." Longarm nodded. "It don't offend me none to get asked, and I hope you ain't offended if I keep my cards close to my chest for a while yet."

Fraser sat silently for a moment, then said, "You know, Marshal Long, I've had an idea while we've been talking. Pour yourself another drink and sit down for a minute longer, if you have time."

"Well, I ain't in all that much of a hurry," Longarm said. "I'll just do that." He went to the cellarette and refilled his glass, then returned to the chair he'd just left. "What's this idea you got?"

148

"You're a skilled investigator, Marshal Long," Fraser said thoughtfully. "And from what I've gathered in talking to Vail, you move fast, you don't waste time, and you don't hesitate to use your gun when you have to."

"I take it that's meant for a compliment, so I thank you, Mr. Fraser," Longarm said quietly, anticipating Fraser's next words. He was not disappointed.

"What I'm saying is that you're just the kind of man our Association can use as a range detective."

"You mean you're offering me a job?"

"A little bit more than a job, Marshal. I have a pretty good idea what the government's paying you, and our men earn a substantial amount more than that."

"I don't guess anybody that's honest ever gets rich on a government salary, Mr. Fraser. The grafters make a lot, and the crooks and swindlers, but that's about all."

"Why stay with it, then, when you can make a great deal more working for us?"

"Oh, I guess I just got the lawman habit. It ain't easy to break once you get it," Longarm replied.

"You can make double your pay as a deputy marshal working for us, Long," Fraser said.

"Well, I don't—"

Fraser broke in quickly, "And I haven't mentioned the bonus I'm prepared to pay you for joining us."

Longarm bought a bit of time by lighting a cheroot. He was aware that Fraser was watching him closely, and didn't waste time in getting the cigar lighted. Then he asked, "You pay all the men you hire a bonus, Mr. Fraser?"

"No. But we do pay one when we want a man badly enough."

"That sounds real good," Longarm said. "But I—"

"You'd want to know how much the bonus is, of course," Fraser broke in. "In your case, I'm ready to pay you a thousand dollars in cash the day you join us."

Longarm whistled. "That's an awful lot of money. I guess you know it's pretty near as much as I make in a year."

"I know what government pay is, yes. But it's not too much of a bonus for a man such as you are. And that's not all I have in mind."

"Maybe you better tell me the rest of it."

"Our chief range detective's getting up in years, Long. He won't be staying with us more than another year or two. With

149

the experience you can get in our particular line of work, you'd be the man I'd appoint to fill his shoes when he quits."

"And I'd imagine that'd mean a little bit higher salary?" Longarm asked, putting more interest into his voice.

"Quite a bit more. You're still a young man, Long. You could hold that job as chief for quite a few years."

"You know, Mr. Fraser, you make the job sound better and better every time you say something."

"Then you'll take it?"

"I won't say no, and I won't say yes, not right now."

"I'd need to know fairly soon," Fraser said.

To delay his answer, Longarm drank the remainder of the whiskey in his glass and puffed his cigar. Fraser sat restively, his eyes fixed on Longarm.

"I don't guess I need to tell you that you're making me a mighty tempting proposition," Longarm said when he judged he'd drawn his time out as much as possible. "You know that just as well as I do."

"Take it, then," Fraser urged.

"Let's put it this way, Mr. Fraser," Longarm replied. "I don't feel like I want to jump into a thing as serious as this."

"Of course you don't," Fraser agreed. "But you will give me your answer right away? Before you leave for La Junta?"

"I won't be pulling out for La Junta right away. It might be a week or more before I go," Longarm told him. "I'll study over it every minute I got to spare in the next day or two, and just as soon as I make up my mind, I'll come back up here and let you know."

Fraser's expression did not change, but his eyes spoke of his disappointment. He said, "You do that, Long. But I hope you won't wait too long before making up your mind. I'd like to have your answer before you leave for La Junta."

Longarm stood up and put on his hat. "Well, that gives me a while to think. I won't be leaving for a few days. And I'll do my best to decide what I want to do before I go, Mr. Fraser. I promise you that much."

Chapter 17

Longarm was thinking hard as he walked along Stout Street on his way back to the federal building. He hadn't been able to resolve his problem when he reached Seventeenth Street, so he turned the corner, walked halfway down the block, and went into Logan's. The barkeep saw him enter and had a bottle of Tom Moore on the bar by the time Longarm reached it. Longarm picked up the bottle and the barkeep handed him a glass.

"Thanks, Eddie," Longarm said. "I got a little thinking to do, so I'm going back and sit at that table in the far corner."

Carrying the bottle and glass, he walked back to the table and lighted a cheroot before filling the glass. He went through the motions automatically, turning over in his mind the surprises of the afternoon.

That's about the smoothest way anybody ever tried to buy you off, old son. Fraser's a slick customer. He didn't say one word that you could repeat in court to prove what he was out to do. If you was to swear he was trying to bribe you, he'd just swear you taken what he said the wrong way, and there wouldn't be no way in the world to tell which one of us was lying. Come right down to it, the judge'd be likelier to believe him, because a thousand dollars is one hell of a big price to pay for a deputy marshal when these Denver policemen is selling out for ten or fifteen dollars a month.

Comes down to what Billy'd believe, too. Him and Fraser being poker-playing friends, that is. Not that Billy Vail would think deep down you'd sell out, but likely he'd get to wondering about it sometimes, even after you told Fraser to take his bribe and go to hell with it. Always be that little niggly doubt in between you and him. And if you was to go tell Billy right now, he'd want to go rushing out and arrest Fraser if he believed you. That'd blow your case sky-high.

Yes, sir, old son, you're right on a tight wire, because now you've laid your bait for Fraser, and he's laid his bait for you, and if he's as cagey as you give him credit for being, he's

going to sniff at that bait a long time before he takes the hook.
Might not even take it at all, then where'd you be?

But it's just like running a bluff in a poker game. You've
shoved in your last chip, and the other fellow raises. All you
can do is fold or play the pot short.

Three drinks and a second cheroot later, Longarm still hadn't
been able to decide how much or what he was going to tell
Billy Vail. He paid his tab and walked the block to the federal
building, but even after he'd mounted the marble stairs to the
second floor and walked much more slowly than usual down
the wide corridor to the office, he was no closer to reaching a
decision than he'd been when he left the Cattlemen's Association office.

Reluctantly, Longarm opened the door and went into the
outer room. The door to Vail's private office stood ajar, as it
did most of the time, and the young pink-cheeked clerk was
at his desk pecking at the newfangled typewriting machine. As
Longarm started toward the door of Vail's office, the clerk
looked up.

"Chief Vail's not in there, Marshal Long," he said.

"Well, he won't be far off, this time of day. I'll just go in
and wait till he comes back."

"You'll have a long wait, then. He won't be back today."

"Something serious must've happened, then. I never knew
Billy to leave here a minute early," Longarm said.

"He did today," the clerk said. "As a matter of fact, he left
almost as soon as he'd gotten back from his noon meal. He
had a bad toothache and he went to the dentist's office."

"And he's still there? It's close to five o'clock."

"He came back for a few minutes. The dentist said his mouth
was too badly swollen to pull the tooth today, so he gave Chief
Vail some medicine to take and told him to go home. I don't
think he'll be in tomorrow, either, because he's got to go get
his tooth pulled at ten o'clock in the morning."

"Well, I might not get in tomorrow myself. I got something
to do that's going to keep me busy," Longarm told the youth.
"I tell you what, when Billy comes in, you tell him soon as I
get back, I'll give him a report on what we was talking about
today."

To Longarm's surprise, the clerk said, "I'll be glad to fix
up your report, write it out for you on the machine."

"Now, that's right thoughtful, but I won't put you to all

152

that trouble. I'll tell you what you can do, though. I need three or four more travel vouchers, so if you'll have 'em ready for me, I'll stop in about ten tomorrow morning and pick 'em up."

Before the clerk could argue, Longarm left the office. He waited until he reached the hall to breathe a huge sigh of relief, and started for George Martin's barber shop to get a leisurely shave before he had his supper.

La Junta was a town even smaller than Vaughn. Longarm had seen it before only from the window of a day coach as he passed through on a train. That had been some time ago, and the town had been called Otero then. It was not quite as he remembered, though the seemingly endless rolling shortgrassed brush-clumped prairie landscape around it looked the same.

As nearly as he could recollect, the depot had been smaller, and located in a different place. The town he recalled had been made up of the depot, a saloon, and a general store, and half a dozen adobe houses. Standing on the station platform surveying his surroundings, Longarm decided the name was about the only thing in the town that had changed greatly.

There were more houses now, perhaps twenty in all, most of the newer ones built with lumber instead of adobe, though the unpainted, weathered boards of the older dwellings differed very little in color from the brown adobe bricks of the original dwellings. However, there was now a main street, and fronting on it were three stores, two saloons, and a rooming house, and across the tracks from the depot there was a livery stable. Having satisfied his curiosity about La Junta, Longarm stepped into the depot.

"You got a manifest yet for a load of steers coming in to them stockpens out from town?" he asked the stationmaster.

"Where'd they be coming from?"

"Now, you'd know that better'n I would," Longarm answered. "All I know is that they're due before too long."

"Then you know more about it than I do," the railroad man said. "If they're being picked up from one of the other lines, I might not get the manifest on the wire until after I've heard the hoghead blow the whistle."

"Well, I'll look in tomorrow, then," Longarm said. "Maybe you'll have it by then."

"You do that. If you've got a herd due, it's bound to be here sooner or later."

Longarm returned to his gear and stood beside it while he lighted a cheroot. He looked reflectively at the livery stable.

This ain't a place where a stranger's going to get by and not be looked at close, old son, Longarm told himself as he turned to gaze down the dusty street. His eyes picked up the glint of the late-afternoon sunshine reflected from the railroad tracks where they curved a quarter-mile from the end of the street to run along the bank of the Arkansas River. *If you got to hang around here two or three days waiting for McCoy, you better find a hidey-hole close by where you won't be sticking out like a sore thumb. Best thing to do is get out close to them stockpens, where you can keep an eye on 'em.*

Gathering up his gear, Longarm walked across the tracks to the livery stable. "Looks like I'm going to need a horse for a few days," he told the liveryman. "Figure you can fix me up?"

"Sure." The liveryman ejected a spurt of tobacco juice and shifted his chew to the other cheek. "Seeing as you got your own saddle, that'll be a dime a day, and you feed the critter. But you got to put up a five-dollar deposit so I c'n be sure you'll bring him back."

"I ain't aiming to run off with no horse," Longarm said. "Not that I object to the five." He dug out a gold half-eagle. "Do you take the rent out of the deposit when I bring him home?"

"Yep. How long you figure to keep him?"

"Oh, maybe four or five days. Depends on if I get located right." He followed the liveryman inside the stable. There were two dust-covered buggies and a wagon standing on one side of the big barnlike structure and three horses in the line of stalls that ran along the other. Longarm looked at the horses with a practiced eye and dropped his saddle in front of the middle stall. "I'll take this roan, he looks biddable."

"Nice animal." The liveryman led the horse out of the stall and picked up Longarm's saddle. "No extra charge for saddling him up. And the bridle and reins go with the horse."

"Well, now, I call that real accommodating," Longarm said. "Maybe you can tell me about them stockpens out east along the river. The folks that run 'em looking for any hands right now?"

"Not as I know of. Funny thing about that place—nobody in town here's got any idea who runs 'em. There won't be a

154

soul out there for weeks, maybe even a month, then they'll be busy as all hell for a week or so, and after that they just close down again."

"You know the foreman's name?"

"Nope. The hands out there rides in on the train with the cattle cars, tends the steers, and when the cattle goes out, the hands goes with 'em. They don't come in town much, just fix up a shakedown at what's left of the fort and keep to theirselves."

"Which fort would that be?" Longarm frowned. "Seems like I recall old Bent used to have a place around here somewhere, but I didn't know about any others."

"Hell, friend, there's more forts along the Arkansas hereabouts than we got any need for," the liveryman replied after he discharged another spurt of tobacco juice. "There's Bent's old fort down below the Purgatoire, and Bent's new fort upriver a ways, right upstream from the town, here. When the Cheyennes was running wild, the Army put up one they called Wise, but the freshets washed it out a time or two, so they moved on downriver and built another one they named Lyons. It got washed out, too, so they moved a ways further down when they built the next one."

"Which is the one you said is close to the stockpens?"

"That'd be the one they called Wise. What's left of it's in a little draw there past the stockpens, sorta hard to see if you ain't looking for it. But if you just ride along the riverbank, you can't miss it."

Stopping at the store nearest the depot long enough to buy a chunk of cheese, a sackful of soda crackers, and a few pounds of potatoes, Longarm followed the liveryman's directions and rode east along the bank of the Arkansas. He passed the stockpens; they looked unused and a bit dilapidated, but adequate to hold a sizeable number of cattle. Except for a tin-roofed hayshed with the straggling remnants of a few bales of hay strewn under its roof, there were no buildings at the pens.

A quarter-mile or so beyond the pens he reached the draw. Its slanting sides showed signs of the scouring they got from rushing water during the heavy rains or freshets from a hard winter's snowmelt. Turning the livery horse, he followed the bank a hundred yards before spotting the eroded adobe walls and sagging roofs of the three adobe buildings that remained of the abandoned fort. A thin thread of smoke rose through the almost-collapsed roof of the least-dilapidated of the three.

Longarm swung out of the saddle, eased the set of his cross-draw holster, and called out, "Hello, inside there! You got any objection to a visitor?"

There was no response to Longarm's hail for a moment or two. Then a tall, husky, swarthy-skinned man came around the corner of the building. He wore city boots and trousers, but his shirt was a riot of color, and so was the neckerchief at his throat. He was neither young nor old, but there was no grey showing in his hair or in his full downturned moustache. After looking at Longarm for a moment he smiled with a dazzling display of white teeth.

"*Bienvenido, amigo,*" he said. "You are come to feex the *corrales,* no? The train, it weel be here soon?"

"Sorry, but I ain't got a thing to do with the stockpens," Longarm told him. "Matter of fact, I'm waiting for the train to get here myself."

"Ah. *Mal suerte!* I am wait three days now."

"Well, from what the stationmaster at the depot in town told me, it might be another three days before it gets here."

"Thees is not good." The Mexican shook his head. "I am too long here now. And you?"

"Oh, I got some business with the folks that's bringing in the cattle." Longarm extended his hand. "Name's Long," he said.

"I am Guzman," the stranger replied, taking Longarm's hand in a firm brisk handshake. "Francisco Guzman. But mostly I am call Pancho."

"Glad to meet you, Pancho," Longarm said. "I didn't look to find anybody around. I was figuring to sorta camp out here while I waited, but since you got here first, I guess I better find another place."

"Ah, no, *Señor* Long," Guzman said. "There is no need you must go—is room for more as one in thees place."

"Well, that's real nice of you. It'll save me going back to town, if you don't mind me staying here."

"No, no! I am don't mind! To have company I am glad!"

"Then I'll just unsaddle and stick around," Longarm said. He freed his saddlebags and bedroll and dropped them on the ground. Guzman picked them up.

"I weel carry in," he offered. "You come when you are finish weeth the horse."

Longarm tethered the horse in the wreck of a building that adjoined the one Guzman was using, and went to join his new campmate. He looked around. The building had an uneven floor of native sandstone, and an almost-intact adobe fireplace in one corner. An iron stewpot and frying pan and enamelware coffee pot rested on a bed of burned-out coals in the fireplace. Blankets on the floor at one side of the hearth indicated Guzman's bed. A canteen hung from a peg in the wall beside the fireplace.

"I got a bottle of whiskey in my saddlebag, if you'd like to join me in a sip or two," Longarm told his impromptu roommate.

"*Gracias*, but I am have bottle *mescal* in blankets," Guzman replied. "I like eet better as wheesky."

Hunkered down by the fireplace, the two men drank. Guzman rolled himself a cornhusk cigarette, and Longarm lighted a cigar. The fact of drinking and smoking together seemed to cement some sort of bond of fellowship between them. They raised their bottles to one another in salute before taking a second drink.

Longarm looked around the battered room. He said, "Looks like you figured you'd have to wait a while after you got here."

"Ah, *sí*. Always, I am have to wait."

"How long you been waiting?"

"Two days only, thees time." Guzman shrugged. "But for me ees worth to wait, I buy cattle more cheap from *Señor* McCoy as nobody else close by. Before, I buy from ranch, but ees all move north, ees too far now, the ranch for me to go to."

Longarm's habitual self-control kept his face expressionless when he heard McCoy's name, but his mind began working faster. To give himself time to think, he asked his companion, "You buying breeding stock for your own ranch?"

Guzman threw back his head and laughed heartily. "I am look like beeg *hacendado*, no?"

"Well, a man can't ever tell," Longarm replied.

"I am buy cattle for butcher shop. I am *carnicero*. Me and my brother, we got *carnicerias*, een Pueblo, een Trinidad."

"You must have a pretty good trade, buying right outa the stockpens," Longarm said thoughtfully. "I never heard about a big cattle dealer selling nothing short of a pretty good-sized herd. I didn't know they'd sell just one steer at a time."

"I tell you about thees thing, *Señor* Long. I make what you call deal weeth *Señor* McCoy. He sell me leetle steer like he don' can sell in estockyard in city, maybe steer they a leetle sick, we butcher queek, so they don' get no worse, maybe die."

"You're buying culls, then. Don't your customers complain?"

"I tell you about thees thing, too," Guzman said. "Ees poor miners we sell to, *hermanos del pais*. Ees lots from them work in coal mines. We got to have the cheap meat."

"And this McCoy sells it to you cheaper than you can get it anyplace else?" Longarm frowned.

"*Sí.* I buy maybe carload at a time, half I take for my *carneciera* in Trinidad, other half go to Pablo een Pueblo. We butcher worst ones queek, sell queek, very cheap."

"You ever hear of apthos fever, Pancho?" Longarm asked. "Hoof-and-mouth disease, they call it up here. I don't know what it's called in Mexico."

"Ah, *sí.* Ees bad for steer. Die slow, make other ones seek, too. They die. Pretty soon, herd all dead."

"You ever buy any steers from McCoy that had it?"

Guzman was silent for a moment. Then he asked, "Why you ask me thees thing? You are of the *policia*, no?"

Longarm nodded. "I'm what you'd call the *policia federal* in Mexico, Pancho. On this side of the border, I'm called a deputy United States marshal."

"You will tell me one thing true?"

"You got my word on it," Longarm said. "Straight truth."

"I will not be put in jail if I tell you truth, no?"

"No. You got my word on that."

Guzman nodded. "Ees good. I know honest man when I am see him. Ask me question. I tell you all you want to know."

Chapter 18

"That's the smart thing to do, Pancho," Longarm said. "You ain't going to be sorry, because if you help me now, I won't have to arrest you."

"*Madre de Dios!* Why you would arrest me? I don' do nothing, only buy esteers from *Señor* McCoy!"

"Even if I ain't got around to looking into it yet, I'm dead sure some of them steers was rustled. What I can prove is that a lot of 'em was smuggled in from Mexico; they're mostly the ones that had the hoof-and-mouth. If you bought 'em, the law says you're guilty as he is."

"But you say you don' arrest me." Guzman frowned. "I don' understand thees thing."

"Because you're on the right side of the law now. Nobody can arrest you, whatever you do from here on out to help me."

"And you don' arrest me for what I do before?"

Longarm shook his head. "No. You don't have to worry about any steers you bought from McCoy before."

"*Bueno.* What it ees you want I do?"

"Nothing, until the cattle train gets here. By then I'll have a scheme of some kind worked up. I need to watch you buy some of them smuggled-in Mexican steers from McCoy. Then I'll arrest him and you can go on back to your butcher shop."

"I keep the esteers I buy, no?"

Longarm thought for a moment, then said, "I don't know, Pancho. They'd be evidence, except I never seen a steer brought into a courtroom. But we'll work out something, even if I ain't real sure right now what it'll be."

"I tell you, Pancho, if I eat another bite, I won't need a thing more except a drink till suppertime," Longarm said.

They were breakfasting off the remains of a stew Guzman had cooked for their supper the evening before, using crackers from Longarm's saddlebags to spoon it from the pot. It was a hearty dish, a pair of jackrabbits Longarm had knocked over

159

with his Winchester in the fading daylight, cheese and potatoes from the supply he'd bought in La Junta, while Guzman had contributed onion and chili peppers and chunks cut from a *chorizo* sausage.

Reaching for his bottle, Longarm washed down the stew with a second eye-opener. He stood up and said, "First thing we'd oughta do is ride into town and see if the stationmaster's got the manifest for that cattle shipment. Damn it, all them trains whistling last night got us up three times, and all three of 'em went right on past without stopping."

"Ees like thees always, the cattle trains," Guzman said. "I get telegram from *Señor* McCoy to come buy esteers, I come from Trinidad and wait one, two, maybe three days for train."

"Once the stationmaster gets his manifest, we'll know. We can saddle up and go whenever you're ready."

"But I don' have no horse, Longarm," Guzman said.

"How in the hell did you get out here, then?"

"I am walk from La Junta. Why am I need the horse? I weel ride from here to Trinidad een the cattle car."

"Well, I guess that makes sense." Longarm nodded. "I just figured you had a horse staked out someplace up the draw."

"Ees better you go," Guzman said. "I am estay, so eef the train ees get here while you are gone, ees one of us to watch."

"I guess that's the only way to do it," Longarm agreed. "I won't be gone long. And I'll pick up a little bit more grub, in case we got to stay here another day or two."

At the depot, the stationmaster recognized Longarm from the previous day. Without being asked, he said, "You can rest easy about the cattle train, mister. I got the manifest about two hours ago. It'll be in before dark this evening."

"Can't you give me a better guess on the time?" Longarm asked. "Before dark covers everything from noon to sundown."

"Don't hold me to it, but I'd say sometime between four and five o'clock, if they don't run any hotboxes and don't have to wait on a siding someplace."

"That's close enough, I guess," Longarm nodded. "Thanks."

Back at the old fort, Longarm told Guzman, "I didn't buy no more grub for us, Pancho. If that train gets here anywheres near when it's due, you'll be on your way home with your steers before it'd be time for supper."

"You weel let me take the esteers, then?" Guzman asked.

"Yep. I been thinking about it a little bit, and I figure if

160

you'll just save me the hides when you skin out two or three of them Mexican critters, that's cnough to go to court with."

"Do I got to go in court, Longarm?"

"Sure. But I'll be there, and there'll be a government lawyer too, so you'll be all right. All you got to do is tell how you bought steers from McCoy, and that there was Mexican brands on a lot of them."

"Is true." Guzman nodded. "I don' be afraid to do thees thing."

"Good," Longarm said. "Now, let's walk up to the stockpens and see how the land lays. I want to be as close as I can get when I jump McCoy and his gang."

"You don' going to get somebody to help you?"

"I figure I can handle it by myself. Likely there won't be more'n three or four, and you'll be there to back me up if things starts to go sour. I guess you got a gun?"

"*Seguramente.*" Guzman went to his rumpled blankets and fumbled in them for a moment before producing an old octagonal-barrel Le Page. He showed the gun to Longarm, saying, "Wheen I bring money to pay for esteers, I don't like to not have gun because maybe I be rob. Ees good *pistola*. I use heem in war, wheen I am *soldado*."

"What war was that, Pancho?"

"Two wars. I fight weeth Juarez to free Mexico from *los Frances*, then I fight weeth Lerdo to free Mexico from Diaz."

"Too bad Diaz won. I never seen him, but I had a few runins with some of his men."

Guzman shook his head sadly. "Ees not good man, Diaz. Ees why I leave Mexico to come here. Eef I stay—" He put his forefinger on his temple and flicked his thumb as though firing a pistol. "Boom, ees feenish."

"We'll try to do all the finishing, this time," Longarm said. "Come on, let's go take a look at them pens."

Almost a quarter-mile behind the abandoned fort, the Santa Fe tracks crossed the draw and curved in a shallow arc to the stockpens. The main line continued in the same shallow curve to La Junta, but a spur had been built to serve the pens. Longarm and Guzman crossed the wide expanse of open land that lay between the main line and the spur, and followed the spur to the stockpens. They stopped opposite the hayshed which stood at the end of the pens. The pens occupied a narrow strip of land between the tracks and the steep slope where the bank of the Arkansas River dipped to the water's edge.

Longarm had seen the same type of pens many times before. They were in the form of a long rectangle enclosed by heavy boards spaced horizontally a foot or more apart and spiked to posts, the top board about the height of a man's chest. Similar fences at right angles to the enclosure divided the rectangle into four roughly square pens, each of them able to hold about two carloads of cattle, roughly fifty head.

There were no loading chutes, just an earth embankment raised between the pens and the tracks. The earthen bank sloped gently upward from the pens to the height of a boxcar's floor and was cut almost vertically along the tracks to leave an open span four or five feet wide which was bridged by duckboards when a car was being loaded or unloaded.

For several minutes Longarm studied the terrain, then shook his head. He told Guzman, "Damned if I see one speck of cover anyplace near enough to be much use. That little skittle of bush down by the river's too far away, and this hayshed wouldn't hide a cat trying to bushwhack a mouse."

"Ees too bad you don't can ride on the train to the pens," Guzman said, pointing to the triangle between the main line and the spur. "Ees only leetle way to cross, there."

"Now, that ain't a half bad idea, Pancho." Longarm studied the space between the two sets of tracks. "The train's going to be slowing down for the switch, and they'll leave the string on the main line while they back the cattle cars onto the spur. It ain't much of a jump between them tracks. I think maybe that's the best way to get where I need to be. Come on. I've seen all I need to here. Let's walk back along that main line and figure out a place where I can get on board."

Hunkered down at the edge of the short trestle that carried the railroad tracks across the draw, Longarm squinted at the sun. Dissatisfied, he took out his watch and checked his guess. He'd been waiting for nearly an hour, and it was almost half-past four now. Unless the stationmaster's pessimistic remark about siding waits and hotboxes had been a forecast, the cattle train should be nearing La Junta very soon.

Returning his watch to his bottom vest pocket, Longarm snaked one of his slim cheroots from the upper pocket and lighted it. He'd been waiting for an hour, and impatience was beginning to gnaw at him. He looked down the tracks to the

162

east, perspective narrowing the parallel rails until they merged into one bright line of steel in the distance. He blinked and looked again. A puff of smoke not as thick as the thread which snaked up from the tip of his cigar had risen above the distant tracks.

Suddenly Longarm's tension flowed away and he felt totally relaxed. He hunched around into a more comfortable position and watched the tiny black dot of the locomotive's boiler growing steadily larger. When he could see the brighter dot of the sun's rays reflected from the headlight, he decided that the time had come to move. If he could see the headlight, the engineer could see him waiting beside the tracks. Standing up, he stretched, then slid down into the draw and stood close to the beams that supported the trestle.

Now the rails were only a few inches above his head, and soon Longarm heard the muted singing that the train's wheels sent along the steel tracks in advance of its approach. The light, high-pitched whine became a grinding buzz, and the buzz separated into a medley of disparate sounds: grinding of steel on steel, clatter of safety chains between the cars, muted thunking of pistons, all linked by the increasingly loud humming of the drivers pulling the train ahead.

When the locomotive had passed, with its flash of red coals from the bottom grate of the firebox and its smell of hot oil, Longarm scrambled out of the draw. The resonating octavo of the brakeshoes reached his ears as he rose above the level of the tracks, and the train began to slow. Standing as close as he dared to the sides of the freight cars passing inches away, he waited while the scent of manure from the cattle cars filled his nostrils and faded away, and the train slowed until it was barely moving as it entered the switch.

Only three or four cars were now between Longarm and the caboose. He could see very clearly the bullseyes of the lantern that protruded from its rear end when he ran along the freight car and jumped to reach its grab bar. His booted feet found the stirrup strap of the underslung step and he swung between the cars quickly, to get out of sight of any brakeman who might be eyeing the string.

Then the train stopped. In the still air the grating of a coupling being opened reached Longarm's ears and he risked peering out for a quick glance ahead. There were two brakemen at the switch and a third walking back toward the caboose, glancing at the journal boxes as he passed each set of wheels. Seeing that the brakie's attention was on the bottoms of the cars, Longarm felt safe in keeping his head out for a moment longer.

He watched while one of the two brakemen at the switch started toward the rear, then stopped as the locomotive chugged and the cattle cars at the head of the string separated and began to move slowly ahead. The brakeman swung aboard the last cattle car, climbed to the top of it, and started walking slowly toward the locomotive. The brakeman walking along the train was close to the cars which sheltered Longarm now. Putting one foot on the coupler, Longarm swung to the opposite side of the train and jumped to the ground.

He landed on his feet, dropped prone, and rolled down the right-of-way grade where he'd be out of sight for the passing brakeman. He heard the trainman's feet grating on the gravel roadbed, and could follow his progress until the man's boot soles snickered against the steel step up to the caboose.

Now Longarm knew he was in the most dangerous minutes of his attempt to reach the spur without being noticed. There was no work to be done by the train crew and the hands who'd be working at the stockpens had not emerged from the car in which they'd been travelling. There was only one place to hide. Longarm rolled up the grade, scrambled across one rail, and stretched out flat on the roadbed between the wheels of the last boxcar.

Lying under the boxcar, its massive axle only inches above his head, Longarm was as good as blind. He strained his ears to hear every sound that would give him a clue. The distant chuffing of the locomotive and the low-pitched whine of steel against steel told him that the cattle cars were being backed onto the spur. The noises stopped after a few minutes and the locomotive began snorting again, at a faster tempo this time; the brakeman had cut the cattle cars loose and the engine was heading back up the spur to the switch. The beating of the drivers changed pitch once more as the engine began backing down the main line.

Over the mechanical noises Longarm could now hear other sounds: men calling to one another, the blatting of cattle now that they were no longer being jostled by the movement of the cars. The sound of voices almost directly overhead took him by surprise.

"Thanks again for letting me ride back here in the caboose

with you," a man's high-pitched nasal voice said. "Too bad about your damned railroad rules. Those two quarts of Green River I wanted to bring along sure would've brightened up the trip."

"Like we explained, Rule G's the one we don't dare bust," a second voice replied. "We might fudge some on the other ones, but no railroader's going to risk his job for life. You need a hand getting down them steps?"

"No, I'm doing all right," the first man replied. "Oh, while I'm thinking about it, here's a little something you men can divide up, just to make up for all the trouble I put you to, like giving up one of the bunks in the caboose and putting that empty boxcar right behind the cattle cars so my men would have a place to stay with their horses. Go on, take the money, and you and the other men split it up."

"Well, you wasn't any trouble, but I'll see that all the boys gets their share. Thanks a lot, Mr. McCoy."

When Longarm heard feet crunching on the roadbed gravel he tried to turn his head at an angle that would enable him to see the elusive man he'd missed so many times in so many places. No matter how he strained and twisted and arched his back, all that he could glimpse was McCoy's legs from the knees down, the bottom third of a pair of striped trousers and a pair of feet shod in fancy-stitched calfskin boots.

As anxious as he was to see the mysterious individual posing as the Real McCoy, Longarm's sense of caution kept him from throwing away months of work and miles of trailing for the sake of a moment's satisfaction. When the clashing of the couplers warned him that the train would be in motion in a matter of minutes, he flattened out again and lay motionless. Out of the corners of his eyes he could follow the movements of the calfskin boots as McCoy started across the space between the main line and the loading spur.

Damned if you ain't finally caught up with him, old son! Longarm told himself as the car above him creaked and began moving. *Now what you got to do is watch out that you don't spook him by trying to rush this deal too fast. Just keep him in sight till it's time to clamp the handcuffs on his wrists! Slippery as that damned McCoy is, he's liable to find a way to dodge outa sight again before you even get a good look at him.*

It seemed to Longarm that a train had never moved more

slowly. The boxcar above him inched along and when it had passed there was another interminable wait while the caboose passed over him. He held his position long enough to make sure that there was no one standing on the back platform of the caboose to see him and give warning before he could reach the shelter of the eight cattle cars that now stood on the spur between him and the stockpens. He turned his head just in time to see McCoy's back disappear around the last car in the string.

As Longarm got to his feet he saw Francisco Guzman leave the haybarn and start along the track, following McCoy. Guzman looked around and saw Longarm, who held his breath for a moment, fearing that his only witness would notice him and wave and give their plan away. Guzman saw him, but made no move except to nod his head an almost imperceptible fraction of an inch before he disappeared behind the end of the cattle cars.

Longarm held his place long enough to give Guzman time to reach McCoy and took advantage of the delay by scanning the string of cattle cars. The freight train had picked up speed and the caboose was already passing the switch. Longarm dismissed it as a possible source of danger to his plan. He started toward the cattle cars.

There was no need for him to try to move silently. The cattle in the cars were blatting louder than ever and their cries, combined with the thudding of their hooves on the car floors and the shouts of McCoy's men making their preparations to unload, would have covered the approach of a herd of elephants.

Longarm reached the last cattle car in the string. Its ends were solid and shielded him from being seen. He stepped up to the corner and peered around. Four men were working at the first car on the spur. It was the boxcar to which McCoy had referred, and they'd placed a duckboard to span the gap between the door and the embankment. They had opened the sliding doors and were leading the horses, already saddled, across the duckboard to the narrow lane between the cars and the stockpens. McCoy had stopped to watch just a few feet from the end of the first car, and halfway down the string Guzman was approaching him.

When Guzman called to McCoy, Longarm could hear him even over the noise the men were making getting their horses

166

across the duckboard. Guzman called, *"Señor* McCoy! I have wait a long time for you! You got the steers you send me the telegram you want to esell?"

McCoy turned and Longarm quickly ducked back behind the car. He heard McCoy's reply, "Well, Guzman! I've got just about a carload of steers that you can have real cheap, if you and your brother can use that many."

"We take all you got, if you make low enough the price," Guzman said. "Only I got to look at them first, you know."

"Sure, sure," McCoy said heartily. "Come on, let's step down there to the pens where you can see them good as they come out of the cars."

Longarm waited until he was sure McCoy and Guzman were at the stockpen fence before he looked again. The men had moved the duckboard to the first cattle car and one of them was walking across it to the car door while the other three stationed themselves to haze the cattle into the first pen. McCoy and Guzman stood at the fence, absorbed in watching as the first steers edged across the duckboard.

Longarm decided it was time for him to move. He stepped across the tracks, putting the cars between him and the pens, and ran toward the head of the string. He counted the cars as he ran and when he'd reached the third cattle car he ducked between it and the car ahead. Looking cautiously around its end he saw McCoy and Guzman inspecting the cattle as they trotted down the embankment and into the first pen.

Even at a glance Longarm could see that about one out of every six or eight of the steers was a Mexican-bred longhorn. Their horns were shorter than Texas cattle, their bodies smaller, and when he got a glimpse of a brand as the steers began milling around in the pen he could see the wavy, uncertain lines that was the mark of brands placed with a running-iron.

Restraining his impatience, Longarm waited, looking out only occasionally, while the first car was unloaded and McCoy's workers moved the duckboard to the car behind which he was sheltered. When Longarm peered out again, McCoy and Guzman had moved along the fence to watch the unloading. They were standing almost directly in front of him, and he could hear them clearly over the noise made by the cattle and the men unloading them.

"Well, you saw the steers out of that first car," McCoy was

saying. "I'd say there's six or eight steers in every car like those little ones you buy, so I'll have about fifty. You sure you can use that many?"

"I say we weel buy all you wan' to sell us, *Señor* McCoy," Guzman replied. "You theenk maybeso I don' got the money? Here, I geeve you to count."

Peering out, Longarm saw Guzman hand McCoy a small leather bag. McCoy hefted it. Longarm decided he'd waited long enough. The requirements of the law had been satisfied. McCoy had been paid for steers smuggled across the border, steers that might be infected with apthos fever. To delay any longer would be risking discovery and a gunfight with McCoy and his men. Drawing his Colt, Longarm stepped from between the cattle cars.

"All right, McCoy," he called. "I'm a deputy United States marshal and I'm putting you under arrest. Put your hands up and stand quiet while I get the cuffs on you!"

Chapter 19

McCoy did not move. He stood frozen, his hand still outstretched and holding the bag of money just handed him by Guzman. He stared at Longarm, disbelief written on his thin face.

Longarm was studying the man he'd been chasing over so many weeks and so many miles. The fake McCoy was of average height, but exceedingly thin, which made him look taller than he was. Actually, he was half a head shorter than Guzman. The striped suit of which Longarm had seen only the bottom trouser legs also added to the illusion of height. His shirt was an incongruous pink, with a high white starched collar and a dark rose-colored cravat. Even at the distance between them Longarm could see the diamond eyes of the steerhead stickpin glinting in the slanting afternoon sun. McCoy wore a cream-colored Plains-creased Stetson with an unusually wide brim.

All these details were registered by Longarm in the space of a few seconds while he waited for McCoy to obey his command. When the steer-swindler made no move, Longarm repeated, "I told you to get your hands up, McCoy! Now do it!"

"Don't get edgy, Marshal," McCoy said at last. "I'm not fool enough to try to run or draw while you've got a gun on me. But I've been as curious about you as I suppose you have about me. I was just taking a good look at you."

As he spoke, McCoy let his hands sag downward a few inches. Longarm belatedly divined his intention. McCoy brought around his right hand in a fast forward sweep and launched the bag of money at Longarm.

Longarm ducked instinctively and triggered his Colt in the same instant, but his awareness of the money bag sailing at him distracted him. The slug from the Colt tore through the thick plank of the fence within an inch of McCoy as the steer-swindler dropped to the ground. The heavy bag of gold and silver coins struck Longarm in the right shoulder. The shock caused him to let his gun hand sag, and the shot he was triggering when the bag hit plowed into the gravel roadbed.

Guzman was clawing at his belt, trying to free the big Le Page revolver from his waistband. The instant McCoy hit the ground he grabbed Guzman's ankles, pulling them out from under him. Guzman started toppling, but grabbed the center board of the fence and began pulling himself erect.

For a few moments after the first shot from Longarm's Colt broke the air, the men unloading the cattle were too confused to take part in the developing fray. Working as close as they were to the blatting cattle, they did not hear the brief conversation between Longarm and McCoy, which in any case had lasted only a few seconds, and the first real clue they had that trouble was starting had been Longarm's second shot.

Then they saw McCoy roll under the bottom board of the stockpen fence and start dodging between the steers that were entering the pen. They also saw Guzman start falling to the ground and at the same time noticed Longarm standing at the end of the cattle car. Seeing that Guzman was out of the fracas, the four riders made Longarm their target.

Revolvers began barking as McCoy's men joined in the fight. Longarm dodged back, taking cover behind the end of the cattle car. He saw McCoy weaving across the stockpen, but could not get a shot because of the cover the steers gave the fleeing man. Longarm used a trick that had served him well before, and jumped for the grab rail high on the car's end. He caught it with one hand, levered himself up to stand on the bar step below it, and began climbing up the end of the car.

While McCoy's helpers were closing in, their eyes at ground level, Longarm leaned around the end of the car and got off a shot which knocked one of the men out of his saddle. Guzman regained his feet and got his massive revolver free at the same time. He snapshotted at one of the remaining horsemen. The heavy twelve-millimeter slug knocked the rider over the horse's cruppers and he landed heavily, arms still flailing.

Longarm had kept his eyes on McCoy, following the fleeing swindler's progress across the stockpen, awaiting an opportunity to shoot. He saw that McCoy was still mixed up with the steers and realized that until McCoy was in the clear he wouldn't be able to get the clean shot he wanted at the fleeing man. He glanced quickly at the terrain on the other side of the stockpens while he waited for his chance to shoot. Beyond the fence the land sloped gently down to the Arkansas River.

There was no cover between the fence and the river, Longarm saw. Nothing except calf-high range grass grew on the quarter-mile that stretched to the water's edge, so he saw no need to hurry. The last thing he wanted to do was to kill McCoy. The running man had too much valuable information locked in his brain, information Longarm wanted and needed to clean up the swindling ring and take into court an airtight case against all its members.

He was positive that questioning McCoy would reveal who had ordered the murder of Elsie Mae Glover, and would at the same time enable him to round up all the participants in the gigantic steer-swindling scheme, which he was sure by now spanned the West from Canada to Mexico.

Steadying his gun hand on the roof of the cattle car, Longarm waited until the fugitive had gotten through the milling steers and was near the back fence of the stockpen. His eyes squared with the Colt's sights, Longarm was absorbed in taking careful aim at McCoy's churning legs. He was tightening his finger on the trigger to squeeze off his shot when the sharp, ringing crack of a rifle cut the air.

Over the notch of his revolver sight, Longarm saw McCoy throw up his arms and stumble forward. A second rifle shot rang out at once and McCoy's body jerked as the slug tore into it. Longarm raised his eyes from the pistol sights. A horseman had appeared from nowhere at the edge of the river. The rider sat with his rifle still at his shoulder.

Some stray thought nagged at Longarm's mind as he looked at the newcomer, but he pushed it aside, concentrating on trying to make out the man's features. The distance was too great and the sun's angle was wrong. The new arrival's face was shaded by a broad-brimmed hat, and his clothing was that worn by virtually every cowhand in the West.

Longarm could not see him well enough to tell anything about him except that he was there, and to realize instantly that the horseman was beyond the range of his revolver. Even as he was berating himself for deciding his Winchester would only be in his way, Longarm was bringing up his Colt. He tilted the muzzle in Arkansas elevation and squeezed off one shot, then another. To his surprise, the rider jerked erect and for a moment swayed in his saddle.

Longarm did not waste time congratulating himself on his shooting. He'd subconsciously counted his shots, and knew his Colt was empty. He was reaching into his pocket for cartridges when the horseman steadied himself in his saddle and raised his rifle again. Longarm dropped below the top of the boxcar and the slug from the rifle screeched inches above his head, skittering across the top of the cattle car, tearing a groove in the tough wood before dropping spent beyond the car.

Without taking his eyes off the rider, Longarm dumped the shell cases from the Colt's cylinder and slid in fresh loads. He snapped the cylinder back in place with a quick wrist twist and brought up the revolver, but he was too late. The rider was far out of range, heading east at a gallop in the wide strip of green between the stockpens and the river.

McCoy lay motionless a few yards away from the rear fence of the stockpen. Guzman and the remaining survivor of McCoy's crew fired almost simultaneously. Guzman's big frame jerked as a bullet found him, but his slug had already found its mark. The last of McCoy's men slumped forward over the neck of his horse.

Longarm reached the ground in a single jump and hurried to Guzman's side. "How bad you hurt, Pancho?" he asked.

"*Es nada, una pica de pulga,*" Guzman replied, then realized he was speaking Spanish and said, "I don' hurt bad. What ees—"

Longarm broke in, "McCoy's shot; looks like he's dead. The rest of his men are out of action. See to things here, Pancho. I'm going after whoever it was that shot McCoy."

There were three horses with empty saddles standing in the narrow space between the cattle cars and the stockpens. Longarm looked at them, picked the one that had a saddle scabbard with a rifle in it, ran to it, and mounted it. The horse reared once, but Longarm quieted it and toed it into motion. He rounded the end of the stockpens and headed for the riverbank.

In the few minutes since he'd spurred off after his exchange of shots with Longarm, the mysterious new arrival had gotten a good lead. When Longarm reached the clear terrain bordering the Arkansas, his quarry was far ahead, still galloping, making good time over the level, flood-scoured strip.

Longarm dug his heels in the strange horse's flank and the animal responded well. It was still fresh, and Longarm kept it at a gallop. Bit by bit it gained on the rider ahead. Longarm

172

could see his quarry plainly, but even with the sun now at his back the face of the man ahead was nothing but a blur.

Far in the distance, Longarm could see the tops of a grove of trees. He was sure the mysterious rider was heading for the cover they would provide, but though he tried to get a bit more speed out of his horse, the animal could move no faster. He kept the fleeing man in sight, but the distance between them remained much the same as the chase wore on.

Gradually the details of the grove in the distance became more distinct, the rider ahead outlined by their dark trunks and low-growing foliage. The trees gave Longarm his clue. A big stand of mature trees was rare along that stretch of the Arkansas, and the only grove Longarm could remember seeing in his travels had been at Bent's old abandoned fort.

Certain now that the goal of the man he was after was the ruined buildings in the grove ahead, Longarm pulled his horse up a bit. The animal had been laboring for several minutes, and Longarm was sure the horse ridden by his quarry must be fading, too. Though he'd gained perceptibly on the rider ahead, Longarm did not press his luck by urging his mount to greater speed. He turned the animal away from the river, taking a course that would put him where he could command both sides of the riverbank from a point beyond rifle range of the grove.

If the man he was chasing grasped Longarm's objective, he gave no sign of it. The fugitive kept moving straight ahead and disappeared into the trees. Longarm maintained his course. He reached the spot he'd planned, south of the grove. The tumbling adobe walls of the long-deserted fort, now broken by long black gaps, were plainly visible between the tree trunks, and on both sides of the grove he had an unobstructed view of the riverbank.

Reining in, Longarm pulled the rifle from its saddle scabbard. It was a twin to his own Winchester, which made him feel easier at once, even if he wasn't familiar with its sighting peculiarities. He checked the magazine and found it was full.

Levering a shell into the chamber, Longarm hooked a knee around the saddlehorn—an unaccustomed luxury he couldn't enjoy when in his own McClellan saddle—and rested the rifle across his thighs. Lighting a cheroot, he settled down to wait.

In spite of his relaxed attitude, Longarm kept both his eyes and his mind busy. While his eyes flicked from one point to another within the grove, he spent his anger against himself.

Old son, you got yourself stuck up shit crick without no

173

paddle. Whoever that killer is, he got away from you when you oughta had him dead to rights. And he ain't no greenhorn at his business, neither. He come to get McCoy and he did it, right in plain sight. Two shots.

Suddenly the nagging bother that had been buried deep in his mind since the gunfight at the stockpens came to the surface and broke his train of thought.

That's what struck you odd, old son! That killer's left-handed. He shouldered his rifle on the wrong side! Now, there ain't no left-handed killers on the wanted list, and if there was one that's been loose in these parts before now, you'd more'n likely have heard. Question is, where'd he come from?

He come here to kill McCoy, and likely you, too, old son. Not any doubt about that. And he knows this part of the country like a book. He didn't waste no time hightailing it for here. He had to know something you don't, or have some scheme in mind you ain't been bright enough to figure out yet. And he ain't fired a shot since he got in that place there. You been made a fool of one time today, old son. You better not let him catch you in another fool's play!

Longarm tossed the butt of his cigar on the ground and swung around in the saddle. Keeping the rifle poised in his right hand, he toed the horse ahead and walked it to the edge of the trees without drawing fire from the grove. Dismounting, he tethered the horse and started toward the ruined fort.

At close range, Longarm could see that little was left of what had been the last outpost of civilization on the Western frontier. A half-century had passed since the Bent brothers built the fort, and for half that time the outpost had been abandoned. Settlers coming to the West, eager for seasoned lumber, had helped themselves to the *vigas* that supported the roof, the lintels above the windows and door, even to the massive beam that had spanned the top of the gates, gates big enough to accommodate a Conestoga wagon.

With their supports removed, the adobes above the openings had eroded and dropped to the ground, leaving only columns where there had once been walls. The walls looked now like snaggled teeth rising from browned gums. Carefully alert, Longarm moved to a corner of the squared structure, where he could look through one of the gaps and see the whole interior at once.

No shot had greeted his approach, and inside the enclosure

nothing moved. There was no noise.

You let him sucker you again, old son, he told himself with suppressed anger. *And if you don't hightail around, he's going to get away clean!*

Running back to the horse, Longarm mounted and rode through the grove. A bend in the Arkansas put its banks within a few feet of the grove behind the fort. The north bank rose in a high, steep slope, and on the baked soil of the slope Longarm saw the drying water-trail left by the killer's horse. He crossed quickly and rode up the high bank. Beyond it, no matter which way he looked, he saw nothing except the waving range grass.

He done it, Longarm told himself. His anger had died and he did not allow it to rule him again. *He knows this part of the country better'n you do, old son. You ain't got the chance of a snowflake in hell of catching him. But there ain't all that many wrong-handed gunmen around. You got a target you can hit now. This case ain't closed yet, not by a damned sight!*

"You're sure you don't need to go into town and have a doctor look at that arm of yours, Pancho?" Longarm asked Guzman, looking at the bandage showing beneath the bloody sleeve of Guzman's torn shirt.

"Ees like I tall you, a leetle scratch. I do not go to La Junta before you get back, I theenk you wan' to look first."

"You thought right." Longarm nodded. "And you done real good here, taking care of what had to be done. But I'd just as soon not have some know-nothing constable or city marshal messing around here before I do my own looking."

Longarm surveyed the scene along the siding. Guzman had dragged the bodies of McCoy's helpers up the embankment and laid them beside the railroad grade, and had tethered their horses. He had left McCoy's body lying as it had fallen, face-down in the half-filled stockpen, but the cattle walked around it as cattle will do when they encounter a strange object. In the first pen the cattle were quiet, but those in the unopened cars were blatting almost constantly.

Looking at the sun, Longarm was surprised to see that it was still high above the horizon. So much had happened in so short a time that he felt as if the day should be over.

"We're going to have to go into La Junta before much longer, and see if we can get somebody to handle these steers," he told Guzman. "I'll do my noseying around, if you want to go in. You can get a doctor to fix up that arm proper while you're there."

"Ees maybe no need to go to La Junta," Guzman replied.

He pointed toward the town. A buggy such as those favored by doctors was crossing the railroad above the switch. It rolled precariously along the sloping grade until it reached to first car on the siding. Longarm could see that a man clad in white was holding the reins.

"Damned if he don't look like a doctor," he agreed. "We better go find out."

As they neared the buggy, they could see that its occupant was a portly man with a cholerically red face. He was looking at the stockpens, but turned to face them as they got closer.

"Looks like you've been having a little private war out here all to yourselves," he said as Longarm and Guzman reached the buggy. "Maybe you'll tell me about it."

"There ain't much needs telling," Longarm replied. "And it ain't your affair, unless you got a badge on."

"I don't have a badge," the new arrival said, "but I might have an interest in what's happened here."

"Well, it ain't no real secret," Longarm told him. "I'm a deputy United States marshal, and I've been on the trail of that fellow you was just looking at, out in the pen. If somebody hadn't shot him, he'd be wearing handcuffs now. He was a fugitive from justice, a steer-swindler that called himself the Real McCoy."

"Then he was something besides a steer-swindler," the man in the buggy snapped. "He was a damned liar, too! Because you're looking right now at the *real* Real McCoy. That's me!"

Chapter 20

For a moment, Longarm looked at the man in the buggy without being able to speak. He found his voice at last and said, "You know, I thought I'd seen you someplace before now. Did you ever run into a man named Cass Macdonald?"

"I sure as hell did, young fellow, but if you're thinking of getting Cass to identify me, you're barking up the wrong tree. Poor old Cass has been dead a lot of years now."

"So I heard. But if you was a friend of his, you'd know what his brand was," Longarm suggested.

"That's a tricky question. Cass had three brands during the time I knew him: the Lazy Z, the Slash B and the O Dot O."

"You're the real Real McCoy, then," Longarm said, satisfaction in his tone. "I worked for Cass when I was considerable younger'n I am now, and I remember you just a little bit."

"If you worked for Cass, you ought to. I bought steers from him, every ranch he ever owned," McCoy replied. "I'm afraid I don't remember you, though."

"I wouldn't expect you to, Mr. McCoy. I wasn't much but a kid then, even if I had fought in the War. It was a while ago, but I never forgot you or your name. For a while, I thought you was a prizefighter turned steer buyer."

"So did a lot of other people. I don't mind telling you I got the idea from the two prizefighters named McCoy. One was a good boxer, the other one was a bum, and the good man started to call himself the Real McCoy. My customers started joshing me about it, so I just started calling myself the Real McCoy. I'll say this, it made folks remember me."

"I know it sure stuck in my mind," Longarm nodded.

"It was a good name. I was proud of it. Still am, which is why I'm here now. I heard somebody was passing himself off as me, so I came to find out about it." McCoy cleared his throat and went on, "Well, Marshal Long, if you're satisfied as to who I am, maybe you'll tell me what in hell's been going on here."

"For a while, I wasn't right sure myself," Longarm replied. "I guess I've got it pretty well sorted out now, though."

"Go on," McCoy invited. "I'm listening."

"I will, but first I better introduce my friend, here. He's called Pancho Guzman. Him and his brother's got a couple of butcher shops over to the west of here, at Trinidad and Pueblo. He come here to buy some steers from the fellow that was passing as you."

"Guzman." McCoy nodded. "I'll bet you've been buying culls from that bastard who's been passing himself off as me."

"Sí, Señor Mc Coy. For three, mebbeso four years."

"Just what I figured, when I heard you're a butcher," McCoy grunted. "Cheapjack brokers always got a butcher someplace to dump culls on."

"You sound to me like you know who that man laying out there was." Longarm frowned.

"I'm pretty sure I do. I won't say positively until I've had a look at him, though."

"If you want to look at him, I'll be glad for you to," Longarm said. "I'm curious about his real name, myself."

"Help me get out of this damned buggy, then," McCoy said, holding his hand out to Longarm. "I don't get around at all good any more. Legs went back on me a few years ago. That's why I had to quit my business."

With the help of Longarm and Guzman, McCoy got out of the buggy. He reached in and picked up two canes that had been lying on the floor, and with the canes helping to support his bulky frame walked slowly down to the stockpen with Longarm and Guzman. Longarm bent down and turned over the fake McCoy's body. McCoy snorted.

"That's who I thought it was," he said. He pointed with the tip of one of his canes. "The thieving son of a bitch has even got on the stickpin he stole from me."

"What's his real name?" Longarm asked.

"I won't guarantee it's the name he was christened," McCoy said, "if he ever was christened at all. But I knew him by the name of Morrison—Cooter Morrison. He used to be my clerk when I was running my business myself. That was when I first started out, in Chicago, before I got smart enough to see that

178

the place for a cattle broker was closer to where the cattle came from."

"You moved to Kansas City, then?" Longarm asked.

"That's right," McCoy replied. He looked at Longarm with a thoughtful frown.

"And you kept on being called the Real McCoy when you moved to Kansas City," Longarm suggested as the old man fell silent.

"Of course. Except that right after I moved to Kansas City I got sick. Some kind of fever. The doctors still don't know much about it, but it damn near killed me, and ruined my legs." He lifted his canes one after the other. "That's why I've got to use these."

"But this Cooter Morrison ran your business while you was sick," Longarm went on encouragingly.

McCoy nodded. "I put him in charge and hired him a girl clerk to do the paperwork. I still had my old friends on the ranches, and in the meat-packing houses and wholesale butcher offices in Chicago, so the business did real well."

McCoy fell silent again, and Longarm prompted him once more by asking, "Why'd you sell out to your clerk, then?"

"I didn't, damn it! I thought I was selling out to a syndicate," McCoy explained. "Morrison and the office girl—her name was Ellie or Elsie, I don't recall exactly—they came to me and told me a syndicate wanted to buy me out. I was tired and sick and not getting any younger, so I sold."

"I don't guess you need to tell me any more," Longarm told McCoy. "This Morrison taken your name and your business, too."

"And abused 'em!" McCoy said angrily. "My reputation is all I've got left, Marshal, and I don't have any use for whoever drags it down. It might not sound nice, but I'll tell you right out, I'm glad he got what was coming to him! I just wish I knew who shot him. I'd shake his hand."

"Maybe not," Longarm told McCoy, his brow wrinkling into a thoughtful frown. "Morrison wasn't in this alone. Whoever got this swindle started just used him as a front."

"And killed him when he got out of line?" McCoy asked.

"That's how I figure it. And I'm going to get on his trail, as soon as I can find somebody to take care of these steers."

"Longarm," Guzman broke in. "Escuse me, but I been

theenking about these cattle while you are gone. Only, I don't have time to tell you before."

"Go ahead and tell me now, Pancho," Longarm said.

"I wan' to buy all the cattle here," Guzman told him.

"*All* of 'em?" Longarm frowned. "You got that much money?"

"No. I have tol' you already, me and my brother, we are not reech. But what else weel you do weeth them, Longarm?"

After a moment's thought, Longarm said slowly, "Well, you sure asked me a good question. I guess I don't have no answer."

"Who are they belong to, now the other *Señor* McCoy ees dead?" Guzman asked.

"I don't have no answer to that, either," Longarm admitted. "The government, I guess. That'd be for a court to say."

"And who weel look after them until the court says? You?"

"Now, you know I ain't got time to look after a herd of cattle, Pancho. I got a case to close up."

McCoy broke in. "Sell him the damn steers, Marshal. Unless you do, you'll be nursemaiding 'em till hell freezes over, if I know anything about courts. I'll tell you what. I qualify as an expert on cattle in any court in the land. I'll give you a value on these for as much as this man can pay, and we can get on our way to wherever it is we're heading."

"Now, hold on!" Longarm protested. "Where'd the 'we' get into this?"

"If you're going after the man who's behind this slimy snake that passed himself off as me, I'm going with you," McCoy said firmly. "I want to know who he is. I want to look through the bars of a jail and see his face back of 'em!"

"Now, you oughta know I can't take you along on official business, Mr. McCoy. It ain't that I don't want to—"

"Shut up a minute, son, and listen to me," McCoy broke in. "You might've been a hand on a ranch, but how much do you know about the cattle business?"

"Not much except what I've learned on this case."

"How much time would you've saved if you'd had somebody like me on hand to tell you things you had to learn the hard way?"

"Quite a bit, I'd imagine," Longarm admitted.

"Then, if you want to wind your case up fast, how much time do you think I can save you?"

"You don't need to say anything more, Mr. McCoy," Longarm said quickly. He turned to Guzman. "Pancho, you just bought them steers. You're responsible for 'em now. Me and the Real McCoy have got to go finish up this swindling case."

"So that's why Mr. McCoy come to Denver with me, Billy," Longarm concluded. The three men were sitting in Vail's office, and Longarm had just finished summarizing the case up to the time he and McCoy had left La Junta. "I found out there's a lot more to buying and selling cattle and moving 'em around to market than I ever figured. There's more papers to fix up than you can shake a stick at. You'd be in pretty much the same boat I am, trying to make sense of 'em, so Mr. McCoy can be a real help to us."

"Yes, I can see that," Vail agreed thoughtfully. "Well, go ahead, tell me what you figure on doing that he can help with."

"Now, Billy, you know I don't like to hash over a lot of things that might or might not happen. I thought maybe you'd be of a mind to come along with Mr. McCoy and me, and give me a hand winding it up."

Vail said nothing for a moment. Then he frowned across his desk at Longarm and said, "What's come over you? This is only the second time since you've been working out of my office that you've invited me to be on hand when you close a case."

"I don't generally close out my cases in Denver, Billy. You ain't around for me to invite most of the time."

"Well, if you want me along, that's fine," Vail said. "Let me know when you're ready to move, and I'll join in."

Longarm looked at the big Vienna Regulator clock on its wall bracket and said, "If you ain't too busy, Billy, now's as good a time as any. There's a hack waiting downstairs, so we can go right on and take care of it."

"You might like to know that the hack fare's not going to cost the government, Marshal Vail," McCoy said. He held up his canes. "I'm paying it myself, because I can't get around as easy as you and Longarm can."

Vail and McCoy got into the hackney cab, while Longarm rode on the outside seat with the driver. The ride was a short one, and as Vail got out and looked around, he said, "This is the Chaffee Building. Did you invite Jim Fraser to be on hand to help close your case?"

"Why, you know him better'n I do, Billy. You'd be the one to do whatever asking is done."

Getting McCoy up the stairs with his canes took a bit of work on the part of both Vail and Longarm, and the quietly luxurious outer office of the Cattlemen's Association was a restful haven when they reached it. Longarm went over to the young clerk and said a few words to him in a low voice. The clerk disappeared into Fraser's private office, and in a few moments the three were inside the office, sitting across the mahogany table from Fraser.

"I don't really know what this is all about, Billy," the Association manager said to Vail. "But I'm sure you've got a good reason for bringing these men up."

"You'll have to get the whole story from Long," Vail said. "I'm here because he thought it'd be a good idea for me to be on hand."

When Fraser turned to him and lifted his eyebrows inquiringly Longarm said, "You know, after you and me had our little talk the other day, Mr. Fraser, I got to thinking about you saying that your chief range detective was going to retire pretty soon. That sorta got me to wondering what he's been doing while all this steer-swindling and smuggling in sick cattle from Mexico's been going on."

"Hoyt Barret?" Fraser frowned.

"I don't think you mentioned his name," Longarm said.

"Hoyt's our chief range detective, so naturally he's been working on both cases," Fraser went on. "I can't see that he's made much more progress than you have, though."

"Seemed to me sorta funny that he ain't," Longarm said. "I just come on the case a couple or three months ago, but I found out quite a bit. If your man's been at it full time, longer than I have, he ought've done a lot better."

"If you feel you need his help, I'm sure he'll be glad to share whatever he's found with you, Long," Fraser said.

"It ain't so much his help I'm after," Longarm replied. "It's—" He broke off when a knock sounded on the office door. "I taken the liberty of asking your clerk to have your man come in while we're here." Raising his voice, Longarm called, "Come on in, Barret!"

All four of the men in the room turned to look toward the door as it opened. An angular man was framed in the opening. He was lantern-jawed, with a slit for a mouth, his face deeply

182

tanned. His cold grey eyes flickered from Fraser to McCoy to Vail and came to rest on Longarm's face. Without a word, his hand swept up, grabbing for his holstered revolver.

Longarm had slipped his derringer from his lower vest pocket when the knock sounded, and had been holding it concealed in the palm of his hand. He levelled the stubby little gun and fired. The bullet knocked Barret backward before he could close on the butt of his pistol. His mouth opened in surprise, but whatever the range detective had intended to say was lost forever. He was dead before he hit the floor.

Billy Vail had started out of his chair when he saw Barret reaching for his gun. Vail had drawn by the time Longarm fired, and he turned now to look at Longarm, his face drawn into a puzzled frown. He gasped, "What in the hell—"

Longarm broke in. "It was me he was after, Billy. He was the one that shot the fake McCoy down at La Junta."

"Now, wait a minute!" Fraser exploded. "You're accusing our chief detective of being a crook and a killer! I demand—" He stopped short when Longarm swung the derringer's stubby barrel to cover him.

Longarm said quietly, "I didn't get a good enough look at your man in La Junta to've sworn he was the killer. But when I got to thinking back over this case, how long the steer-swindle's been going on, it come to me that your outfit must've been working on it quite a while, Fraser. You give me the lead I needed, only I didn't know you was doing it at the time."

Fraser had regained his self-control. He turned to Vail. "Your man's lost his mind, Billy! Now he's accusing *me* of being in cahoots with Barret! You've known me long enough to know the kind of man I am! Tell that fool deputy of yours—"

"Shut up, Jim!" Vail snapped. "Long's no fool. I want to listen to what he's got to say before I do anything. Now sit down, and we'll all listen to him." He waited until Fraser had settled back into his big thronelike chair, then holstered his revolver and turned to Longarm. "Go ahead, tell us what you've got in the way of proof," he said.

"It ain't that I got much to tell you, Billy," Longarm said quietly. "I was counting on Fraser to give us the proof. I'd be willing to bet a pretty we'll find everything we need to put him away if we'll just look in that fancy desk behind him, there."

Vail faced Fraser. "It's up to you, Jim. You can either open

183

that desk and let us search it, or I'll get a federal warrant to go through it. Make your choice."

Fraser smiled. "You're more than welcome to search my desk, Billy. I'll guarantee you won't find anything in it that'll back up Long's stupid accusation. Look for yourself. The desk's not locked."

Vail got up and walked around the table. He stared at the massive Wooten desk. It was closed, but after looking at it for a moment, he stepped up to it and swung the sides apart. He looked at the multitude of drawers and turned to face Longarm.

"This was your idea, Long," Vail said. "What am I looking for in here?"

Before Longarm could reply, McCoy spoke up. He said, "I'll tell you, if you don't mind, Marshal Vail. That's why Longarm asked me to come along." Levering himself slowly to his feet, McCoy hobbled on his canes to the corner of the table. "You'll want bills of sale. They'll show brands and where cattle were bought and sold, and how many. Look for railroad manifests showing where cattle were shipped, and how many. With those figures, it'll be easy enough to figure out how the swindlers worked."

Longarm said, "It'd take you and me a long time to figure all that stuff out, Billy. Mr. McCoy can do it fast, seeing he knows the business. Fraser was just using that story about hoof-and-mouth to cover up what was really going on."

"It's going to take a while to go through all these drawers, though," Vail said.

Longarm stood up. "I sorta got a hunch I can save you some time looking."

He stepped over to the Wooten desk and opened the drawer that he'd discovered when he was searching its twin in Kansas City. When he closed it with a hard push, the back section that covered the hidden compartment fell open with a snap. Longarm walked around the desk and reached into the niche. He produced a thick sheaf of papers which he held out to Vail.

"I imagine Mr. McCoy can find what we're looking for in these," he said.

"Damn you, Long!" Fraser exclaimed.

He swivelled around in his chair, lifting his hand from the table drawer as he turned, raising the revolver he'd sneaked from the drawer to cover Longarm, whose hands were filled with the papers he'd taken from the compartment.

McCoy lifted the tip of the cane in his right hand and poked it into Fraser's ribs. He pressed the embossed band below the cane's handle. The report of the shot that sent a bullet into Fraser's heart broke the sudden hush that had seized the room. Fraser slumped out of his chair to the floor.

"That's the first time I've ever had to use this crazy contrivance," McCoy said calmly. "I wasn't really sure it'd work."

"You saved my bacon, Mr. McCoy," Longarm said. "I'm right grateful."

"Don't be, son," the Real McCoy said. "From what I saw and heard, that fellow laying down on the floor was the brains behind this whole scheme. He's the one that took away my good name, and when a man's in my fix that's about all he's got left. I was just taking back what belongs to me."

Watch for

**LONGARM
AND THE HANGMAN'S NOOSE**

sixty-sixth novel in the bold
LONGARM series from Jove

coming in June!

5